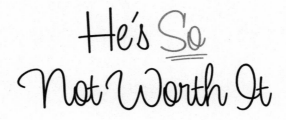

Also by Kieran Scott

He's So Not Worth It

kieran scott

SIMON & SCHUSTER BFYR
New York London Toronto Sydney

SIMON & SCHUSTER BFYR

An imprint of Simon & Schuster Children's Publishing Division
1230 Avenue of the Americas, New York, New York 10020

SIMON & SCHUSTER BFYR is a trademark of Simon & Schuster, Inc.
For information about special discounts for bulk purchases, please contact Simon &
Schuster Special Sales at 1-866-506-1949 or business@simonandschuster.com.
The Simon & Schuster Speakers Bureau can bring authors to your live event. For
more information or to book an event, contact the Simon & Schuster Speakers
Bureau at 1-866-248-3049 or visit our website at www.simonspeakers.com.
Book design by Krista Vossen
The text for this book is set in Andrade.
Manufactured in the United States of America
10 9 8 7 6 5 4 3 2 1
Library of Congress Cataloging-in-Publication Data
Scott, Kieran, 1974–
He's so not worth it / Kieran Scott. — 1st ed.
p. cm.
Sequel to: She's so dead to us.
Summary: Told in two voices, Allie and Jake continue to be bombarded by family
issues and pressures from the "Cresties" and their poorer counterparts as they spend
a summer dealing with the fallout of their breakup.
ISBN 978-1-4169-9953-9 (hardcover)
[1. Interpersonal relations—Fiction. 2. Social classes—Fiction. 3. Dating (Social
customs)—Fiction. 4. Family life—New Jersey—Fiction. 5. New Jersey—Fiction.]
I. Title. II. Title: He is so not worth it.
PZ7.S42643Hes 2011
[Fic]—dc22
2010046494
ISBN 978-1-4169-9958-4 (eBook)

FIRST
EDITION

For Matt and Brady

Daily Field Journal of Annie Johnston
Saturday, June 26

Position: Golf cart parked across the circle from the entrance of the Orchard Hill Country Club/Shannen Moore's birthday extravaganza.

Cover: If anyone asks, I lost a diamond earring while out on the links today and I'm checking all the carts before busting out the metal detector on the back nine.

Observations:

10:05 p.m.: Subject Chloe Appleby exits the front door in tears. Uniform: pink dress, high heels, party hair. The two lazing valets hop to attention. One reaches out to her for a ticket, which she doesn't have. Subject Hammond Ross drove her, of course. Subject Chloe starts back inside, thinks better of it, takes a step toward the parking lot, turns a heel, and almost goes down. One of the valets gamely grabs her arm and keeps her from hitting her butt. (Assessment: Subjects Chloe and Hammond had a fight. A big one.)

10:06 p.m.: Subject Hammond Ross comes barreling through the door in a panic. Uniform: Hugo Boss pinstripe suit, pink tie. Dutifully matching the girlfriend, of course. He sees the valet holding on to Subject Chloe and tears her away. She shoves him and shouts, but I can't make it out from this distance. (Note: I briefly consider firing up the golf cart and gunning it across the sea of marigolds at the center of the circle to get within hearing distance, but fear that might attract a bit too much attention.)

10:07 p.m.: Subject Chloe slaps Subject Hammond across the face so hard I can see the fingerprint-shaped marks from here. (Note: Keep the camera phone on at all times, idiot!)

10:08 p.m.: Subjects Mr. and Mrs. Appleby finally appear from inside. Subject Mr. Appleby has a few stern words for Subject Hammond, who skulks back inside. The valet has the Applebys' car for them in approximately seven and a half seconds. The Applebys peel out. (Query: What the hell did Hammond do in there?)

10:09 p.m.: Ally Ryan walks out with her mother and Subject Gray Nathanson. None of them are speaking. Ally looks like she just ate a bug. She keeps swallowing over and over again like she's trying to keep it down. The valet gets Subject Dr. Nathanson's car in approximately eight and a half seconds, and they're gone as well. (Query: WTF is going on and what does Ally have to do with it?)

10:10 p.m.: I try Ally's cell phone. It goes straight to voice mail.

10:15 p.m.: Subject Jake Graydon jogs out and looks both ways, then talks to the valets and runs a hand over his hair. He tugs out his cell phone and dials, holds it to his ear for a split second, then curses. He tries again. Same result. (Assessment: He's trying to call the same person I'm trying to call.)

10:20 p.m.: Subject Jake gives up and hands the valet his ticket. The valet gets his car in approximately two minutes. (Note: Response time is clearly slower for the children of the members than for the members themselves.) Subject Jake's taillights hesitate at the end of the long drive. And hesitate. And hesitate. Finally he turns right, headed for the crest. Headed away from Ally. (Assessment: I missed something huge. Note: Next year, get an invite to Shannen Moore's birthday party.)

Ally

I had imagined my reunion with my father so many times over the past two years, I had every last detail down. I knew how many breaths of surprise I'd take upon seeing him. How long my strides would be as I raced across the distance that separated us and into his arms. I knew that he'd pick me up and twirl me around exactly three times before setting me down again, pushing my hair back from my face, and saying, "I missed you, bud."

In my mind, it had always looked like some sappy Disney movie. Him with a big, toothy grin. Me with my feet kicked up, my skirt flying. The sun was always shining and the birds were serenading us with a happy tune. It was the kind of scene that would bring tears to moviegoers' eyes everywhere.

Except I didn't actually wear a lot of skirts. And the sun had gone down hours ago. Plus, the only sound outside the car was the annoying beeping of a truck backing up. Also, it had never occurred to me that when we all saw each other again, no one would feel like smiling. In fact, the moment I spotted my dad on the front steps of the condo my mother and I shared in the Orchard View Condominium community, all I could imagine doing was shoving him as hard as I could.

"Oh my God," my mother said from the front passenger seat. Outside the window, my dad slowly rose to his feet. He was wearing pressed khakis and a crisp, white button down with varied stripes. His salt-and-pepper hair was cropped short on the sides and pushed back from his face on top. His shoes gleamed, and he wore the silver and gold Rolex my mother's father had given him on the day of their wedding. Since leaving Orchard Hill in shame and destitution two years ago, my mom had sold most of her good jewelry to help pay the bills. Apparently that plan had never occurred to my dad. "I'm not really seeing this," my mother said. "Tell me I'm not seeing this."

Her hands shook as she reached for the clasp on her seat belt.

"Melanie, just take a breath and calm down," her boyfriend, Gray Nathanson, said. He put the car in park and covered her fingers with his large hand. "You don't want the first thing you say to him to be something you'll regret."

"Something I'll regret?" My mother's voice sounded like it was coming to us through a tin can tunnel. "I'm not going to say anything. I'm just going to kill the bastard."

Yeah. A Disney movie this was not.

Gray said my mother's name, but she was already out of the car. I found I couldn't move; my legs had gone dead. I watched through the window of Gray's luxury SUV as my father's eyes followed my mother's approach and suddenly registered fear.

"How could you?" my mother screeched, slamming his chest with both hands. Like mother like daughter. My dad staggered back a couple of steps and Gray hustled out of the car.

"Wait here," he said to me, slamming the door shut behind him.

For some reason, that directive was what finally got me moving. I undid my seat belt and scrambled out onto the pavement. A couple of lights flickered to life around me, and I saw concerned neighbors peeking through the slats of their blinds. Great. I gave it five minutes before the Orchard Hill Police Department descended on my little family reunion. As if there hadn't already been enough humiliation tonight.

"Gray? What the hell are you doing with Gray Nathanson?" my father said as I approached.

Gray had one hand on my dad's chest, holding him back as my father talked about him like he wasn't even there.

"What the hell am I—? Are you kidding me, Christopher? Where the hell have *you* been for the last two years? Who the hell have *you* been with?" my mother shouted.

"I haven't been with anyone! I've been trying to get my life back together!" my father shouted back.

"Oh really? That's funny! Because I thought your life was with us! Have you been here all this time and I've just missed you somehow?"

Gray put his other hand on my mother's shoulder. "Why don't we all just calm down, go inside, and—"

"I have a better idea. Why don't you shut the fuck up and let me talk to my wife?" my father demanded, shoving Gray off of him.

Gray finally lost his composure. His face turned purple and his fists clenched, the tendons in his neck stuck out. My heart thumped with panic. My dad was tall and toned, but thin. Not exactly the fistfighting type. Gray worked out every day and was a lot stronger-looking than my dad. If hooks and jabs started flying, my father would be toast. I had to do something.

"Dad?" I croaked.

All three of them turned to look at me. They had clearly forgotten I was there. Gray's fists relaxed. My mother's eyes flooded with tears. My dad blew out a breath, tilted his head, and said, "Hey, bud."

He even managed to smile. It was almost exactly like I'd imagined it. Except—

"No!" my mother shouted, slicing a finger through the air. "*No!* You do not get to call her 'bud.' You don't even get to *look* at her! Not after you haven't so much as called her for her birthday or for Christmas or for *anything* in the past two years! Not after what happened to her tonight, thanks to you." My mother was hysterical now, the tears streaming down her face as she blindly, haphazardly groped for my hand.

My dad's face was blank at first, then concerned. "Wait . . . what happened to her tonight?" He repeated. "What do you mean 'What happened to her tonight'?"

Nothing much. I was just completely blindsided and humiliated when Shannen Moore played a video at her birthday party for half the junior and senior class and most of my mom and dad's former friends to see. A video of her, Faith Kirkpatrick, Hammond Ross, and Jake Graydon "happening upon" my father as he worked behind the counter at a deli in New York City. Up until the moment it unfolded on the huge screen over the dance floor, I'd had no clue where my father had been for the past two years, whether he was alive or dead, whether he'd . . . I don't know . . . gotten himself a new identity and moved to Paraguay. I found out at the exact same time as everyone else in the room that he'd been slinging bologna less than fifty miles away all this time. Just making sandwiches and pouring coffee and wiping counters. Living life as if my mother and I had never existed.

Wait, strike that. A few people had known *before* me.

Namely, the people in the video, who had filmed it last winter: Shannen, Faith, Hammond, and Jake.

"We are going inside now. *We* are." My mother grabbed Gray's hand as well and basically yanked us both up the stairs. She fumbled with her keys until Gray finally took them from her and opened the door. He ushered me inside ahead of him while my mother let the screen door crash behind us. She turned around and glared down at my father, who, at that moment, looked smaller than he ever had in my life. "You can stay out there and rot."

I watched my father as the door closed on his stricken, disappointed face. My mother ran to her room and slammed that door as well, leaving me and Gray alone in our cramped entryway. He put his hands in his pockets and looked out the tiny window set high in the door.

"No one would blame you if you wanted to go out there and talk to him," he said.

"Oh really? I think my mom would disagree," I replied, somehow speaking past the thick, wet paper towel that had jammed itself in my throat.

"She's just upset right now," Gray said. "But he's your father. She knows you two should have a relationship."

I swallowed hard. There was a long, skinny window of cut glass next to the front door, which you could only see through if you angled your eye just right, and even then you could only catch a sliver of the outside world. I stood on my toes and tilted my head to see my father frustratedly pacing in our parking lot. He moved out of view, then back again. Covered his face with his hands, muttered something under his breath. Finally, he turned and walked away, toward the exit of the complex, whipping out a cell phone as he went.

Just like that. He was here and then he was gone again.

"I think I'll just go to bed," I said weakly.

Gray gave me a sympathetic smile. He looked like he maybe wanted to reach out and squeeze my shoulder, and I was relieved when he restrained himself. I liked the guy, but I didn't much want anyone touching me at that moment. Definitely not a father figure touching me in a fatherly way. Not now.

I walked to my room, closed the door, and sank down onto the edge of my bed, clutching the blanket at my sides. I was still wearing the black cocktail dress I'd bought specifically for Shannen's party and I suddenly felt like tearing it off my body in shreds. What a waste of a week's paycheck. I couldn't believe I had been so naïve. So stupid and gullible and oblivious. Less than five hours ago I'd been standing in front of the mirror in this very room, grinning at my reflection, giddily anticipating Jake Graydon's arrival so he could squire me off to the biggest party of the year. Five hours ago Jake was my almost-boyfriend. Five hours ago I was almost friends with Shannen and Hammond and Chloe Appleby again. Five hours ago life was on its way to being good. It was on its way to being great. One might even say perfect.

It is amazing how in five short hours, everything completely and irrevocably turned to crap.

Daily Field Journal of Annie Johnston
Sunday, June 27

Position: Window stool at the Apothecary.

Cover: Trying out tinted moisturizer at the counter. Oddly (and to the saleslady's obvious annoyance), none seem to exactly match my skin tone. Perhaps because the cheapest three-ounce bottle is priced at $22.50.

Observations:

1:05 p.m.: Subject Chloe Appleby arrives. Uniform: pink skirt, white T-shirt, silver thongs, ponytail, larger sunglasses than usual. (Assessment: Clearly mourning the death of her relationship with Hammond. Note: Confirmation of this was all over Twitter this morning. Ally has still not answered her phone.) Subject walks to the sunscreen aisle, stops, and stares at a Clinique bottle. (Note: Shisheido is her brand of choice. Assessment: She's not handling this breakup well.)

1:21 p.m.: Subject Chloe Appleby still staring at Clinique bottle. Subject Shannen Moore arrives. Uniform: cutoff shorts, rubber thongs, wrinkled Three Dots T. Subject freezes when she sees Subject Chloe, turns around, and walks out. Subject Chloe never sees her. Unless she hid her reaction behind those big-ass glasses and just faked it. (Assessment: Chloe totally saw her.)

1:45 p.m.: Subject Chloe has replaced Clinique bottle and moved on to nail polish. Subject Hammond Ross walks by the window. Uniform: plaid shorts, polo shirt, Nike sport sandals. Subject Hammond spots Subject Chloe. He stops. Turns. Hesitates. Walks in. Subject Hammond approaches his prey.

Hammond: "Hey, babe."

Subject Chloe slams the NARS bottle she was considering down on the shelf and storms out. Several jars hit the floor and two of them break, ruining Subject Hammond's Nikes. Pinched-face saleslady forces Subject Hammond to pay for two sixteen-dollar bottles of nail polish. He shoves the door open so hard on the way out, it smacks against the window, and the Botoxed customer next to me actually changes expression.

(Personal Note: It's a good day.)

Ally

"Don't worry, bud. I have a plan."

My father sat down on one of the two stools at the breakfast bar in the one-bedroom apartment he'd invited me to come check out with him in downtown Orchard Hill. The stools were the only furniture in the entire place and the one he'd chosen tipped as he sat down on it, the legs clearly uneven. The kitchen behind him had four cabinets, one stove, and no dishwasher, and the living room carpet was dotted with several nonspecific stains. Still, my dad had just signed the lease that now sat on the countertop next to him, so apparently this square apartment, those ancient stools, and even the scary stains were somehow part of his plan.

"A plan for what?" I said.

For explaining why you left? Or why you're back? A plan for winning Mom back? For getting her to break up with Gray? For winning *me* back? The words were on the tip of my tongue, but my lips wouldn't open. I'd always been able to talk to my dad about anything. Just not, apparently, the most important things of all.

"A plan for getting our lives back to the way they're supposed to be," he said, rubbing his hands together.

"Oh," I said. "Right."

I leaned back against the whitewashed wall of the living area, trying to figure out where to look. I couldn't believe I felt this awkward around my dad. But then, when you don't see someone for two years and they suddenly step back into your life, I suppose awkward makes sense. For so long I had wished he would come home, but now I could hardly wrap my brain around the fact that he was here.

"First of all, I've got a new job. Two new jobs, actually," he said. "Charles Appleby has decided to open a day-trader's shop and he's asked me to come on board. I'll be starting at the bottom, of course, re-proving myself, but at least it's a foot in the door. But before I can start making trades I have to retake my Series Seven Exam, which means taking night classes, so in the meantime I've landed a gig as manager at Jump, Java, and Wail!"

I stared at my father. He couldn't be serious. He was going to be working at the coffee shop where everyone from school and their parents bought their soy lattes and triple-shot espressos every day? Where the people whose money he'd lost two years ago—most of whom, by the way, had *not* gotten over losing it—popped by for their morning cup of joe? Did he not see a problem with this plan?

"You're kidding," I said finally, because I had to say something.

"I know. Charlie's been amazing these past couple of years," my father said, missing my point entirely. "He's really been a true friend to me, putting me up in the city . . . giving me that job at the deli. And when I came to him a couple of months ago and told him I was going to try to start over, he really listened to what I had to say. It means a lot that he's willing to give me this second chance."

It was so ironic I wanted to laugh. Chloe's dad listening, giving him a second chance. Meanwhile, when I tried to explain to Chloe what had happened between me and Hammond over two years ago—why we'd kissed and how it had meant nothing—she didn't want to hear a word.

"Um, yeah, that's amazing," I said.

I slowly crossed the room to the wall of windows—the tiny place's best feature—which overlooked Orchard Avenue. Mature trees lined the sidewalks and there were flower boxes in front of almost every window. Down below, a white Mercedes pulled into a parallel parking space, hit the curb, pulled up and back, hit the curb again, then stopped. A woman got out, her dark hair perfectly framing her tan face and gold sunglasses. She looked at her back tire, which was half on the sidewalk, muttered something under her breath, and stormed through the front door of the Apothecary, which was right beneath my feet.

The Apothecary, where all the wealthy Crestie moms went to procure their night creams and cellulite solutions and magic age-reversing vitamins.

"And then, once I pass my Series Seven, I can start trading full time, making back all the money I lost," my dad continued, strolling over to join me. "Who knows? Maybe one day we can even get our old house back."

My throat closed over and I hiccup-coughed into my hand. Jake Graydon and his family were currently living in our old house. I had a sudden vision of me reclaiming my old bedroom and tossing Jake's stuff out onto the street, while he looked on, all helpless and dejected. In my current frame of mind, the image was highly gratifying. Impossible, I knew, but gratifying.

"Shouldn't you be telling Mom all this?" I said, glancing up at my dad.

"I should be telling both of you all this," my father said,

putting his arm around my back and his hand on my shoulder. "Unfortunately, your mother won't answer my calls."

I shrugged away from him, and his face fell, but just for a moment. "So . . . what? You want *me* to tell her all this?" I asked, sounding belligerent.

"No. Of course not." He took the apartment keys out of the pocket of his gray pants and fiddled with them. "Though it might be nice if you could, possibly, convince her to call me."

My teeth clenched as a surge of anger coursed through me. I turned to the window again and held my breath for as long as I could. I *was not* this person. I had spent the last two and a half years trying as hard as I could not to be this person. Trying not to think about my dad at all. Because whenever I did think about him, I felt this awful mix of rage and confusion and longing and sadness and insecurity burning inside my stomach. So I had just . . . put it aside. I'd just not let myself go there. And I'd become *so* good at it—the not thinking. So good that I'd actually been able to fool the world into believing I was a perfectly normal, well-adjusted, happy human being. I'd even kind of convinced myself.

But now that he was here, it was impossible not to think about everything that had happened. And that meant feeling it. All of it. All the time. Well-adjusted? Ha. Try malfunctioning.

My life was a total and complete wreck because of him. All my old friends hated me, which wouldn't have even mattered if I still had Jake, but that blew up in my face, thanks to my dad, too. And now, what? He was asking me to do him a favor?

The thing was, I'd also missed him. I'd missed him every single day and had daydreamed every other hour about what it would be like when he came back. And now here he was.

So how was I supposed to deal with it? Was I supposed to be angry or happy? Excited or indifferent? Because right now, I was everything.

I took a deep breath and tried to relax. Tried to choose to be hopeful. Because if he'd come back now with this elaborate plan, he must be serious about staying. He must be serious about trying to get things back to the way they'd been before—back when we were all one happy family. That was what I decided to believe.

"I like the view," I said, changing the subject.

You could see the spire of the Episcopal Church down on the other side of Oak Street, which cornered the building, and the hills beyond were all green and rolling, like something out of a Thoreau poem.

"It's nice, isn't it?" he said.

On the sidewalk down below, Quinn Nathanson and her friend Lindsey walked along eating frozen yogurt, shopping bags swinging from their wrists, totally carefree. At that very moment, Quinn's dad, Gray, and my mom were out shopping for new bedding for Gray's shore house. For his bed. The bed they would share for the summer.

Puke.

Every time I thought about the two of them together—the way they held each other's hands during dinner, how they were always exchanging knowing looks, how he touched the small of her back whenever they walked through a door together—I felt an awful panic rising up in my throat. Maybe I didn't feel like doing my father any favors, but I had a bad feeling that my mother wasn't going to be picking up the phone to talk to him on her own any time soon. And with Gray in the picture, the longer my mom and dad didn't talk, the worse off we all were.

"Okay," I said with a sigh. "I'll talk to her for you."

"Thanks, bud." He leaned in and kissed the top of my head. "So!" He clapped his hands together and took a step back. "How's everything been? How was school this year? I hope you're still playing basketball." He walked over to the counter again and picked up the lease.

"Yep. We had a good season."

"And school?"

"It was . . . good," I lied.

Except for the last few days. If I could just go back and make the last few days un-happen, I'd be fine. Then I wouldn't go to Shannen's party, she wouldn't show that awful video, I'd never know that Jake knew all along where my dad was and didn't tell me, and Jake and I would be together and happy right now, planning our two months down the shore.

I opened my mouth, the fourteen-year-old in me—the one whose dad was her best friend—wanting to pour it all out to him. To tell him what had happened with the Cresties and with Jake Graydon, the guy who'd crushed my heart and had yet to call, text, or even e-mail to apologize. But I forced my lips shut again. Because I wasn't that fourteen-year-old girl anymore. And he wasn't my best friend anymore either.

My dad shoved the papers into a brown leather messenger bag. I tugged my cell phone out of my pocket and checked the screen for messages. Not a one. Not from Jake, not from Chloe, not from anyone.

"And I hear you're going to be spending the summer down the shore?"

His voice was excited. Maybe too excited. Like he was

trying too hard to sound okay with it. I guess when you come back to town to win your family back it's kind of a bummer to hear they're moving away for two months. I wondered how he'd heard. Probably from Mrs. Appleby. The woman did love to gossip. I wondered why she hadn't told him about Gray. Probably didn't want to spoil the delicious surprise. Evil witch. I swallowed hard and tucked the phone away.

"I don't really want to go," I told him.

Understatement city. I loathed the idea of going down the shore, of spending the summer watching my mom and Gray live like a couple, of hanging out with the Cresties every day—them thinking I wanted to be there, that I still wanted, on any level, for them to accept me as one of their own again. Because I didn't. I was over it. Why I'd ever wanted any of them back in my life was beyond me.

But worst of all I'd have to see Jake all the time and deal with that spirit-shattering awkwardness. Deciding whether or not to go places based on whether or not he would be there. What to wear, how to act, what to say. Ugh.

"But Mom is going so . . . I guess I have to."

Suddenly, my father's face lit up. "Or maybe not."

"What?"

"You could stay here!" he said, his eyes sparkling. "With me!"

I stared at him, feeling a quick flutter of excitement. If he was inviting me to stay, then he couldn't be planning on bailing again, right? "Really?"

"Yeah!" He dropped his messenger bag and walked a few paces past me toward the bedroom. "You could have the bedroom for the summer and I'll sleep on the couch." He laughed and put his hands on his hips. "When I get one."

My throat tightened suddenly. I saw the entire summer play out before my eyes. Me and my dad in this tiny apartment, having shallow conversations and pretending everything was fine. Me wondering if he was ever going to explain. Him constantly asking me how my mother was doing. The whole thing seemed uncomfortable and sad.

"Uh . . . yeah, I guess. I mean, I'll have to ask mom," I hedged.

"This is going to be so great!" My father walked over and enveloped me in a hug. His signature, tight, no-holds-barred hug. He smelled different and suddenly it hit me like a speeding car to the chest. He'd been out there somewhere, all this time, working and talking to people and smiling at strangers and smelling of new cologne. All this time he'd been out there and I'd just been here. Waiting for him. When he released me, I felt relieved. "I'll call your mom and leave her a message. Since we both know she won't pick up," he joshed, as if we were old pals telling an inside joke about a third buddy of ours.

"Um, okay," I heard myself say.

"Great. We'll spend the whole summer hanging out, catching up. We can go fishing! It'll be just like old times."

My dad walked into the kitchen, pulling out his phone. I turned toward the window again and leaned my forehead against the cool glass. The Mercedes woman got in her car with her pink paper Apothecary bag, slammed the door, and peeled out, almost taking out a lady with a jogging stroller in the crosswalk.

A summer down the shore with all my sworn enemies a shell's throw away, or a summer in this apartment with the man I wasn't entirely sure I could trust. As I heard my father start to leave a voice mail on my mother's phone, I started to wonder . . .

Was there an option C?

Jake

Before Ally Ryan moved back to Orchard Hill, I never didn't know what to do. Now it was all the time. It was like I *always* didn't know what to do.

And it was starting to piss me off.

Like, was I supposed to call her, or not call her? She'd told me she didn't want to see me anymore. Did she mean it? Or was I supposed to, like, go after her? And if that's what I was supposed to do, did I really want to be that guy? The guy who begged a girl to take him back?

The only thing I knew for sure was that every night I did want to be that guy. Lying in my bed, listening to the crickets, thinking about what she was doing, I was like, *Fuck it, just call her.* Then every morning, I'd wake up and be relieved I hadn't done it. Because Jake Graydon doesn't beg for girls. What was I thinking?

Then I'd spend all day obsessing about her, and as soon as I was in bed again, the cycle started all over.

As I drove over to Hammond Ross's house the Monday after the shit hit the fan, all I could think about was the cycle. And whether or not I had the balls to break it. It had been about forty-eight hours since my best friend Shannen Moore had shown that video of us finding Ally's dad at that deli in the city. Forty-eight hours since she'd made me look like some kind of lying, secret-keeping jerk to Ally, then told me she basically did it because *she* liked me. Yeah, that part I definitely was not ready to deal with. But I was starting to sort of feel like I could maybe talk to Ally.

Possibly.

"S'up, man?" Hammond loped across his front yard and got into the passenger seat of my Jeep. His blond hair looked longer than it had during the school year, and he was already tan. "Why are we driving to Faith's again?"

"Because we can," I said.

He smirked. Fist bump. "Nice."

Ever since I got the Jeep for my seventeenth birthday I drove wherever I could. I would've driven from my door to the mailbox to get the mail if my mother didn't pounce on it the second it came. I hit the gas and two seconds later we were pulling up in front of Faith's house. When I swung the car into the driveway, I saw that Chloe Appleby's white convertible was there too.

"Shit," Hammond said. "Did you know she was coming?"

"Faith said it was just us," I told him.

I should've known something was up when Faith had called me that afternoon. She'd never called me before unless she was trying to track down someone else. The story was, her mother had all these leftovers from a church thing she'd hosted and she wanted us to come over so they wouldn't go to waste. Had she invited Chloe, too, or had Chloe just shown up? Hammond made no move to get out of the car, so I didn't kill the engine.

"You talk to Chloe yet?" I asked.

"Once," he said. He reached forward and picked at some invisible speck on my dashboard with his thumbnail. "Long enough for her to officially dump my ass."

There was an odd twist in my chest. "Sorry, man."

"I can't believe she broke up with me because I kissed some girl two years ago," he said. He shoved himself back in the seat, his hands limp in his lap.

Again, the twist. Hammond hadn't just kissed some girl. He'd kissed Ally Ryan.

Two years ago, I said to myself. *Before she even knew you existed.* For some reason, it still didn't make me feel better.

"She didn't even let me explain what happened," Hammond said. "She could've at least heard me out."

That was what I was afraid of, why I really hadn't called Ally. Because I didn't want her to just hang up on me. I wanted her to let me explain. And I was scared shitless that she wouldn't let me. That we were so far gone, she wouldn't even listen. And if we were that far gone, I didn't want to know.

Which made me a wuss. Which also pissed me off.

"Come on, dude. Let's go in," I said, turning off the engine. "Get it over with."

Hammond stared at the arced, red front door of Faith's stone house. "Yeah. Yeah. All right."

We got out and walked inside without knocking. The only door we ever knocked on was Shannen's, and that was only because she never wanted anyone to come in, so she only ever came out. The lights were on down in the kitchen, and the door to the basement was open. We heard voices from the top of the stairs. Hammond looked like he wanted to be somewhere else, so I figured I should go first. I jogged down the steps and suddenly wished I was, too. Because Chloe wasn't the only surprise guest. Shannen was there also.

"Dudes! Faith got the new Extreme Sports!" Todd Stein stood up from the wraparound couch with an Xbox controller.

"Get your asses over here so we can school you," his twin brother Trevor said.

Todd was in brown shorts and an orange T-shirt. Trevor was in orange shorts and a brown T-shirt. Their blond hair stuck out all over, like they'd just woken up, which considering summer had started, was completely possible. Trevor popped a mini quiche into his mouth, then laughed, showing us the mangled bits of food on his tongue. So at least the claim of leftovers was real.

"What's up with them?" I asked, lifting my chin.

In the corner by Faith's prized dollhouse, Faith gestured at Chloe, whose eyes were on the floor, and Shannen, whose eyes were on me.

I sat down next to Todd and looked at the TV.

"Chick drama," Todd said, tossing me the third controller. On the screen, two snowboarders raced down a slalom hill.

Hammond was still at the bottom of the stairs. Now he made his move, walking slowly across the carpeted room. Todd and Trevor shouted in protest as he blocked their game for a split second, but he didn't notice or care. When he got to the girls, Faith stopped yammering and, aside from Trevor and Todd's chewing and the sound effects coming through the surround sound, the place was silent.

"Chloe, can I talk to you?"

"Does he really need to be here?" Chloe asked Faith. She didn't even look at Hammond.

Faith bit her lip, fiddling with her car keys for some reason. "Come on, Chloe. Can't you at least just talk to him?"

"Fine." Chloe rolled her eyes and scoffed. She grabbed her bag off the couch and started for the door. "If he's staying, I'm leaving."

"Chloe, wait," Faith called.

Chloe stopped right in front of the TV and Todd's boarder hit a tree.

"Oh, man! What the hell, Chloe?"

I paused the game.

"Look, I didn't come here to be ambushed," Chloe said, whirling on Faith. "You said it was going to be just the two of us. Then *she* walks in." She gestured at Shannen with her bag. "And now Hammond? What are you trying to do?"

"I'm trying to keep the group from completely self-destructing! Doesn't anybody care about that but me?" Faith said, turning her palms out. Her long blond hair hung down around her shoulders and for once in her life, she wasn't wearing two tons of makeup. Even her outfit was different from usual. Plain brown shorts and a white tank top. No popsicle-colored minidress or too-hip jewelry or ridiculous heels. "If it makes you feel any better, I told the guys it would be just them, and Shannen, too. None of them knew."

"Oh, good. So you're the only liar in the room," Chloe said, crossing her arms over her chest. "Oh, wait! Shannen and Hammond already *proved* they were liars."

"Chloe—," Shannen began.

"No. You don't even talk to me," Chloe said, lifting one finger from her bag. "You knew for two years that my boyfriend cheated on me, but you never felt the need to tell me until it fit into one of your stupid anti-Ally plots."

Then she turned on Hammond. "And you . . . you've liked her all this time, haven't you?" Her bottom lip trembled so badly I felt embarrassed. "What was I, just some, like, pseudo-Ally? Someone to hang out with while you pined and prayed for her to come back?"

Hammond's jaw was set as he stared at Chloe. Was that true? Did he still like Ally?

"That's not how it is," he said. "You know it's not."

He tried to take her hand, but she snatched it away.

"I don't know anything, obviously," she said. Then she took in a breath. "Thanks a lot, Faith. I didn't have enough public humiliation this week. I really appreciate it."

She stormed up the stairs and a few seconds later the front door slammed.

Faith looked like she was about to cry.

"I think I'm gonna walk home," Hammond said.

I started to get up from the couch. "I'll take you."

"Guys, come on," Faith said. Pleaded, really. "I still have the food, and I really—"

But Hammond was already gone. I stood up straight. The idea of staying here with Shannen, who I had nothing to say to, and a tearful Faith was not happening.

"I'd better go," I said. "Sorry Faith."

And I was out. On my way to the door, I heard Todd ask if it was okay if they kept playing.

Outside, Hammond was nowhere to be seen. Chloe's car was gone. I got in the Jeep and reversed out of the driveway. As I drove down the hill toward town, I suddenly knew for absolute sure that I had to call Ally. Of everyone I knew, she was the only person I actually *wanted* to hang out with. Who cared if I had to grovel to be with her? What was that old saying? Something about the ends justifying the means? At the first stoplight I came to, I grabbed my phone and let my thumb hover over the A button. But I froze.

I couldn't do it. I was too fucking scared. God, I hated myself.

The light turned green. Cursing under my breath, I dropped the phone on the passenger seat and hit the gas.

Daily Field Journal of Annie Johnston
Tuesday, June 29

Location: Orchard Hill Country Club lobby.

Cover: Applying for a summer job as a ball girl. As if I'd ever show that much leg

Observations:

10:01 a.m.: Subject Faith Kirkpatrick arrives. Uniform: gauzy, see-through cover-up, silver sandals, string bikini, huge straw sun hat. Subject strides past without seeing me. (Note: I am, after all, invisible.) At end of hallway leading to locker room, Subjects Corrine Law (graduated senior) and Tiara Weston (finished freshman year at Duke by the skin of her teeth [see random gossip item #142 in appendix B]). Subject Faith gives them a bright "Hi, guys!" Subjects Corrine and Tiara reply with less enthusiastic "hi's" and keep walking. Subject Faith visibly embarrassed, proceeds to locker room. (Assessment: Faith is a loser among Cresties. Personal Note: Payback's a bitch.)

Location: Orchard Hill Country Club poolside.

Cover: Applying for a summer job as a lifeguard. As if I can swim.

Observations:

10:31 a.m.: Subject Faith lies on a lounge chair. She takes out her phone and dials.

Faith: "Hi, Chloe! I'm at the club pool! Come by if you get a chance! I have prime real estate between the snack bar and the warm water corner! Call me!"

Subject hangs up. Frowns. Dials again.

Faith: "Hi, Shannen! What are you doing later? We should get together before I leave for the shore! Call me!"

Subject hangs up. Frowns some more. Dials.

Faith: "Hammond! It's Faith! Come to the club pool! That lifeguard you guys like is on duty! Bring the twins! Call me!"

Subject hangs up. She looks at her phone. Considers. Sighs. Places it next to her thigh. (Note: It needs to be in grabbing distance for all the callbacks she's not going to get.) Subjects Corinne and Tiara walk by. Neither acknowledges Subject Faith. (Assessment: Faith Kirkpatrick has no friends. Also, she's destined for frown lines. Personal Note: Nice.)

Jake

"Jake? Can I see you for a moment, please?"

My mother stood at the door of my room. There was a piece of paper in her hand. I had no idea what it was, but there was something ominous about it.

"What's up?" I asked.

"Downstairs."

She turned around and went. Yeah. Very not good. I shoved myself off my bed and followed, walking through the cloud of flowery perfume that always trailed her. Her jewel-covered flip-flops left tiny footprints in the heavy carpeting of the hallway and made slapping sounds as she walked down the stairs. Why did I suddenly feel like those slapping sounds were the soundtrack of doom?

In the kitchen, my mother walked to the other side of the island and placed the paper down in front of me. Now I could see it was my report card.

Shit.

"Three Cs, a C minus, one B, and an A," she said. "In gym."

The dark red helmet of her hair kind of trembled. Never a good sign.

"Yeah, but that C minus was totally unfair," I said, leaning forward into the island across from her. "Mr. Caswell is a complete douche."

My mother flinched. "Language."

"Sorry. It's just—"

She held up her hand. The huge diamond on her ring finger

31

swung around to face me. "Jake, I just talked to your father and we've decided that there's only one thing we can do here."

"What?" I swallowed hard.

"You're grounded."

"What!?"

"For the summer."

"*What!?*"

Grounded for the summer? What did that even mean?

"No more Mrs. Nice Guy, Jake," she said, walking over to the fridge and yanking it open. She took out the glass pitcher filled to the brim with water, ice, and sliced lemon, then let the door slam. "Between this report card and your SATs, you're going to be lucky to get into Bergen Community next year, let alone Fordham."

"But mom—"

"There are no buts here," my mother said. The ice tinkled as she set the pitcher down on the counter. "It's about time you start taking your life seriously. I've already called this new SAT tutor Connor's mother recommended and secured her services for the summer, and tomorrow morning you're going to go out and get a job."

I blinked. She might as well have just dumped the whole pitcher over my head. "A job?"

"We need to prove to the admissions people that you're a serious, well-rounded person." She turned her ring back around so the rock was face up, then laid her hands down flat on the granite counter. The lights overhead were reflected in her shiny pink and white fingernails. "In this economy, sloth is frowned upon, Jake. You need to show them you're willing to work for what you get."

She wasn't making any sense. "But I can't go out and get a job here. We're leaving for the shore on Thursday."

My mother cleared her throat and turned her back to me, plucking a glass out of the cabinet. Everything inside me sank.

"Mom, you can't—"

"Your *brother* is leaving for the shore on Thursday," she said. Her hand shook a little as she closed the cabinet door. She paused for a minute and drew herself up before turning around again. Like she was gathering her strength for the boxing ring. "He's going to be staying with Jason's family, and your father will go down some weekends. We, however, will be staying here."

"No," I said. I walked around the island and stood in front of her. She held on to her glass, touching the opening at the top with her flat palm over and over, like she was playing a bongo. "Mom, no. You can't ground me from the shore."

"Do you think this is fun for me, Jake?" There was something almost menacing in her eyes and she spoke through her teeth. "If you can't go, I can't go."

Yeah. Mom was not happy. If she had to stay here with me it meant losing out on quality bonding time with all her Crestie girlfriends. The lobster bakes, the sailing trips, the farmers' markets. She lived for that shit. So maybe, just maybe, all she needed was a push in the right direction.

"Well then forget about this and let's both go!" I said, already seeing three moves ahead—and I never saw three moves ahead. "I can get an SAT tutor down there! I can get a job down there!"

"And you'll also be up all night partying with your friends and running around meeting girls," my mother shot back. She set the glass down, braced her hands on the granite for a moment, then poured herself some water. "No way, Jake," she said resolutely. "There are just too many distractions down the shore. I need you focused this summer."

She picked up her drink and started for the sliding doors, which led to our patio and pool. I walked over to the table and dropped down in the nearest chair. My hands propped up my head as I stared through the glass top at my bare feet. This had to be a nightmare.

"Oh, and I also signed you up for an American Literature class at BCC," she said. "It starts in a couple of weeks and according to your vice principal, if you ace that, they'll change your C minus to a B plus for the year."

I let my hands drop. "So while all of my friends are down the shore surfing, partying, and hanging out, I'm going to be working, studying, and reading?"

"If you wanted to have fun this summer, you should have worked harder during the year," she said flatly.

"If you'd warned me this was going to happen, maybe I would have."

She shook her head. Smiled like I was so stupid. "Well, then consider this a warning for next year."

I glared after her as she walked off toward the pool. This could not be happening. I was not going to spend my entire summer stuck here with her while Hammond, Chloe, Shannen, Faith, and Todd and Trevor were hanging out down the shore.

And Ally. There went any chance in hell I had of making up with Ally.

I shoved away from the table, grabbed my car keys, and stormed out the front door, slamming it so hard she'd be sure to hear, even all the way out back. It wasn't until my feet hit the pavement and their bottoms were scorched off that I realized I had no shoes on. Fuck it. I could drive without shoes.

As I floored it out the driveway, I almost careened into a white contractor's truck that was turning into Chloe's. The guy behind the wheel cursed at me, but I just kept going. All I wanted to do was go and see Ally.

I stopped at the bottom of Harvest Lane and cursed again. I couldn't go see Ally. She was five minutes away, but I couldn't go see her because Ally didn't want to see me.

I put the Jeep in park, slammed my hands against the wheel, and tried to breathe. The sun was beating down on my face, and when I looked at my reflection in the mirror, there were beads of sweat on my forehead.

This sucked. Everything, everything, everything sucked.

And now, even if a miracle happened and Ally and I made up, it wasn't going to be any five minute drive to see her. I was going to be three hours away from her all summer long.

Ally

"Dude, that is so not right," David Drake said, laughing through a mouthful of a Nathan's hamburger. Marshall Marino was dipping his onion rings into his Häagen Dazs coffee ice-cream shake and popping them, dripping wet, into his mouth. Disgusting. But oddly intriguing.

"You have no idea what you're missing, man," Marshall replied, slurping some shake off his chin.

Annie leaned her elbows on the table, shoving back her zillion rubber bracelets as if she was pushing up long sleeves.

For the past few days she'd been experimenting with dark eye shadow, so when she narrowed her eyes at Marshall, they almost disappeared. "Are you, perhaps . . . pregnant?"

David and I laughed as Marshall flung an onion ring at her. I sat back in my chair and sighed. This was what summer was all about. Hanging out in a frigidly air-conditioned mall, eating junk food with my friends. Not sitting in Gray's shore house listening to Quinn sing show tunes, watching Gray and my mom make out, wondering what new torture the Cresties were devising for me two houses down.

"What's your deal, Sigh-ey McGhee?" Annie asked.

"What?" I blinked and sat up straight.

"You just sighed, like, four times in a row," David pointed out.

Marshall confirmed with a nod of his head as he sucked half his shake down through the straw.

"I was just thinking . . . maybe if I stay with my dad, I could get a second job here," I said, leaning my elbows on the table. "I could just spend all my time out of the house, working, and kind of . . . power through the summer. Then, I not only wouldn't have to live with my Mom, Gray, and the cheerleader, I'd also barely have to deal with my dad and all the awkwardness."

Annie rolled her eyes as she sipped her soda. "That sounds like fun."

I rolled my eyes back and stole an onion ring from Marshall. "Well, I'd hang with you guys, too."

"I'm for that plan, then," Marshall said, giving me a joking wink.

"Your mom hasn't said anything to you about it yet?" David asked, his feet bouncing under the table.

I shook my head. "She said she got the message and we'd talk about it later. So now I'm both dreading and looking forward to *later*. Whenever that ends up being."

I had tried, as promised, to talk my mom into calling my dad and hearing him out—I had even hinted at his grand master plan—but my mother had basically shut me down. She'd said she would call my dad when she was good and ready. When I'd asked when that might be, she'd turned up the volume on the television so loud my eardrums hurt.

"Ally, all I'm hearing here is that you want to avoid all the conflicts in your life," Annie said, placing her soda on the table and lacing her fingers over her stomach.

"Oh, boy. Here we go." David crumpled a napkin. "This happens every summer. She's been watching *Dr. Phil* again."

"Shut it, Drake," Annie snapped, her eyes disappearing again. Then she looked at me, her expression eerily neutral. "What you need to ask yourself is (a) what do you really want? and (b) what do you need to do to get it?"

My smile faltered a bit. Because what I wanted was for my parents to get back together. And I wasn't going to get it if they were apart all summer, no matter what kind of plans my dad had up his sleeve.

"Can we go now?" I said, looking at the guys.

"Most definitely." Marshall rose from his chair, shooting Annie a disturbed look. She was still eyeing me carefully, as if waiting for me to bare my inner soul.

"You stop watching *Dr. Phil*," I admonished. "Cuz you're freaking me out right now."

Annie shook her head as she got up, sliding her tray from the table. "All I know is, if you don't talk to them soon, you're gonna bottle it all up till you pop. And when you pop, it's not gonna be pretty."

"Everyone always says that, but it's so not true," David said as he shoved his tray into the garbage. He'd cut his hair so short for the summer you could see his scalp, and it shone under the fluorescent lights. "I say, clam the hell up, put on a happy face, and get through the next year. Then you'll go away to college and you'll never have to see these people again."

"So . . . the approach your sister took," Annie said, sipping her soda while simultaneously emptying her tray.

David lifted his shoulders. "Yeah."

"The sister you never see and totally resent."

He blushed, but lifted his shoulders again. "Well, yeah."

"Sure. Good plan," Annie said, facetiously.

She dropped the tray atop the can with a clatter and turned, her plaid skirt flouncing behind her.

"I like David's plan," I said. "It lacks confrontation. And I, personally, am anticonfrontation."

"Speaking of confrontation . . . ," David said under his breath.

We all spotted her at the same moment. Faith Kirkpatrick. Her blond hair was back in a tight ponytail, and she wore a floral minidress that left zero to the imagination with a trendy little vest tossed over it. Her wedge sandals were so tall it was a miracle she hadn't bumped her head on the banner advertising the Books-A-Million summer reading sale. Dangling from one hand were her car keys, on a Coach leather key chain, even though she had a purse and all those shopping bags. As soon as she saw us, she stopped and almost tripped. Where the hell were Chloe and Shannen? I'd hardly ever seen Faith without them all year. They were like her permanent accessories.

"Hey, Ally," she said. Then she squinted briefly at my friends. "Guys."

For a moment I felt off balance. Like I'd slipped through a wormhole into an alternate reality. It was the first time she'd greeted me without an insult since I'd been back.

"Excuse me. I see that book I wanted to read," Annie said, grabbing David and Marshall's wrists. "You know, the one about the rich bitch who drops her best friend for no apparent reason and becomes a vapid airhead overnight? Let's go."

Faith shot Annie a sarcastic smile as she dragged the guys away. Annie and Faith had a bit of a history. As in, they used to be best friends until Faith decided it was more important to impress Chloe and Shannen and she dumped Annie like last year's It bag. And because of that three-year-old injustice, I was now without an entourage.

But Faith hadn't word-slain Annie, either. Which was also odd.

"So. What's up?" Faith asked casually. Like we were just two friends bumping into each other at the mall.

"Seriously?" I said, raising my eyebrows. I glanced past her at the crowd of hungry kids and harried moms, wishing she'd move on before her friends caught up with her. I didn't know whether I'd have to deal with Chloe or Shannen or both, but "none of the above" was the option that appealed. "You've been a bitch to me all year and you're leading with 'what's up?'"

"Ally, you know I had nothing to do with what Shannen did, right?" she said, sounding almost fed up. Like she was already over me accusing her, even though I'd yet to actually accuse her—of that anyway. "I mean, I was there when the thing was taped, but she never told me what she was going to do with it."

"But you knew it was nothing good," I said, crossing my arms over my chest.

"Well. It's Shannen," she replied under her breath, looking warily around as if the potted plant next to us had ears.

Translation: When Shannen decided to do something awful, there was no talking her out of it. Which wasn't the greatest excuse, but it was one we'd all used at some point in our lives.

Silence reigned. Faith twisted her ankle down and up, down and up, laying the side of her wedge sandal flat on the floor, then righting it again, over and over. She twisted her mouth into a sideways pucker. Her keys jangled as she scratched an itch above her eye.

"I'm really sorry, okay?" she said finally. "I *know* I've been a bitch to you. I know. I just . . . I was so mad at you. When you left it was like *there goes my best friend!* And then you never even called. And Chloe and Shannen basically ignored me for, like, *ever*. I was a complete outcast for, like, weeks. Which, by the way, is *not* fun. And then everything happened with my parents and I just . . . I hated you for not being here."

She tilted her head and gnawed on her bottom lip.

"None of that is my fault," I said. Except the not calling part. Which I used to feel guilty for. Until she sank her fangs into my neck my first night back in Orchard Hill last summer.

"I know! I know, okay?" she pleaded. "When I saw your face the night of Shannen's party. When she . . . you know . . . showed the thing?"

I narrowed my eyes. "Yeah . . . ?"

"Well, when I saw your face I realized . . . this whole thing sucks for you, too."

I bit back a sarcastic laugh. The girl was a genius!

"It's just, I never really thought about it that way before."

I supposed I shouldn't have been surprised. Empathy had never been Faith's strongest quality. She felt all her emotions to the ten-millionth degree, but rarely seemed to grasp the fact that other people had feelings too.

Suddenly I felt very, very tired. I found the nearest empty table and sat down. Faith followed me.

"So, do you hate me still?" she asked.

I looked up at her. Her blond hair was perfectly backlit by a spotlight to form a halo. Hilarious.

"I guess 'hate' is a strong word," I said.

The thing was, Faith always had been kind of a follower, and I knew in my heart of hearts that most of the torture I'd been put through the past year had been Shannen's plotting—that Faith had just been along for the ride. Plus, at the moment, there was something weirdly vulnerable about her and it took the wind right out of my indignation.

"Thanks." She didn't sit, but hovered alongside the table. Like she sensed she shouldn't push it.

"Don't mention it."

She gave me a genuine, if tentative, smile, and I couldn't help remembering the way Faith was before I'd left. Fun, imaginative, but most of all, needy. That was why I'd been so surprised when she was the first to bite my head off last year. Faith with a backbone had been a shock.

"So you're staying at the Nathansons' this summer?" she asked.

My stomach swooped with dread. "My mother is. I'm undecided."

Faith's already Bambi-esque eyes widened. She finally sat across from me, dropping her bags and leaning forward. Her keys clanged against the table. "Oh, no! You *have* to come."

"Why?" I asked.

"Because . . . it's totally gonna suck this year," Faith said. "Shannen and Chloe aren't talking. Chloe and Hammond aren't talking. Jake's not even *coming*. Who am I supposed to hang out with?"

Okay, I wasn't even going to get into the hypocrisy of that question. Like I wanted to hang out with her? Like I was really going to swoop in and save her from a socially bereft summer? Maybe I didn't hate her, but I wasn't about to become her BFF. Really there was only one part of that ramble I was interested in addressing. The part that had made my breath catch.

"Jake's not going down?" I asked.

"No," she said with a pout. "His mother went all strict on him and grounded him for the entire summer. He's staying in Orchard Hill."

Every inch of my skin tingled, and not from the overzealous air-conditioning vent behind my head. Jake was going to be here all summer. And the Cresties were not.

Suddenly the idea of staying with my dad was a lot more appealing.

Ally

As I walked into the condo that night, mentally rehearsing my arguments for staying in Orchard Hill, I started to wonder if I was emotionally deficient in some way. Was I really going to let the fact that Jake Graydon was staying here make my decision for me? He'd basically lied to me for months. He'd let me babble on about how much I missed my dad and ramble pathetically about how I had no idea where he was, and the whole time *Jake* had known. He'd known exactly where I could find my father, and he hadn't told me. When I thought about the number of times he could have just said something, the number of times I'd made a fool out of myself in front of him, it made me want to break something.

I slammed the door behind me so hard the old fashioned knocker on the outside of it—the one the designers had added to give the newly built condos that old-school Orchard Hill charm—swung and banged back against it. I took a breath and thought about Jake. Really thought about him. I thought about that thing he'd said on the night of Shannen's party, before the birthday girl had sent my world crumbling down around me.

"Yours," he'd said. "From now on."

My knees, right there in the tiny hallway of my overly warm condo, went weak. It was like I could feel his breath on my neck. The perfect words still prickling in my ear. So, I guess there it was. That was why I wanted to stay. I wanted to see if what he'd said that night actually meant anything to him. I wanted to find out if I could get past those months of secrecy. I wanted to know if he was worth forgiving.

"Ally?"

"Hey, Mom."

My mother walked over from the living room and stood at the end of the hall, between me and the kitchen. I moved past her and dropped my bag on the table. She was wearing a white polo-shirt-style dress and no shoes. The second school ended every year, my mom sported nothing but sundresses until September rolled around again.

"Did you eat at the mall?" she asked, opening the refrigerator. "I was just going to make some dinner."

Before I could answer, the phone rang. My mother froze for a moment, staring into the fridge. I saw her knuckles turn white as she gripped the handle tighter. Then she took out a plate of raw chicken cutlets and placed it carefully, almost deliberately, on the counter. As if it took all the power within her not to hurl it at the wall.

"Are you gonna get that?" I asked, sensing that I shouldn't go near the phone.

"Nope."

"Aren't you even going to check the caller ID?"

"I know who it is," she said, removing the cling wrap from the dish and balling it up.

On the third ring, I walked to the phone. It was my dad.

"He's called every two hours all day," my mother said as she tossed the cling wrap into the garbage and let the lid slam. "And I swear, Ally, if you ask me why I'm not picking up for him, I might scream, so please just let it go."

My face stung at being admonished for something I hadn't done. But I *had* been about to do it, so I said nothing.

My mom blew out a breath, leaned back against the counter, and smiled at me tightly. "So. Food?"

"I'm not really hungry now, but if you make extra I'll eat it later." I swallowed my ten thousand dad-related questions and glanced into the deserted living room. There was a packed suitcase on the floor. Just seeing it made me feel hollow inside.

She was really going. The question was, was she going to make me go with her? "No Gray? No Quinn?"

She took out the grill pan and placed it on the stove. "I thought it should be just us tonight. Since I'm leaving tomorrow."

I froze. Did she just say "*I'm* leaving?"

"Wait . . . I thought you said you hadn't talked to Dad."

She rested her hands on the counter for a moment, then turned to face me, running her thumb along the back of one of the chairs. "I wanted to make sure this is what you really want first."

My throat tightened. What I really wanted was for her to stay home *with* me. For her to pick up the phone the next time my father called. For him to explain everything away, and for it all to go back to the way it used to be. For us to be a family.

"I know you don't want to be around your old crowd this summer, Ally," she said. "But you won't necessarily *have* to see them."

"Yeah, right," I scoffed. "Come on, Mom. You have to remember what it's like down there."

What it was like when all the Cresties were on LBI was one giant, two-month-long slumber party. All the families had houses on the same stretch of private beach in Harvey Cedars. Every night there were cocktail parties and barbecues and swimming in the ocean and boating in the bay. Every night people crashed at random houses, or passed out on someone's boat. On weekends, one or two of the dads showed up at whatever house had claimed the most people from the night before, toting bags of bagels and elephant ears and steaming cups of coffee. You couldn't not hang out with everyone. They were in your face every minute of every hour of every day.

Which used to be really fun. But now it sounded like the worst form of torture. Every year, it all culminated with the Kirkpatricks' end-of-summer brouhaha—an elaborately themed event that often raged on for three days. Yeah. I couldn't *wait* for that.

"Yes," she said. "I do."

She looked disappointed. Hurt.

"Why don't we both stay home?" I suggested hopefully. "We could get a membership at the town pool, see movies, go shopping. . . ."

The word hung in the air. Shopping hadn't been much of a pastime for us the last couple of years. And the pool membership was probably expensive. But maybe I could help pay for it. And then Gray would be three hours away, and my dad—and Jake— would be just five minutes up the street.

"That is not an option," my mother said, turning back to the stove.

"But, Mom—"

"Ally, Gray invited us to the shore, and I've already accepted," she said, twisting the knob to turn the gas on under the grill pan. "I've prepared him for the fact that you might not come, which was difficult enough for him to hear, but—"

"Why?" I asked. "Why does he care whether or not I'm there?"

"Because he cares about *you*," she said, like it was the most obvious thing in the world.

Well, I don't give a crap about him, I thought, but didn't say. As boyfriends went, if my mother had to have one, Gray was all right. But now my dad was back and all I wanted was for Gray Nathanson to go away.

"He's very disappointed that you might not come, but

he understands," my mother continued, dropping slices of chicken into the pan, where they sizzled and spat.

"Understands what?" I asked, irked. What did I care whether or not Gray understood me? Why did *she* care whether or not he did?

"That you haven't seen your father in two years. That you want to reconnect with him."

"What about you? Don't you want to reconnect with him?" I demanded.

My mother half groaned, half sighed as she turned on the water in the sink to wash her hands. "We're not talking about that right now, Ally."

"Why not? I thought we could talk about anything," I said, sounding both pathetic and annoyed.

She turned the water off with a bang and grabbed a towel. "Not this."

I got up from the table, my sudden anger so fierce it wouldn't let me sit still. How could she keep shutting me down like this? Didn't she understand that I wanted to talk about my dad? That I *had* to? Why was she being so selfish? I turned toward my room, envisioning a good door slamming and some quality time with my iPod, but my mom stopped me in my tracks.

"Wait."

I didn't turn around. I needed to hear what she had to say first.

"Fine. If it means that much to you, you can stay with him," she said quietly. "I mean, if that's what you really want to do."

I hesitated. For a moment I scarcely believed that she'd actually agreed. But then it sank in, and nervous flutters filled my chest. Staying meant being near Jake. It meant giving him a chance. And my dad a chance too.

But there was something else. An odd shiver of nervousness crept over my shoulders. As I turned to look at my mother, I suddenly realized it also meant being away from her after two and a half years straight of being there for each other every day, through everything. I was seventeen years old, and the idea of being without her scared me.

But going down the shore with her and Gray and Quinn like one big happy family, and being thrown together with Chloe, Shannen, Faith, and Hammond every single day . . . that idea *horrified* me.

"Yeah," I said, somehow managing to look her in the eye. "That's what I want to do."

Daily Field Journal of Annie Johnston
Wednesday, June 30

Location: Jump, Java, and Wail!

Cover: Eating a chocolate chip muffin. Actually, that's not a cover. I just love them so.

Observations:

9:35 a.m.: Subject Jake Graydon peeks through the front window. Keeps walking. Uniform: light blue, short-sleeved button-down; pressed dark khaki shorts; mandals. (Query: What's he doing up this early on a summer day? According to records, the earliest Jake-spotting last summer before he left for the shore was 11:55 a.m.)

9:37 a.m.: Subject Jake Graydon walks by again.

9:38 a.m.: Subject Jake is back. He takes a breath as if for courage, and yanks open the door. The bell ring seems to startle him, even though he must have heard it fourteen million times before.

9:39 a.m.: Subject Jake approaches counter. BCC's favorite alt-rocker wannabe, Chase Delia, awaits. Talk about polar opposites. This should be fun.

Jake

"Hey, man. What can I get ya?"

The scruffy dude behind the register at Jump, Java, and Wail! stopped rubbing the counter with his grimy cloth. His red hair stuck out around his head like a lion's mane. His eyes were rimmed with purple eyeliner. He pressed both fists into the countertop and leaned toward me. There were letters tattooed across his fingers, but they were upside down and I couldn't read them. His brown apron had a white smear across it. The pimple on his chin looked set to pop. He smelled like Southern Comfort and coffee.

What the hell was I doing here?

"Um . . . you hiring?" I mumbled.

The guy pulled back. Like he was surprised. He ran the gross cloth through his hands a couple of times while backing away from me. Almost like he thought I was gonna jump him or something.

"Hang on a sec," he said.

I spent the entire fifteen seconds he was gone holding onto the counter's edge with both hands. Otherwise, I was gonna bolt. When he came back out, the world kind of tilted in front of me. Because he came back out with Ally Ryan's dad.

"Hello! What can I do for you?" he asked cheerily.

He didn't recognize me. Which meant I could breathe again. He was wearing a brown and gold JUMP IF YOU LOVE COFFEE! T-shirt and a big-ass smile. Like he was the greeter at Great Adventure and not stuck in some crappy local coffee place.

What was he doing here, anyway?

"Um, yeah . . . I . . . I'm looking for a job? For the summer?" I said.

I sounded like a tool. Lion dude laughed under his breath and shook his head. Luckily, a couple of customers came in to distract him, because if he kept laughing at me right now, I was gonna have to walk around the counter and dead leg him.

Mr. Ryan smiled. "Come with me."

He walked down the counter, grabbing a piece of paper from a drawer on the way, and gestured at the small round table in the back corner. The one no one ever sat at because what's the point of hanging out at Jump if you're not gonna hang with all your friends and people watch from the huge window up front?

"Have a seat."

I did. He sat across from me. My back was to the door. He smiled at me expectantly. I was starting to feel hot.

"I'm Chris Ryan," he said, offering his hand.

"Jake," I said as we shook. I cleared my throat. "Jake Graydon."

"Ever been on a job interview before, Jake?" he asked.

Was it that obvious? "No, sir."

He chuckled. "While I appreciate the sentiment, you don't need to call me sir. Mr. Ryan's fine, and maybe if we get to know each other better, Chris."

"Okay," I said. I'd had adults tell me to call them by their first names before, but I never really thought they meant it, so I'd never actually done it.

He put the paper in front of me and turned it around with his fingertips. Then he added a pen from his pocket. It was an application. "Why don't you just fill out the first section?"

"All right." I cleared my throat and started writing. I paused when I came to the part asking for my address. Which was his *old* address.

"So . . . never had a job before?" he asked.

"I used to cut lawns in middle school," I told him.

Fuck it. What was I gonna do, lie about where I lived? I wrote down my address.

"Well, that's something," he said.

I finished up with the basic info and handed back his pen. He picked up the application and I averted my eyes. There was nothing to look at but the brick wall. On it was an artsy, framed poster of a coffee cup, with three wavy lines of steam rising up from it.

"You live at number two Vista View Lane?" he asked.

My eyes were now on the table as I nodded. "Yes, sir. I mean, Mr. Ryan."

"That's my—I mean . . . I used to live there," he said.

I nodded again. Looked him in the eye. "Yeah, I mean, yes. I know."

His eyebrows came together. "You do?"

"I know Ally?" I said. God, I sounded like English was my second language.

"Oh!" His body relaxed. "How do you know her?"

My throat was so dry there were armadillos crawling across it. "Um, we're friends. From school. She was my backslapper for soccer."

"You play soccer? That's great," he said. He double-clicked the pen, then made a note on my application. "It's good to get involved in school activities. Keeps you out of trouble."

"I swim, too. And play lacrosse," I said.

He leaned back in his chair, clicking the pen again, and grinned like we were suddenly old friends. So he still didn't remember me. He had no clue that I'd been there that night when Shannen had made that stupid video of him. "Jake Graydon . . . I don't think she's mentioned you."

My stomach sank. Great. Just great. That was so what I needed to hear right then.

"But we're not here to talk about Ally," he said. Another pen click. He rested his forearms against the edge of the table, hovering over my almost-blank application. "We're here to talk about you."

The bell over the door rang and a bunch of loud people entered. Loud, young voices. Like people I might know. I didn't turn around.

"If you want to work here, Jake, you're going to have to be willing to work odd hours," he said. He turned the application over and I saw that there was a spot to check off which days you could work. "The place is open from five a.m. to midnight every day, so your shifts will be all over the place. How does that sit with you?"

"It sits fine," I said.

But there was no way I was *ever* coming in here at five a.m. Up front there was a huge group laugh. My neck was on fire. What if someone recognized me sitting here with the manager and an application? Did I really want to work here, where I'd be seeing people from school all the time?

This morning, when my mother had asked me where I was going to apply, Jump, Java, and Wail! just came out of my mouth. Because I hadn't thought about it at all. Because I had hoped she was going to change her mind. But then, as I was walking down Orchard Avenue, I realized that there was nowhere better. I didn't fold my own shirts, so I wasn't about to fold them at the Gap all summer. The deli was out, because mayonnaise-based salads make me hurl. And the library? Uh, no. And then, I was here.

"Any days you can't work?" he asked.

"Nope," I said. "Oh, except I'm gonna be taking a class at BCC in a couple of weeks. I'm not sure which days it meets yet."

"A college class over the summer, huh?" His eyes lit up, and I realized he thought I was taking it voluntarily. He made another note. "That's good."

"Yeah," I said. Did I really come off as someone who wanted to study over the summer? I wasn't sure how I felt about that.

"I need someone who'll be responsible, show up on time, and not mess around with their friends when they come in."

"I wouldn't do that, Mr. Ryan," I said.

Mostly because if anyone I knew came in here, I'd be hiding in the back.

"And you can't be twittering and texting and all that, either," Mr. Ryan said. "This is a place of business. We have fun here, don't get me wrong, but we all have to respect each other, and that means respecting the job."

"Yes, sir," I said with a nod.

But what the hell was he talking about? The place sold nothing but coffee and muffins. It wasn't the Pentagon.

The bells above the door rang again. Mr. Ryan looked up and did a double take, and then his jaw went slack. I turned around, just in time to see Mrs. Stein, Todd and Trevor's mom, spot Mr. Ryan. Her skin turned gray.

"What the—?" she blurted.

Mr. Ryan shoved himself to his feet as she stormed over. She clutched the strap of her purse for dear life with both hands.

"Sarah. Hello! I—"

"Hello? Is that all you've got to say to me? What are you even *doing* here?"

I'd never seen the twins' mom so pissed. Not even the time they'd used the hood of her car as a skate ramp. I sat there and sort of stared at the sides of their legs, my heart pounding. Everyone in the place was staring at us.

"I'm sorry, Sarah, but can we do this another time?" Mr. Ryan said in a professional voice. "I'm in the middle of—"

"What? You're not just going to blow me off. Not after all this time! Do you realize my family lost their home because of what you did?"

From the corner of my eye, I could see people whispering behind their hands. A few kids from school were texting. Otherwise, the place was silent.

"I didn't know that. And I'm very sorry. But you must realize I did nothing malicious," Mr. Ryan explained. "It was all a horrible mistake. My family was affected by it too."

"You can't just gamble with people's livelihoods, Christopher!" Mrs. Stein blurted. "With people's *lives*!"

Mr. Ryan put his hand on her arm. "I understand why you're so upset, Sarah. If you'd like to wait for me in my office, you can shout at me all you want. . . ."

She glanced at the door behind the counter, which he was now steering her toward. For the first time, she noticed what he was wearing too. "Your office? You . . . you work here?"

"At the moment, yes," he said.

She snorted a laugh and shook her hair back. "Thanks

anyway. I think I've done all the shouting I need to do. But you can bet I won't be coming back in here anytime soon."

Her eyes flicked to me for the first time, and I did the only thing I could think to do. I raised a hand weakly and smiled. "Hi, Mrs. Stein."

"Jake," she said, appearing confused. Then she turned around and flounced back out to the street.

Mr. Ryan blew out a sigh as he sat. Gradually, the life returned to the coffee shop. "I'm sorry you had to see that."

"That . . . that's okay," I said.

"There are some people in this town who are not very happy with me," he said, his eyes going distant as he looked down at my application. I felt sort of sorry for him right then. The guy had just made a mistake. Yeah, that mistake meant millions of dollars for a lot of people, but . . . it was still a mistake. "Anyway, where were we?" He glanced over the page. "Ah. Right. So . . . tell me why you think I should hire you, considering you have no experience," he said. He held the pen over a bottom section labeled "notes." His hand was shaking.

I stared at him for a second. Was he kidding? What kind of experience did a person need to pour coffee?

"Um, well . . . I'm here because I want to prove to my parents that I can be responsible," I improvised. Because telling him my mom made me come here so I could prove to college admissions boards that I was responsible probably wouldn't sound too good. "I don't want to be just another one of those rich kids who has everything handed to him," I said. "That's not me."

The pen didn't move. He narrowed his eyes. He wasn't

buying it. He was about five seconds away from calling my bluff and booting my ass to the curb.

But then, he smiled. "Good answer." He stood up and offered his hand. "You're hired."

"Really?" I asked, standing as well. I realized my palms were sweating and I rubbed them on my chino shorts before shaking his hand. "Thanks."

He gripped my hand tightly and didn't let go. "I'm taking a chance on you, Jake. Don't let me down."

Dude. The guy sounded like something out of an army movie. It was *coffee*. As in, crushed beans and water. Lighten up.

"I won't, sir," I said, trying to sound grave. He gave me a look. But not an admonishing look. More like, *Dude. Get with the program.* "I mean, Mr. Ryan."

"Good. You can start tomorrow. Eleven a.m. work for you?" he said.

Eleven was a little early, but I guess it could have been five. "Sure."

"Good."

He finally released my hand and slapped me on the shoulder. He looked past me toward the door, then out the window, up to the right. I wondered if he was waiting for Mrs. Stein to come back with a posse or something.

"Sorry," he said. "I'm actually just waiting for Ally to show up." He glanced at his watch. "I'm hoping to talk to her mother when she drops her off, but they're late."

I couldn't breathe. "Ally's coming here? Now?"

"She's supposed to be, yeah," he said. "I was going to take my fifteen to hopefully chat with her mom and then help her carry her stuff over to my apartment, but if tradition holds, it's about to get seriously busy in here. I'd rather not leave during a rush."

I barely heard the last part. I was too busy shaking my head to get all the Ally-related information to fall into place, to make sense.

"Carry her stuff?" I said.

"Yeah. Ally's staying with me for the summer," he told me. "I got an apartment across the street. Hey . . . maybe you could help her bring her stuff over. As a kind of favor to your new boss?"

My face burned. "Uh, yeah. Sure. I could do that."

Ally was staying with her dad for the summer. In walking distance to Jump, Java, and Wail! Where I was going to be working. She was *not* going down to LBI. She was *not* going to be three hours away. Instead, she was going to be right across the street and we were going to be thrown together all the time. She'd come visit her dad at work, I'd give her free coffee. Sooner or later she'd *have* to talk to me. She'd have to forgive me.

This was the best day ever. Thank God my mom had grounded me.

Ally

"Now remember, Ally. If you need anything—anything at all—you can call me anytime," my mother said as Gray drove his silver Land Rover up Orchard Avenue toward Jump, Java, and Wail! She kept turning around in the front seat, her sunglasses pushed back atop her head, holding her hair away from her face. Quinn sat next to me, some musical soundtrack turned up to an ungodly volume on her iPod. The entire car was filled with the sickly sweet scent of her watermelon gum. The back was crammed with canvas Lands' End bags, filled to the brim with everything from sunscreen to beach towels to exercise equipment. Apparently when Gray packed up his shore house at the end of each summer, he left nothing behind for the next.

"I know, Mom. Thanks," I said.

Gray slowed down and hit his blinker to make the left onto Grove Lane. Jump was right on the corner, and already a few girls from school were hanging outside in their short shorts, sipping iced lattes. Suddenly Quinn pulled out her earbuds and the sound of a wailing voice filled the car, backed up by, like, a hundred trumpets.

"Did you guys know that *Bye Bye Birdie* is actually a spoof?" she asked, her blue eyes bright. Quinn had not stopped talking about *Bye Bye Birdie* for the last month. She was going to be playing the lead in the show at some big local theater down the shore. Which was supposedly why Gray had taken the entire summer off to stay down there. Usually he only did weekends. As much as I knew he loved Quinn, I had a feeling he was actually taking an entire summer off so he could shack up with my mom. "They were spoofing what happened when Elvis Presley went to war. Did you know that Elvis Presley was *drafted?*"

My mom and Gray exchanged an amused look, like *Isn't our daughter oh so precious?* It made my stomach turn. Because last time I checked, Quinn was not my mother's daughter. Staying in Orchard Hill for the summer was the best choice I'd ever made. Because I couldn't watch *that* every day for the next ten weeks.

"Yes, I believe I read that somewhere," Gray joked, his long blond bangs flopping over the tops of his Ray-Bans.

The traffic opened up and he made the turn, pulling into one of the fifteen-minute parking spaces alongside the store. I jumped out, tugging my gargantuan duffel bag with me.

"Thanks, Gray!" I shouted as my mom got out of the car.

He lifted a hand. "Have fun!"

My mother took my hands, kissed my cheek, and gave me this half-pout, half-smile. "You sure you're okay with this?"

"Yes, Mom. I'm sure," I said patiently.

"Okay, then." She gave me a bear hug. "Be safe! And call me tonight."

"Wait," I said, my heart falling. "You're not coming in with me?"

She glanced toward the coffee shop warily. "Ally—"

"What if dad wants to talk to you about . . . I don't know . . . rules or something?" I said.

She laughed. "You're not exactly high-maintenance."

"But, Mom," I said, feeling desperate. This was my one and only chance to get my parents back in the same room together for the rest of the summer. "Just for a minute?" I glanced at the side window of Jump, willing him to come out.

"Ally, I told you," she said, stepping closer to me and lowering her voice. "I'm not ready to talk to your father yet."

"Well, when will you be ready?" I asked, irritated. *After you've eloped with Gray?*

"I don't know," she said seriously. Then she blew out a breath. "Enough of this. I'll talk to you later. Be good, okay?"

"Just wait one second," I said, taking a couple of steps toward the door. "I'm sure he'll—"

And that's when I spotted them.

Jake Graydon was standing with my father at the back of the shop, and they were chatting like old friends. They hadn't noticed me yet, probably because my dad was too busy belly laughing at something Jake had just said into his ear. My father, the guy who kept so many secrets from me I couldn't even count them, and Jake, the guy who'd kept the biggest secret of all.

What. *The hell.* Was this?

Jake was supposed to be out of my life, not hanging out in it when I wasn't even around. It was just so wrong. Like my feelings didn't matter at all. Like he still thought he belonged, no matter what I said. And talking to my dad like best buds? *I'd* barely even talked to my dad in two years.

What were they saying about me?

Wait a minute, Ally. Calm down. It's not all about you.

Except what else could they possibly be talking about?

Just then, my dad looked through the window, saw me, and waved. He started out the front door, sidestepping a mother and daughter who were hovering by the fixings area. Jake followed after him.

My mother sighed, oblivious. "Ally, we have to go—"

"Wait," I said, my voice shrill. My mind was reeling and suddenly I didn't even care if she spoke to my dad. I just didn't want her to leave me alone to deal with . . . this.

"Ally! Hey!"

My dad walked over and gave me a quick kiss on the cheek. Jake hovered there, hands in the pockets of his shorts, a doofy smile on his face.

"Hello, Melanie," my father said.

She shot me a half-fed-up, half-sad look. "Hello, Chris."

Dad looked through the car window and lifted a hand at Gray, like they were all long-lost friends having a roadside chat. Everyone was very civil, all of a sudden. I glanced at Jake, feeling nervous and awkward and confused and annoyed. What the hell was he doing here?

And why did he have to be so freaking *gorgeous*? His spiky brown hair was gelled up a little in front, and the bright sky peeking through the canopy of tree branches overhead made his light blue eyes practically glow. He was wearing a short-sleeved button down shirt and khaki shorts with leather sandals. Kind of dressed up for a random summer day, but it worked on him. Who was I kidding? Everything worked on him.

"Hey . . . are you okay?" he asked as my dad started peppering my mom with questions about the shore—how long were they staying, did they have any big plans, etc., etc. Jake put his hands on his hips as he looked at me with concern. He had really long arms. Long and tan. The kind you just want to sink into. I tore my gaze off them and looked him in the eye.

"Not really," I snapped sarcastically.

Jake glanced at my parents and tucked his chin. "Did I do something? What's wrong?"

"What's wrong is that I can't take people talking about me behind my back anymore," I blurted. I was surprised, and pleased, by how in control I sounded. Because the voice in my head was growing panicky. I was so sick of feeling stupid. Feeling like the only one who had no idea what was going on.

He blinked and touched my arm, nudging me slightly away

from the car. My dad was still talking to my mom, but she was staring over his shoulder with her jaw clenched, like she was concentrating very hard on not punching him in the face. "You mean, me and your dad? We weren't talking about you."

I laughed. "Yeah, right."

"We weren't!" he protested. "I was just applying for a job."

Pfffttt. That was the incredulous sound my lips made at that announcement.

"I was!" he said, his eyes wide at my unbelievable unfairness.

"Sure. You're getting a job," I said dubiously. "Why would you be getting a job?"

"I know, I know. But I have to," he said. "My mom grounded me for the summer and she's making me jump through all these hoops. I gotta get a tutor and take a class and—" He started ticking things off on his fingers and I sort of couldn't believe it. How could he think it was okay to launch into a casual conversation? He was just like my father, trying to act like everything could be how it was before, without so much as an apology—without so much as an acknowledgement that he'd done anything wrong. Did he think all was forgiven? Because it definitely was not.

"You know what?" I interrupted. "You're mistaking me for somebody who cares."

His jaw dropped. Okay. That was maybe a little bit harsh. But what did he expect me to do? Play along and act all flirty and interested, as if he'd done nothing wrong? As if he hadn't broken my heart? I had just spent an entire year taking crap from everyone around me and I wasn't going to do it anymore.

I turned around and dragged my bag back toward the car.

"Did Ally tell you I'm going to retake my Series Seven this

summer?" my father was saying. "I should be trading again by the end of August."

"No, she didn't tell me that, Chris. How nice for you," my mother said facetiously. "I really hope you're not going to become one of those fathers who uses their daughter as a go-between instead of dealing with things himself."

"Well, when you refuse to answer my calls . . . ," my dad said with a chuckle.

Much to Quinn's surprise, I opened the side door again, threw my bag inside, and got in.

"Come on, Mom. Let's go," I said out the window.

"What? Ally . . . I thought you were staying with me," my father said.

"I changed my mind," I told him.

My mom barely bit back a grin. "She changed her mind," she said with a shrug. Then she got in the car as well and slammed her door. "Gray," she said as she buckled her seat belt. "Let's go."

"But I . . . shouldn't we talk about this?" my father said.

I felt bad for bailing on him like this, but I couldn't stay there a moment longer with the two of them—the two guys who'd broken my heart. Just seeing them standing there together made me want to cry or shout or throw things.

"I'll call you later," I told my dad.

Then Gray pulled out into traffic and we were gone.

"Are you okay?" my mother asked. "What did Jake say?"

"I don't want to talk about it," I said. I put my sunglasses on and hunkered down for the long drive.

"Oh, but look at him. He looks so sad," Quinn lamented, gazing out the back window at Jake. I shot her a look that, in a perfect world, would have killed her dead. She popped the bubble that hung from her mouth, wisely averted her eyes, and put her earbuds back in.

Suddenly, I couldn't get away from Orchard Hill fast enough. I needed something. Something to help me stop feeling this way. Like there was some kind of roiling, hot poison in my chest, just waiting for the perfect moment to spew forth. Maybe what I needed was a change of scenery. Something new.

My phone beeped and I leaned forward to slip it from my pocket. It was a text. From Faith.

R U coming down??? We can go 4 manicures!!!

I turned the phone off and curled my knees toward the door. Unfortunately, all that was waiting for me at LBI was more of the same old same old.

Jake

The grating scream of buzz saws greeted me as I turned onto my street. As if I wasn't already tense enough. There were four separate trucks and a Jaguar parked outside Chloe's house. A plumber, a carpenter, an electrician, and an air-conditioning specialist. I didn't know who the Jaguar belonged to, but I'd bet money it was an interior decorator.

Looked like Mrs. Appleby was bored again.

I pulled into my driveway, and Shannen stood up off the front step. Fuck. I put the car in park and leaned my head against the wheel for a second. Took a breath for patience. This was so not what I wanted to deal with after the Ally disaster.

"Hey." She shoved her hands into the back pockets of her shorts as she arrived at my window.

"Hey." A sudden clatter of wood made me flinch. "What's going on over there?" I stalled.

"Chloe talked her mom into having an addition put onto her room," Shannen said, sweeping her long bangs out of her eyes. They fell right back again. "She's gonna have her own media room and a walk-out deck. I got all this from Faith, of course, since Chloe's still not talking to me."

I looked down at my keys in my lap. She sounded all bitter. Like she didn't remember that there was a reason Chloe wasn't talking to her. So weird.

"Are you?" she asked.

"What?" I said.

"Talking to me?"

"Yeah," I said. "I mean, sure. I'm talking to you right now, right?"

She rolled her eyes slightly and placed her hands on top of the Jeep's door, clutching it. "You know what I mean."

Actually, I didn't.

"I just feel so stupid," she said, shaking her head.

There was a long moment of silence. If you didn't count all the construction noise.

"So . . . what do we do now?" I asked.

She laughed, but it was more like one part exhalation, one part laugh. "I guess you could tell me what you think."

"What I think about what?" I asked.

Another laugh. I'd never heard Shannen laugh this much in a conversation. Her face was all red and she tipped her head forward so her hair hid most of it. "About . . . what I told you at my party," she said. "About, you know . . . how I feel."

Right. Suddenly I wanted to be anywhere else. I would've even gone back to the street with Ally yelling at me rather than have this conversation.

I mean, on the one hand, Shannen had been my best friend for two years. But on the other hand, she completely destroyed Ally, taking me, Chloe, and Hammond out in the process, and *then* decided to tell me that she did it all because she liked me. Because she wanted Ally out of my life. Because, basically, she was jealous.

So, not only had she been psycho evil on my behalf, but basically, it was all my fault. If Shannen didn't like me and if I didn't like Ally, none of it would've happened.

Also, Shannen was like a guy to me. A friend. Not that I couldn't see she was hot. I'm not blind. But I wasn't going to hook up with her just because she was hot. Because what would happen after that? Nothing good.

She was staring at me. Waiting for a response. She was going to make me say it.

"I'm sorry, I just don't . . . I thought we were friends," I said.

Her hands slid down the door, then tucked under her arms. She took a step back. "Oh."

"I'm sorry, Shan," I said, shrugging. "I just don't think of you that way. And you know, I mean . . . you know I like . . . someone else."

"Ally." She said the word like it was laced with jagged glass.

"Yeah." I exhaled and flipped the visor down, then back up again. Down and up. Down and up. "Not that it matters. She did the weirdest thing before. I was over at Jump talking to her dad and she—"

"Are you kidding me?" Shannen blurted, just as the

high-pitched sound of the saw pierced my eardrums again.

"What?" I asked.

"Do you really think I want to hear about your romantic problems with Ally Ryan?" Shannen shouted, bending at the waist. There were angry tears in her eyes. Suddenly I felt like the rat bastard both she and Ally clearly thought I was. "God! You are such an asshole, Jake."

Then she turned around and stormed off. I almost made a move to follow her, but what was I supposed to say? I wasn't going to tell her I was in love with her, because I wasn't. So I just let her go.

I leaned my head back against the headrest and blew out a sigh. This day was just getting better and better. Any second my mom was gonna come out the front door and tell me I had to take cooking classes, too, or learn how to knit. I just wanted everything to go back to the way it was before last weekend. I wanted Shannen to be my friend and Ally to like me still. Was that so hard?

My phone beeped. My stomach did that weird, hopeful swooping thing it did whenever it heard a beep these days. Was the text from Ally? I fished the phone out of my pocket. The text was from Chloe.

R U O K?

Huh? I looked over at her house. All I saw was bushes.

I can see u!

I texted back.

How?

Stand up.

All righty then. I hoisted myself up and stood on the seat of my car. My head and torso sticking up through the roll bars.

There was Chloe, standing on what was basically half of a deck. It had been built outside her room. There was a big hole in the wall behind her, and I could just see her pink wallpaper inside. She waved. I waved back. Then she started texting again. A second later my phone beeped.

I'm bored. Wanna go 2 movies 2morrow?

I blinked. Chloe had never asked me to make plans alone before. But I guess with Faith, Hammond, and the Idiot Twins down the shore, and her not talking to Shannen or Hammond anyway, I was all that was left.

I'm in but gotta ? mom 1st.

Cool. Txt 18r.

I put the phone back in my pocket, feeling slightly better. My mom couldn't say no to one night of vegging in front of an action movie. My SAT tutor wasn't coming until Friday and the class didn't start for a couple of weeks, so there was nothing to study yet anyway. And I'd gotten a job. So I was ahead of the game. In her book anyway.

As I jumped down from the Jeep, I saw a familiar guy get into the electrician's truck and drive off. He looked over as he got to the end of my driveway and gave me a nod, so I nodded back. When I saw the name Halloran on the back of the truck, I realized why I knew him. Will Halloran: running back on the football team. Guess his dad was an electrician or something.

I wished my dad had some job I could apprentice at. I bet stringing wires at Chloe's house would be a lot more fun than schlepping coffee at Jump. And at least then, no one would expect me to go to college. I could just take over the electrician business when my dad retired. No muss, no fuss.

Everyone thought that living on the crest was easy, but

being a Norm definitely had its perks. Number one being, that if I were a Norm, Ally Ryan never would have had a reason to hate me.

Ally

By the time we got down to LBI, I was tired, cranky, and guilt-ridden. As I watched the familiar scenery fly by—the chowder stands and fudge shops, the random businesses selling boogie boards and sunscreen and plastic shovels—all I kept seeing was Jake's forlorn expression as we pulled away from Orchard Hill. Why did I have to be so mean? Now he was never going to try to apologize, which meant I'd never get the chance to forgive him. But did I even want to forgive him? Maybe I should just move on. That's what healthy people supposedly do—put the people who hurt them behind them. Besides, being with him meant being with his friends, and that was not a place I wanted to be. Especially not after everything they'd put me through over the past year. But still . . . every time I thought about him, my heart caught. Didn't it realize what he'd done?

Stupid heart.

I banged my head lightly against the car window as the view outside shifted. We were headed north on the island, away from the hustle and bustle near the causeway and onto the tree-lined stretch of the Boulevard. A woman rode along on a cruising bike, her wide-brimmed straw hat tugged back by the breeze, a tiny black dog sitting in the wicker basket on her handlebars. A far-too-tan guy in a BMW convertible pulled out of a driveway with a huge private beach—no trespassing sign tacked to a pole. Up here, where the biggest of the beach houses lived, there were more of those signs than there were people. A few seagulls cawed overhead, and I found myself hoping one would poop on the guy's fresh wax job. Finally, Gray pulled into the winding, white pebble driveway that led to his house.

I was so tired of not knowing how I felt. Whether I was mad at my father or relieved he was back. Where I wanted to live for the summer. Whether or not I should be with Jake. I pulled out my cell phone and considered a text, but what would I say? *Sorry? Call me? Miss you?* It all seemed way too pathetic and not quite right. Then the SUV emerged from the evergreen trees and I forgot all about my phone.

"This is your house?"

"This is it," Gray said.

I couldn't believe it. This was *the* house. My single favorite house on LBI. It was shaped like a long, shallow triangle and set up on stilts, like many of the houses on the island, to protect it from flooding and storm water. From the beach, this house looked like a huge, hovering alien craft—all windows from top to bottom, with three levels of decking and several sets of stairs to the beach. When I was little and we'd go for strolls in the sand, I had always wanted to walk by the spaceship house.

My mother and Gray got out of the car. Quinn flipped open a mirror and reapplied her lip gloss. Outside, my mom and Gray held hands and walked right past the wide wooden steps to the front door.

"Wait. Where're you going?" I asked, getting out and slamming the door. The cool wind off the ocean immediately whipped my hair across my face.

"Hello? Delicate process over here! You just shook the whole car," Quinn said through the open window.

Mom and Gray turned in toward each other to look over their shoulders. "To the Rosses' for the party."

"Oh. Well. Can you just let me inside first?" I asked. My feet crunched the pebbles as I walked over to them. My mom and Gray exchanged a look, then released each other.

"I'd really rather you come with us," my mother said, tucking her hair up under a straw visor.

I glowered. "What happened to 'I don't have to see anyone I don't want to see'?"

Quinn got out of the car. "Ready!" she trilled, jogging over to us.

"Just for a little while?" my mother implored. "I'm sure the party will be big enough for you to go unnoticed." She linked her arm around mine and held it fast. "Besides, they're going to have a ton of food. Aren't you hungry?"

My grumbling stomach betrayed me. Gray had refused to stop at any one of the many Burger Kings on the parkway, and Mrs. Ross did always have the best barbecued ribs. I looked down at my outfit—wrinkled camo cargo shorts and a white T-shirt. I was so not dressed for a party, but that was hardly my fault. I'd thought I was going to spend the day on my dad's new couch watching reruns and waiting for his shift to be over so we could order takeout before he headed off to class. But then, what the heck did I care what the Cresties thought of my clothes? My stomach grumbled again and I sighed.

"Fine," I said, slipping my sunglasses on. "But I'm only staying long enough to eat."

"There ya go!" Gray said, reaching out to ruffle my hair.

I flinched, surprised. Gray and I had always kept a respectful distance from each other. When had we crossed that line into invasion of personal space being okay? He didn't seem to notice my discomfort, and my mom just smiled, so I let it go. As long as it didn't happen again.

We walked up the beach to the Rosses' house. The sun was high in the sky and blazing down on the crashing waves. It was my first glimpse of the LBI ocean in years, and a thousand memories hit me like a tsunami. Burying my dad up to his neck in the sand with my mom's expert assistance, the summer between third and fourth grade when they'd both helped me and my friends make a four-story sand castle that had stood for almost a week, all the kite flying, ball throwing, and volleyball playing. Every memory contained my mom and dad.

"Ladies first," Gray announced, standing aside so the three of us could tromp past him onto the steps leading up to Hammond's house.

I glanced sideways at him. Suddenly, in that Ralph Lauren shirt unbuttoned one button too low, with the string attached to his sunglasses around his neck, carrying an eco-friendly cloth bag full of clanking wine bottles, he looked like a complete tool. A poor-man's Chris Ryan.

A few people on the deck greeted us with raised glasses. Smoke poured off the barbecue, which was being manned by some hired dude in a Hawaiian shirt. As I looked out at the view from the deck, I remembered that night five years ago when my parents had renewed their vows right outside Faith's house, which was a few houses down from Hammond's. The Rosses had insisted on hosting the pre-party, and Mrs.

Ross, Mrs. Moore, Mrs. Appleby, and Mrs. Kirkpatrick had acted as bridesmaids. All the women had gotten ready here, at the Rosses', then walked over to the ceremony, the five of us holding my mom's delicate lace train. Hundreds of white candles had been placed in the sand to form an aisle, and my dad had been standing at the end of it, on a huge heart made out of seashells that my friends and I had spent all day painting red. At the time, I'd thought it was the most romantic thing in the world—all my dad's idea, all for the woman he claimed he'd always love and always do anything for. So how was it possible that less than three years later, he could have ditched her?

Didn't she want the answers to these questions too?

"Hon? Are you okay?" my mother asked.

I hadn't realized I'd stopped moving. They'd gotten ahead of me, and she had to come back to snap me out of my trance.

"It's too windy out," I told her. "I'm gonna go inside."

She nodded and I made a beeline for the living room. Most of the other kids were in there as well, playing video games in the sunken conversation pit near the stone fireplace or huddled around the leather-topped wet bar in the corner. I realized my mistake the second I was through the door, but it was too late to turn back now. I'd been spotted.

"You came!"

Faith put her plastic cup down on the coffee table and skipped up the two wide steps from the pit. She was wearing a tiny red minidress, which rode up high enough to expose her underwear when she threw her skinny arms around me. (I could tell by the way the Idiot Twins and their friends reacted, with widened eyes and high fives.) A few girls from the year above us—Victoria Mihook, Tandy Lassiter, and some new girl I'd never met—shot us cursory looks from the bar area and went back to texting.

"Omigod, thank you *so* much for changing your mind," Faith said as she leaned back.

As if I'd come here for her.

"Where are Shannen and Chloe?" I asked, wanting to get my nemeses in my sight line.

Her eyes widened. "Didn't you hear? They're not coming down."

I blinked as the possibility that this could be true rushed through me like a calming breeze. "What?"

"Chloe's mom's, like, completely renovating Chloe's room, so they're staying home. But really, it's probably because Chloe doesn't want to be around Hammond," Faith said, lowering her voice and glancing back over her shoulder to where Hammond sat with the other boys cheering at the huge plasma screen.

Unbelievable. Chloe didn't want to be around Hammond, so her mother not only agreed to stay home for the summer, but gifted Chloe with a freshly renovated bedroom. But when I wanted to stay home for the summer because I'd been publicly humiliated in front of practically everyone I know, my mom's response was "I'm out."

"What's to drink?" I said, walking past Faith toward the bar.

"Oh, there's lemonade, iced tea, soda." She paused at the end of the bar. "Not, like, *drink* drink, just drink. Right?"

The older girls looked at me. Part of me wanted to grab a Corona just to shock them, but it wasn't in me. I'd never been drunk in my life and I wasn't about to start just because I was pissed at my mom—and Jake, and my dad. I took a bottle of Minute Maid lemonade from the well-stocked minifridge. The girls lost interest in me again and went about their business.

"What about Shannen?" I asked, shaking the bottle.

"Her parents sold her house a couple of years ago, so Shannen usually stays with Chloe, but . . ."

"Right. They're in a fight," I said, swigging the tart lemonade. It cooled me instantly, taking the edge off my tension. "So why doesn't she stay with you?"

Faith averted her eyes and shrugged. "She said she might come down later in the summer. . . ."

There was something in her voice that made me doubt she really believed this. Part of me was curious as to why, but if she wasn't about to share, I wasn't about to pry. Honestly? I didn't care why Shannen wasn't there, I was just happy to avoid her. And as much as I wanted to get the chance to explain everything to Chloe, I was more than happy to avoid that for the summer too.

Over in the pit, the Idiot Twins shouted, then laughed. Hammond slapped Trevor on the back in a congratulatory way. Hammond and I hadn't spoken since the revelation of our hook up at Shannen's party. I wondered if he was going to acknowledge it or, like everyone else these days, pretend it never happened. I saw him glance over at us, but he didn't nod or smile. He simply popped a macadamia nut into his mouth and leaned back on the plush couch, with his arms crooked behind his head and his ankle across his knee. I noticed how good his arms looked, and quickly busied myself, fishing some ice out of the ice bucket at the end of the bar.

"Isn't it so weird, how Hammond always seems hotter down the shore?" Faith said.

I blushed and dropped two ice cubes into my bottle. Did she really think I was checking out Hammond? Because I hadn't done it on purpose. It was merely an accidental ogling.

"Okay, spill." She put both hands on the bar stool behind her and hoisted herself up. Her legs crossed at the ankle and she smoothed her hair over one shoulder. "You have to tell me all about your hook up."

I gulped my lemonade. "My what?"

"Your hook up with Hammond!" Faith said. She laced her fingers together on the bar and leaned forward in a way that made me think of Kelly Ripa or the chicks on *The View.* "What did you guys *do* exactly?"

"You're serious," I said.

"Yes I'm serious! I mean, Hammond's like a brother, don't get me wrong, but was it hot? I bet it was hot."

"So . . . let me get this straight," I said, setting my bottle down. "You freaked because I didn't come to Chloe's sweet sixteen, but sticking my tongue down her boyfriend's throat . . . that's not a problem for you."

Faith screwed her face up like I was nuts. "Okay, first of all, Hammond was still in love with you then, so we *all* know it was him who stuck his tongue down *your* throat. I think even Chloe knows that. Which is why she's so pissed off. I give her a couple of weeks before she forgives you entirely, by the way."

I wasn't sure which was more shocking: the fact that she had it entirely right about that night, or the fact that she was talking so casually about it.

"So did he attack you or what?" Faith asked conspiratorially.

"Ally, you have to come outside! My dad's looking for you!" Quinn appeared out of nowhere, a swirl of pink and white, and grabbed my arm.

"What? Why?" I asked.

"His friend Rick Morris is out there and he wants to meet

you!" Quinn tugged on my wrist like a toddler begging her mother for ice cream.

"Who the heck is Rick Morris?" I asked, holding my ground. Quinn may have been aggressively cute, but I had more strength in my big toe than she had in her entire scrawny body. And when did Gray start demanding I meet his friends, anyway?

Quinn released me and put her hands on her hips, like she was about to launch into a halftime cheer. "He's a scout for the UNC women's basketball team."

I glanced past her out the plate-glass windows. My mother and Gray were chatting up a towering guy with squared shoulders and the biggest smile I'd ever seen. UNC was one of my top five choices. I'd kill to play on their team. Butterflies crowded my stomach, and I automatically smoothed my hair behind my ears. Crap. Now I did care about what I was wearing.

"Faith. I gotta go," I said.

"I'll come with you!" she said, sliding off the stool.

It was needy Faith all over again, and momentarily I missed the oblivious bitch she'd been all year. I put a hand out. "I'll find you later, okay?"

Though I didn't really intend to find her later. Faith and I were no longer friends. The sooner I reminded her of that, the better. But this was no time for a scene. And with Faith, that conversation would *definitely* be a scene.

"Oh. Okay. I get it. Big meeting," she said, backing up again. She bumped the stool with her butt and it jostled Victoria Mihook's seat. Tori gave Faith a glower, which made Faith look like she was about to pee in her pants. "We'll go for a drive!" she said to me, trying to sound casual and failing miserably. "I have my car!"

"Okay," I said.

"Promise?" Faith called after me.

"Promise," I muttered. But I didn't even know what I was saying. I was already going over my last season's stats in my head.

"There she is!" Gray boomed as Quinn ushered me onto the deck. He reached out an arm, slung it over my shoulder, and squeezed. I tried not to cringe. "The pride of the Orchard Hill High basketball team!"

I kept my smile on for my mother's sake—and for Rick Morris—but it was difficult. Gray finally released me so I could shake Rick's hand, and I was able to breathe again, but now I felt like I needed to keep a wary distance from my mom's boyfriend. What was with all the fatherly touching? What had changed between the night of Shannen's party and now? I hoped he didn't think that me coming down here was some sort of sanctioning of his relationship with my mom—or that I'd somehow chosen him over my own father. But as Rick started to ask me about my season, and Gray and my mother looked on proudly, I had an awful, sinking feeling in my gut—a feeling that it was too late. For all of us.

Daily Field Journal of Annie Johnston
Thursday, July 1

Position: CVS.

Cover: None. I work here, bitches.

Observations:

10:47 a.m.: Subject Jake Graydon pulls into the parking lot. The top's down on his Jeep. He throws his arm over the passenger seat to look over his shoulder as he backs into a space. He kills the engine and looks around, like he's expecting applause. Yes, we're all impressed with your driving prowess, golden boy. Hang on while I click your Like button.

10:53 a.m.: Subject Jake is still sitting behind the steering wheel. Hmm. I wonder who he's waiting for.

10:57 a.m.: Subject Jake gets out of the car. Uniform: Orchard Hill High athletic shorts, white T-shirt, sneakers, Ray-Bans. Subject Jake peeks through the CVS window while walking casually by. He tries the door at Stanzione's Pizza. Looks momentarily flustered upon finding it locked. (Note: It's not even eleven a.m., smart guy.)

10:58 a.m.: Subject Jake casually strolls by again.

11:01 a.m.: And again.

11:02 a.m.: And again. (Query: Can this guy ever enter a place without staking it out first?)

11:05 a.m.: Subject Jake grows a pair and walks through the door. He looks at me, flinches, and heads straight for the back of the store. Where the condoms live. (Note: God, please let him buy condoms. Ringing up that transaction would make my summer.) After one complete circuit of the place, Subject Jake heads for the door. He hesitates a second, looks at me again. Seems to consider saying something, then thinks better of it. As he starts to walk out again, I speak.

Me: She went down the shore for the summer.

Jake: Oh, I thought . . . I mean, I know. That's not why I'm here.

Me: You thought she might have changed her mind.

Jake (defensively): No.

He walks up to the counter, picks up a random roll of mints, and slaps them down.

Jake: I just needed these.

I ring him up.

Me: You do have some awful breath.

He pays.

Jake (sarcastically): Thanks a lot.

He walks out, leaving the mints behind.

11:08 a.m.: Subject Jake cranks up the stereo in his Jeep and tears out of the parking lot. (Assessment: Somebody's in lo-ove.)

11:08 a.m.: I pop a few of my free mints. (Assessment: Spearmint rocks.)

Ally

"Ally, I'm sorry, but would you mind taking your feet off the table?"

I looked up to find Gray looming over me with bright red lobster-shaped pot holders covering his hands. He held them up like he'd just scrubbed in for a surgery and was letting the water drip off.

"Sorry." I let my Converse drop onto the white area rug under my feet, one of several that had been carefully and strategically placed throughout the great room to protect the rare Australian bamboo floors I had already heard far too much about.

Gray gritted his teeth, pulled his lips back, and sucked in a hiss. "Actually, would you mind taking off your shoes? I just had a cleaning service come in to do all the rugs."

I bit down so hard on my tongue I tasted blood. "Sure."

Laid out on the couch to my left, Quinn lifted the remote and changed the channel, flipping from MTV to ABC Family. I hooked my finger inside the back of my shoes to remove them. I could actually feel Gray's breath on my hair. I sat back again, but he still hovered. Finally, I had to look up at him. He gave me an impatient glare.

"What?" I asked.

He rolled his eyes, removed one pot holder, and put his hands out. "I'll just take those."

He meant my shoes. "Oookay." I bent over and plucked my Chuck T.'s off the rug, noticing for the first time how grungy and worn they were. Still, he took them from me without wincing and put them inside the closet next to the front entry. As he closed the door, I noticed that the shoes my mom was wearing earlier were in there, along with Quinn's sandals, which she'd kicked off upon returning from her first rehearsal. I didn't know this was a no-shoes house. Why hadn't someone just told me?

"My dad's a little anal about the beach house," Quinn said as soon as her father was safely on the far side of the island that separated the huge gourmet kitchen area of the great room from the living area. My mother returned from the bathroom right then, and I sank lower in my seat. He'd waited until she was gone to come over to me, hadn't he? The revelation made me feel icky and conspicuous. "You'll get used to it," she added.

But I didn't want to get used to it. Her dad was not my dad. And I didn't like that he was acting like he was.

I looked around the great room. When we'd finally come inside the night before, I'd seen enough to realize the place was very beautifully decked out with modern furniture and carved wood sculptures and other expensive trappings, but now I noticed the details. Like that there was a stack of round glass coasters on every single table. Like the bristled floor mats outside each of the sliding doors. Like the complete and total lack of magazines, books, beach towels, boogie boards, lawn chairs, umbrellas, and all the other beach-related paraphernalia that was usually strewn around a true LBI house. This was not the kind of place in which a person could kick back and relax—not like *our* shore house used to be.

When the doorbell rang a moment later, I flinched. Quinn jumped to get it.

"Hi, Mr. and Mrs. Ross!" Quinn trilled, standing on her bare tiptoes to accept a cheek kiss from Hammond's mom.

"Quinn! You get lovelier every time I see you," Mrs. Ross said.

Hammond and his brother Liam, who was basically a taller, skinnier, but still hot version of Hammond, stepped in behind their parents. They were followed by Faith and her mom and little brothers. All of them shuffled their shoes off before Gray and my mother had looked up from their pasta pots. Hammond lifted a hand in my direction.

"Hi, Ally!" Faith called, standing on her toes. "You have to show me your room!"

"Take her upstairs, Ally," Gray said congenially. "Show her around your new digs."

They're not my digs and you are not my father, I thought, but wasn't brave enough to say. Instead, I rolled my eyes, got up from the couch, and headed for the sliders to the beach.

"Ally? Ally, where are you going?" my mother called.

"I'm gonna go call Dad," I replied. "You know, the guy you're still married to?"

I closed the door behind me, shaking from my, admittedly, low blow. But honestly? Maybe she needed a reminder. Maybe they both did. I looked around for my flip-flops, which I'd definitely left out here earlier, but they were nowhere to be seen. Probably squirreled away by the shoe police.

I hurried down the steps anyway. It wasn't until my feet hit the cool sand that I could breathe again. I curled my toes, gripping the sand, then releasing it, letting it tickle the balls of my feet. Freedom was mine.

Then my phone beeped. I yanked it out of my pocket. It was a text from Faith.

WTF was that? R U O K?

I rolled my eyes and deleted it. Someone couldn't take a hint. For a minute, I considered actually calling my dad, but last night's conversation with him hadn't gone all that well, what with me lying through my teeth about why I'd changed my mind at the last minute, and him being oddly quiet in return. Besides, every time I thought about him and Jake together, I felt betrayed. What had Jake said about me? Did my dad realize Jake had been there the night Shannen had taken that video? Were they hanging out at Jump right now, wiping down the counters, talking about my crazy, fickle exit yesterday? The very idea made me want to hurl my phone into the ocean as far as I could.

Instead, I took a deep breath and walked a few yards toward the water, away from the house. Then I turned my steps north, following the edge of the dunes. The sound of the breaking waves cooled my nerves, and the stars overhead were like winking little friends, welcoming me back after my long absence. I took another deep breath and blew it out very, very slowly.

I loved the shore. Always had. I just currently couldn't stand the people who came with it.

A sudden whoop and a shout caught my attention and I froze. Squinting in the relative darkness, I could just make out the shadowy outline of about half a dozen people laughing and shoving each other closer to the shoreline. There were a couple of beer bottles—which was totally illegal, but common anyway—and an open box at their feet. While I stood there staring, someone noticed me and pointed me out. The hairs on the back of my neck stood on end. The beaches up here were private, but trespassing was a favorite pastime of some of the locals (who claimed they should own the beach since they lived here all year), and of some of the environmental types (who claimed all beaches belonged to everyone). So was this someone's older brother or sister and their friends—someone I knew—or were they strangers?

I faced forward and started walking again, feeling like an open target. Any luck, they'd just ignore me and stay where they were.

I was about thirty yards away from them, drawing up even, when the security light over the deck on the Schwartzes' house lit up like a spotlight and completely blinded me. There was a rustle in the reeds and someone came barreling out onto the sand, slamming right into my side.

"Damn! Watch where you're going," he said.

I blinked a few times, purple spots floating across my vision from the light. All I could tell was that he was broad, and there was a case of beer balanced on one shoulder.

"Oh," he said, looking at me. "Hey."

As the spots began to clear from my vision, I saw that he had shaggy blond hair under his backward baseball cap, and that he was already seriously tan. His Hawaiian-print bathing suit hung low on his hips, and his white T-shirt was sweaty in spots, clinging to his torso. Square face, broad shoulders, thick calves. Just looking at him, the word "solid" came to mind. And beautiful.

"Do I know you?" he asked.

"Um, no. I don't think so," I said. "I just came down with my family last night, so—"

"Wait. Is this *your* house?" he said, looking over his shoulder at the Schwartzes'. Before I could answer, his jaw dropped, amused. "Oh, shit!" he shouted. "Dudes! We're totally busted! One of the rich bitch bennies is here! Apparently we're on *her* beach."

My face burned as his friends closer to the water laughed. "I never said it was my beach," I hissed. "I don't care what you do."

I started past him, my arms crossed over my chest and my hands stuffed under my arms.

"Sorry," he called after me. "Just most people would bust my ass."

"It's fine," I said, just wanting to get away. "Have fun."

"No, wait."

I rolled my eyes and turned around to face him. "What?"

He dropped the box on the ground, ripped it open, and pulled out a Coors Light, which he held out to me. "Peace offering."

"No, thanks," I said.

"Come on. It looks like you could use one," he said.

I cocked one eyebrow. "Oh, and you know me so well?"

"I feel we've really connected," he replied teasingly.

I smirked. My eyes darted to the beer. I glanced back toward Gray's house, and took it.

He smiled. "I'm Cooper."

"Ally," I said.

"So, you're a weekender or what?" he asked.

"I'm down for the summer." I toyed with the tab on the can, flicking it with my thumbnail. "That's my mom's boyfriend's house," I added, pointing past his shoulder.

"Ah. I see." He had this glint in his eyes as he nodded, like he'd just completely figured me out. It both annoyed and intrigued me. "So come on."

"Come on where?" I asked.

"Come hang out with us, summer girl," he said, tipping his head toward his friends.

I considered for a moment, feeling tingly with possibility. But I'd never been one to party with strangers. And if the cops came and we got busted with alcohol, we'd all be screwed. My instincts were just telling me to bail when something caught his eye. I looked up to find Hammond speed walking toward us as best as he could in the sand.

"Hey," he said as he approached. "Everything cool?"

"Yeah," I replied, embarrassed. "Fine."

He shot Cooper a suspicious look and stepped closer to me, sort of squaring off with him. Cooper eyed him up and down, clearly amused.

"You know you're not supposed to be here," Hammond said.

My face burned with humiliation as Hammond played right into the "rich bitch bennie" stereotype. Cooper laughed and sipped his beer. Behind him, a couple of his friends had noticed Hammond and were loping toward us. Great. Just what I needed: a brawl on the beach.

"What are you doing here?" I asked Hammond.

"I just . . . your mom wanted me to see if you were okay," he said.

"Aw! How sweet!" Cooper said. "He's your mom's messenger boy!"

Hammond glowered. I could practically taste the adrenaline sizzling in the air between them.

"You know, I can have the cops here in under ten minutes," Hammond said.

I rolled my eyes. "Ham, go back to your family."

Cooper snorted. "Your name is *Ham*?"

Hammond, to his credit, ignored him. "Come back with me."

He was being protective. Which was sweet on some level. But I didn't need his protection.

"Thanks, I'm good right here." I walked past Cooper, toward his friends who were now mere steps away, trying to head off any confrontation. "You coming?" I shouted back to Cooper.

Cooper slowly took another sip of beer, looked at Hammond, then stooped to pick up the case. He tucked it between his arm and his hip. "Yeah. Let's go. See ya later, *Ham*."

His friends had paused next to me. One was a stocky guy with a buzz cut and huge arms. The other was a girl with blond braids wearing a bikini top and board shorts. We sized each other up, and waited for Cooper.

"All good?" the guy said.

Cooper nodded. "All good. Ally, this is Dex and Jenny. Jenny's my sister. Dex is just some loser we let hang out with us because his dad owns the Fishery and he gets us free clams."

"Ha-ha," Dex said. "Haven't heard that one before."

"That's all you got?" Jenny asked. "Coors Light?"

"It's all I could grab," Cooper replied. He swung the heavy case off his shoulder and kind of tossed it at her. She almost buckled under the weight. "Beggars can't be choosers, Jen. Next time you can do it yourself if you're so picky."

Cooper and Dex walked ahead of us as Jenny jostled the case until she got both arms under it. I moved to help her, but she shook me off.

"I got it." She rolled her eyes. "Brothers, right?"

"Yeah," I agreed, not knowing what else to say.

"So, you gonna hang out with us?" Jenny asked.

"I guess," I said.

"Yay!" She wagged her hips hugely as she walked me back toward the group, the box of beer cans shifting precariously. "Another gi-irl! Another gi-irl! Another gi-irl!" she sang. She dropped the beer on the ground next to the first, half-empty box, and slapped her hands together. "The testosterone around here is so thick it's like a frat party at Hooters during the NFL draft. *All* the time."

I laughed as the guys teased her. Over her shoulder, I watched Hammond trudge back to Gray's house, his shoulders slumped, and hoped he wouldn't tattle on me. He looked back at me once, but kept going, and I saw his cell light up as he texted someone. Gravity reversed itself as I realized he could very well be texting Jake, telling him that I was spending my second night at the shore with some random guy and his friends getting drunk.

But then . . . what did I care? Suddenly I'd had enough of doing what everyone expected of me—of being good, predictable little Ally. No one else ever cared about doing what *I* expected of *them*—not Jake, not my mom, not my dad. So let Hammond tell Jake whatever. Maybe it would be a good thing if he thought I was moving on.

"So, Ally." Cooper slung his heavy arm over my shoulder as he chugged. "Tell us all about yourself."

I smirked, hoping that Hammond was watching, and took the smallest sip from my beer. "What do you want to know?"

Daily Field Journal of Annie Johnston
Thursday, July 1

Position: Walking toward the park with David, en route from Scoops.

Cover: None.

Observations:

10:22 p.m.: Subject Chloe Appleby emerges, laughing, through front door of the Golden Marquee movie theater across the street. Uniform: floral sundress, strappy sandals, date-hair. Subject Jake Graydon steps out behind her. Also laughing. (Note: I miss what happens next because I walk right into a light post, drop my ice cream on my foot, and momentarily black out. When I come to again, David is laughing his ass off, my new sandals are ruined, and Subject Chloe and Subject Jake are gone.)

Jake

I'd been working at Jump, Java, and Wail! for exactly fifty-seven minutes. There was already a patch of sweat on my neckline, I'd cut my finger closing the pastry case on it, and gotten screamed at for trying to serve a doughnut I'd dropped on the floor. Apparently no one around here had heard of the five second rule.

Fifty-seven minutes and I'd considered quitting thirteen times.

"Can't you just pour me a coffee? How hard is it? The cups are right there."

Make that fourteen.

"Want me to come around and do it for you?"

No. I want you to shut the fuck up and stuff that yoga mat you're toting up your ass. Which, I'll admit, was a fine ass. But still.

"I told you, this is my first day," I said through my teeth. "I can't handle the coffee."

The woman snorted through her skinny nose. She tapped her hands against the glass case, her huge diamond ring clanging around. "You can't handle the coffee. Takes a big man to admit that."

I paused with my plastic-gloved hand hovering over the muffins. Was she mocking me? Was this adult person mocking me?

I glanced over my shoulder at Chase, who was taking orders, and Leena, who was making the coffees. I was supposed to be getting Leena an apple cinnamon muffin for her customer, but she didn't look like she was waiting on it.

"Fine," I said to yoga bitch. "Large coffee with milk?"

"*Skim* milk."

Her cell phone rang. I glanced at my coworkers again. No one was paying attention to me. I grabbed the regular coffee from the burner and snagged one of the large cups. I poured it half full with coffee, then bent to the refrigerator, which I'd seen Leena open a dozen times. In it were four silver containers clearly labeled: whole milk, two percent milk, skim milk, and cream. Which had more fat in it, whole milk or cream? I didn't have time to overthink it. I grabbed the whole milk and dumped it into the coffee. The woman was still gabbing on her phone when I handed it over.

"How much?" she said, holding her hand over the receiver.

"S'on me," I told her with a big-ass smile.

She looked me up and down, and all of a sudden she was flirting with me. "Thanks. I'll be back."

Then she winked, picked up the cup, and walked out. Outside the glass door, I saw her take a huge chug of it. Nice.

A few guys from school walked in, including Will Halloran. Snagged. I lifted my chin at them. They looked confused. And then, Leena was all up in my face.

"Excuse me. Did you just make a coffee, then give it away?" Leena demanded.

"I, uh—"

Over her shoulder, I saw Will and his pals looking on.

"You are on muffin duty. Nothing else, all right?" Leena scolded me. "And I believe I asked you for an apple cinnamon."

Did those guys really just hear this woman tell me I'm on muffin duty? From the cackling, it looked that way.

Fifteen times.

What should I do? Tell her off? Make a joke? While I was still trying to figure out how to save face, she reached past me, took a muffin, and stormed away.

"And you're gonna pay for that coffee!" she threw over her shoulder.

Son of a—

Sixteen times.

At that moment, Ally's dad stuck his head out from the office. "How's it going out here, Jake?"

"Fine," I replied, hoping no one would say otherwise. "Great."

"Good. Keep it up. When I'm done back here, I'll come train you on the coffee machine." And then he was gone.

I wondered what Ally was doing right then. Sleeping in, probably. Dr. Nathanson's shore house was sick, with a hot tub on the roof and an infinity pool on the second level looking over the ocean. Maybe she was in the pool. I wondered if she was a bikini person or a one-piece. Probably a one-piece, but let's make it a sexy one-piece. . . .

"Hey, Graydon."

I looked up. Will and his two football buddies were in front of the muffin case. One of them was Andy Lu, a linebacker I knew from trig. Kind of a jackass. He talked back to the teacher like he thought it was hilarious, when, really, it was just embarrassing for both of them and annoying for everyone else. The other was Rory Crane, the quarterback. He was okay, mostly. He lived in one of the bigger houses on the Norm side of town. I'd been there once for a group project; his mom had served us crudités for some reason.

"What's up, guys?" I asked.

"I hear you're on muffin duty," Rory said with a laugh.

I sighed through my nose. Seventeen times.

"You guys want something?" I asked.

"I wanna know what you're doing working here," Andy said, leaning his beefy arms on top of the case. The thing actually sagged in the middle. "Whaddaya, need a weekend car or somethin'?"

Lu and Crane laughed. Will rubbed his eyebrow.

"Jake! I need a marble loaf and a bran muffin!" Leena shouted.

"I'm on it!" I shouted back.

"Get on it faster," she replied.

Lu and Crane cracked up again.

"Come on, man," Will said. "Leave him alone. Dude's working." He smacked Lu on the chest with the back of his hand, and the three of them moved back to the line.

I shot Will a grateful look, grabbed the muffin and the marble loaf, and shoved them in a paper bag. I cursed under my breath, hating my mother for doing this to me. As I dropped the bag on the counter, my phone beeped. Chase's eyes darted to my hand as I pulled it out of my pocket, but he said nothing. Probably because he was texting every chance he got.

I checked the screen, turning back toward the muffin case. It was from Chloe.

Had nightmares thx 2 u. Next time I pick the movie.

I laughed under my breath. Chloe had claimed to be totally

fine with seeing the latest end-of-the-world flick. And it was good. The special effects were awesome. But I guess it was too realistic for her. She kept hiding her face and knocked over my popcorn when that meteor had come outta nowhere and flattened that dog. I texted back.

Fine. No subtitles.

The office door opened again and I shoved the phone away. Mr. Ryan came over and slapped his hand down on my shoulder.

"All right, Graydon, you are about to learn the intricacies of a good cappuccino."

"Uh. Great," I said.

Will and his buddies had made it to the counter, and I was glad I wasn't going to be running for their muffins. In fact, I was feeling a lot better than I was five minutes ago. Chloe and I had had fun last night. And she wanted to do it again. Maybe this summer wouldn't suck entirely.

Ally

"Make me a vanilla, chocolate, and coffee banana split."

I looked at Mitch Daly, the proprietor of Take a Dip ice cream. Then I looked at the clock. It was 10:30 in the morning. He couldn't be serious. But he didn't blink.

"Um, okay. I can come behind the counter?" I asked.

"You're gonna hafto if you're gonna make me a banana split," Mitch said. Then he kind of inhaled a laugh, his shoulders and massive stomach rising and falling as one.

Excellent point. I stepped behind the counter and looked

around. There was less space back there than I would have thought—only about three feet of red tile floor between the ice-cream freezer and the counters along the back. Mitch had already set up for the day, so the ice-cream scoops were floating in warm water in little silver buckets that hung from the sides of the freezers, and the covers had been removed from the huge tubs of ice cream. I had never made a banana split before, but my dad used to make them for us all the time. How hard could it be?

I plucked one of the long, plastic bowls from the dispenser. Mitch crossed his beefy arms and laid them atop his Santa-style stomach. There was a black tattoo on his left forearm depicting a frog keeled over next to a beer bottle, its eyes tiny x's and its tongue hanging out, trailing flat into a puddle of beer.

Which begged the question: Did I really want to work for this guy?

"You might want to start with a banana," he suggested.

"Right."

There were two bushels of bananas hanging from a metal holder on the counter. I ripped one off, peeled it, and looked around for a cutting board. Not finding one, I used a paper plate. Behind me, Mitch clucked his tongue, but said nothing. Feeling hot all down my back, I procured a knife from a drawer and cut the banana in half down the center, then cut both halves lengthwise. I placed them in the bowl like a hot-dog bun, just the way my dad always did. As I turned for the ice cream, Mitch stood on his toes to see over my shoulder. His stomach just grazed my back.

This was definitely the oddest job interview I'd ever suffered through.

I started with the vanilla, making sure to use a different scoop for each ice cream so as not to taint one flavor with the other, which was always one of my pet peeves. Mitch grunted his approval at this move. Once all the ice cream was scooped, I closed the freezer, but the heavy door slipped from my sweating palm and slammed at the last second, almost taking my fingertip off.

"Oops. Sorry," I said.

Mitch simply closed his eyes for a moment, as if praying for patience. My throat was completely dry, and it felt like it was somehow coated in the same sickly sweet smell that clung to everything in the place. I turned around and looked at the row of syrups against the back wall. There was chocolate, butterscotch, caramel, marshmallow, strawberry, and a warming vat of hot fudge. Crap. Which one went on a banana split?

I looked up, quickly and casually scanning the colorful signs advertising the million different combinations one could order at Take a Dip. There was a two-scoop sundae, a three-scoop waffle cone, a ten-scoop bikini buster. But the classic banana split was nowhere to be found.

"Um?" I looked at Mitch quizzically. "Which toppings would you like . . . sir?"

"Hot fudge and whipped cream," he said.

"Right."

I doused the ice cream with hot fudge, dripping a few huge globs of the stuff on the counter. Biting my tongue, I hit the fridge, grabbed the first can of whipped cream I saw, and sprayed. It exploded everywhere. Literally everywhere. Pellets of whipped cream dotted my shirt, the glass doors of the fridge, the ceiling fan lazily spinning above our heads, . . . and Mitch Daly's face.

"Oh my gosh. I'm so sorry!"

Clearly I was not getting this job. I wondered if the CVS by the causeway was hiring. At least I had experience. But there were no tips at CVS, and summer jobs down the shore were all about the tips.

Slowly, Mitch extracted a filthy rag from the back pocket of his grungy shorts and wiped his face.

"S'okay," he said, licking his lips. "Happens all the time. You gotta hold it upright."

He reached over and straightened the silver bottle in my hand, so that it was perpendicular to the floor and my elbow was sticking up at an unnatural angle. I said a quick prayer and tried again. The whipped cream came out nice and slow, in perfect ridged beauty. After adding a generous mound to the top of the sundae, I placed the can back in the refrigerator and handed him the bowl.

"Cherry?" he said.

"Right. Cherry." There was a topping bar in an open case between the two freezers. I plucked a cherry out by its stem and placed it atop the sundae. Then I stepped back, wiped my hands together, and realized I was nervous. I wanted Mitch Daly's approval. What was wrong with me?

He turned the sundae this way and that, inspecting it from all angles. He even held it up and checked underneath.

"Not bad," he said finally. "Technically, the customer also gets one dry topping." He tilted his head toward the toppings bar, with its stunning array of choices, everything from sprinkles to crushed nuts to mini M&M's to chopped Thin Mints. "But it's okay. I'm watching my calorie intake this summer."

He reached for a plastic spoon, dipped it in, and took a huge, whipped cream—laden bite. His T-shirt rode up, exposing a swirl of black hair around his belly button. I wondered if this man actually knew what a calorie was.

"Can you start this afternoon?" he asked, his mouth full. "I already had somebody call in sick."

"Yes! Definitely. And my summer is *wide* open, so as many shifts as you can give me, I—"

He held up his hand, the spoon held between his thumb and forefinger in an oddly delicate manner, to stop me.

"We'll see how you do," he said gravely. "The ice cream game . . . is not for everyone." Then he turned and walked down the aisle toward the door, which led, I assumed, to the storeroom. "Pick out a shirt from the case out front. You get one free and if you want extras, you can buy 'em at half price. And be here at two for a four-hour." He kicked open the door. "And clean up that counter before you go."

The door slammed behind him. I breathed out and looked through the windows at the fluorescent lights twisted into the shapes of dripping ice-cream cones and chocolate-covered bars and funnel cakes. I was gainfully employed. By a man who ate ice cream for breakfast.

I swiped a rag from one of the bars that hung from the back cabinet doors, wet it, and cleaned up my mess. The case to which Mitch had referred was a double-doored bookcase filled with folded Take a Dip T-shirts in a variety of colors, which were available for purchase at the low, low price of fifteen bucks. But lucky me—I got to take one, gratis. Already this job had benefits. I chose a blue short-sleeved with a strawberry cone on the back and the words DIP THIS scrawled above it. On the front, above the left breast, was the Take a Dip logo—a girl in a bikini diving into a vat of chocolate ice cream.

I balled the shirt up and turned to go, but paused when I saw Hammond peeking through the locked glass door, his hand above his eyes like he was on a boat at sea scanning the waves for the shoreline. My jaw automatically clenched. He stood up straight when he saw me approach, and took a step back. It was almost like he expected me to be there.

"They don't open for another hour, you know," I said, stepping out into the heat.

"Oh. Weird. I thought they opened at ten," Hammond said.

I let the door close and lock. Hammond's Explorer was the only ride in the parking lot. The cruising bike I'd borrowed from Gray's garage leaned against the brick wall next to it.

"So, what was up with you and those locals last night?" Hammond asked, pushing his hands into the pockets of his plaid shorts. He leaned back against the wood railing of the porch, which wrapped around the side of Take a Dip and was slam-packed with people almost every night of the summer.

"Hammond, did you follow me here?"

"What? No," he said.

He totally did.

"You know how obsessed I am with their Moose Tracks," he said.

"Right. Don't tell me. Jake, Chloe, and Shannen aren't coming down, so you need someone to hang out with," I said. "It's so nice to be everyone's fourth or fifth choice."

Hammond laughed. "Like you've ever been anyone's fourth or fifth choice."

I blushed, and wondered if he even realized what he just said.

"Well, if you're planning on being all up in my grill all summer, good luck," I said, trying to skate past the awkward moment. "Looks like I'm going to be spending most of my time here."

"Oh yeah?" Hammond looked up at the wooden sign above the door, all freshly repainted for the summer. "Then maybe I'll get a job here too."

"Yeah, right," I said.

"What? What's so funny?" Hammond asked.

"You don't work," I replied. *And half the reason I wanted to get a job was so that I wouldn't have to be around you and your little friends.*

He lifted a shoulder. "Maybe I'll give it a whirl. I do have to start saving some money for college. Since, you know, my entire college fund magically disappeared."

My throat closed over. The smile fell off Hammond's face. Apparently he'd momentarily forgotten that it was my dad who'd magically disappeared his college fund, and that it had caused all of us more than our fair share of misery over the last couple of years.

"Right, so . . . I'll just go fill out an application."

He tried the door. Which was still locked.

"You have to call the guy," I said, taking out my phone. I dialed Mitch's office number, which I'd found in the paper that morning. He answered on the third ring.

"Take a Dip!"

"Hi, Mitch. It's Ally Ryan."

Dead silence. Except for the slurping of ice cream.

"Ally Ryan? You just hired me?" I said, giving Hammond a confused look.

"Oh, right. Didja clean up the counter?" he asked.

"Yeah. I'm actually outside with someone else who wants to apply," I said.

There was a heaving sigh, followed by a loud squeal. Then I saw the office door open out of the corner of my eye. Mitch stuck his head out.

"What's his deal?" he asked, checking Hammond over from the other side of the shop.

"His name's Hammond," I said. Hammond lifted a hand in a wave. "He's . . . a good guy."

Hammond raised his eyebrows at me, pleased. What was I going to do, tell the manager that Ham was a jerk after he'd just reminded me my family was responsible for the fact that he needed a job this summer in the first place? Not likely.

"All right. I'm comin'," Mitch said.

"Thanks."

I turned my phone off and tucked it away as Mitch lumbered across the small shop.

"You so love me," Hammond said with a grin.

"Yeah." I scoffed a laugh. "We'll see if you still think that after your interview," I said sarcastically.

Suddenly he didn't look quite so cocky. I would've given my left pinky finger to see Hammond fumble his way through a banana split, but I had to go. I didn't want him thinking I cared.

I just hoped he'd screw it up worse than I had. Because there was no way I was working side by side with Hammond Ross in three feet of space all summer long.

As I jogged down the steps toward Gray's bike, the man himself turned his Land Rover into the parking lot, its massive tires crunching over gravel. My mom was in the front seat, and

I caught a glimpse of Quinn's blond hair as he turned the car sideways in the lot, taking up almost the entire space. I froze with my hand on the handlebar. My mom's window eased down.

"How'd it go?" she asked, resting her arm on the windowsill.

"Fine. I got the job," I said.

"Great! Hop in! We're going to LBI Pancake House for a late breakfast."

The back of the Land Rover opened automatically, letting out a hiss. Gray got out of the car and walked around as if to help me with my bike. My fingers tightened around the grip. This whole scenario felt way too "one big happy family" for me, and I knew why they were doing it. They were trying to prove to me that just because I stormed out on them last night, it didn't mean I wasn't going to have to spend time with them this summer. They weren't giving up that easily.

"I'm not hungry," I said, looking past Gray's shoulder at my mom. "I was going to go for a bike ride."

"So you can go after breakfast," Gray said.

He put his hands on the handlebars, right next to mine. When I looked at him, poison darts flew from my eyes. "I said, I'm not hungry."

I wrested the bike from his grip and straddled it, awkwardly maneuvering around him.

"Ally," my mother said. "Come here, please."

I felt hot all over, and my throat was so tight I could barely breathe. But I turned my back on her and started to peddle toward the street. "I'll see you guys later," I called, my voice strained.

"Ally!" my mom shouted, seriously pissed now.

But I didn't turn back. I tore out of there as fast as I could, and turned down a side street hoping to make as many turns as possible so they wouldn't be able to follow me. My mother may have decided she wanted to spend all her time with Gray and Quinn Nathanson, but she couldn't force me to do it too. I'd never wanted a sister. And I already had a father. They were just going to have to be one big happy family without me.

Ally

How much ice cream did u eat?

I smirked at Annie's text and leaned back on the soft lounge cushion to text back. The view from Gray's deck was not at all bad, especially now, as the sun was setting behind me, glittering golden over the water. It was Friday evening and I was freshly showered after my first shift at Take a Dip, which had actually been kind of fun. Somewhere during the third hour I'd realized that making sundaes and cones lent a certain giddy satisfaction—the kids' grins as they used both hands to take a dripping double-dip from my fingers, the glimmer of life in exhausted parents' eyes when they saw their mango milk shakes. I felt like I was making people happy, which was rarely the case when slinging Depends undergarments and Pepto at the CVS back home.

There had been a rush on the place around three o'clock that had lasted until four, but I was out of there at six, when the dinnertime lull was on. From what my coworker Sandy had told me, it was the evening shift that was the real killer—started around seven and didn't stop till after eleven. Mitch didn't have me scheduled for one of those until late next week. Apparently he liked to ease in the newcomers.

The unfortunate part was spotting Hammond's name on the schedule. Guess he hadn't flubbed as badly as I'd thought on the banana split test. Our first overlapping shift was scheduled for the Fourth of July. I was already trying to think up ways to get out of it. And then I came home to find my mother and Gray coming inside from the outdoor shower, all wet and giggling, and found that, somehow, I just could not be in the same house with them. They were now inside, throwing together some kind of trendy summer salad in Gray's state-of-the-art kitchen, listening to light rock on the stereo system, while Quinn was off at rehearsal. Thank God for the deck. Although, I was surprised that my mother had yet to come out here to talk about how I'd bailed on them that morning. Maybe she'd decided to just ignore it. Hopefully.

I texted back.

None.

Liar!

LOL. I figured if I started, I wouldn't be able to stop. So when r u coming down?

Tmrw late morning. Mom needs car in a.m. to drop off recycling. BTW have good Crestie dirt.

My heart thumped and I stared at the screen. How could she have good Crestie dirt? Ninety-eight percent of the Cresties were down the shore or in Europe. She couldn't mean *Jake* dirt, could she? Had she talked to him? Had he asked about me? Had he told her why he hadn't called?

I swallowed back the urge to ask. I did not want to appear

interested in what Jake was doing. Because I wasn't.

Cool.

The sliding glass door behind me zipped open, spilling out a blast of cold air and overproduced synthesizer. Crap. Looked like my reprieve was over. Here came the lecture.

"Ally? You have a visitor," my mom said.

Or not. I turned around in my chair, expecting to see either Faith or Hammond—my two LBI stalkers. I almost dropped the phone when Cooper stepped out the door next to my mother. He was even more beautiful in daylight: a white T-shirt showing off his insane tan, his blond hair long enough to curl under his ears. I realized suddenly that I never thought I'd see this guy again—and that I was very happy to be proven wrong.

"Hi," I said.

"Hi."

His grin almost knocked me out of my chair. My mother shot me an intrigued and expectant look. Her hand was still on the door and she stood sideways, because Cooper's shoulders nearly filled the opening. He had a beach towel around his neck, and wore brown and tan Billabong swim trunks and flip-flops.

My phone beeped, but I didn't even look at Annie's text. I just texted back.

Gotta go. Hot boy arrival.

There. That'd make her think I didn't care what Jake was up to.

"What's up?" I asked Cooper, standing. I smoothed my cotton shorts over my thighs and cleared my throat, wishing I'd dried my hair after my shower.

"I came by to see if you wanted to go for a swim," he said.

"Uh, yeah. I could do that," I said.

He'd remembered where I was staying. He'd stopped by. In all my years of coming down the shore, no local boy had ever noticed me. Not once. The packs of local kids always had this aura about them. They were almost never fully clothed, and had zero qualms about it. They could ride their bikes barefoot and ocean-wet, while toting long boards under one arm. Whenever they walked into a surf shop or the fudge place or a pizza joint, they knew someone behind the counter and would make plans to go places we'd never heard of even though the island was so small there was no way we hadn't heard of everything.

That was probably why I'd never considered hanging out with a local crowd to avoid the Cresties. It was an unimaginable alternative. But now, with Cooper standing there in all his beach-boy perfection, it definitely seemed like a viable—not to mention, very attractive—option. I felt this sort of warm satisfaction that he'd come to find me. It was as if I'd broken some kind of secret code.

"Let me just go get changed."

Cooper turned sideways so I could slide between him and my mom. I shot her a smile—normally cute boys were something we bonded over—but she didn't smile back. Instead, she followed me over to the stairs. Gray didn't look up from the tomatoes he was slicing in the open kitchen.

"Ally?" my mom called. "Can I talk to you for a minute?"

"Yeah. I'll be right down," I shouted over my shoulder as I jogged up the steps. Inside the room I'd been assigned for the summer—cream walls, peach bedspread, Formica furniture—I yanked open the bottom dresser drawer and pulled out my two bathing suits. The blue Speedo was out of the question. It smashed everything down and made me look like a boy. The other—a striped tankini from last summer—left something to be desired, but at least you could tell I had female parts. I yanked my T-shirt off over my head just as my mom walked in.

"God! You scared me!" I said, holding the shirt against my chest for a second.

"I'm sorry, but would you care to explain?" she whispered, closing the door behind her.

"Explain what?" I asked. I turned my back to her to change.

"That boy," she said impatiently. "Who is he? How do you know him?"

"His name's Cooper," I said as I shimmied into the bathing suit top. "He's a local."

"So . . . what? We're just hanging out with random local boys now?" she asked.

My skin bristled at her comment. Why did the word "local" sound so negative when she said it?

"Is there something wrong with local boys?" I asked. "Is he not rich enough for you? Because guess what, Mom, we're not rich either. Or did you forget that?"

I whipped my T-shirt off my bed and pulled it on, then quickly reached back to braid my hair, sliding in front of the full length mirror on the closet door.

"Ally," she said with a sigh.

"Besides, it's either hang out with him or have no friends all summer, because I am *not* hanging out with Hammond and Faith no matter how many times you try to throw us together," I said.

My mother stepped up behind me, her face hovering just over my shoulder in our reflection.

"This has nothing to do with money, Ally. You know that," she said, just barely holding on to her patience. "It's just that we know nothing about him."

I tightened the rubber band around my braid and let it snap. "Well, I know one thing. I'd rather be on the beach with him than standing here having this conversation with you."

I grabbed my flip-flops and a towel out of the closet and started past her, but she stopped me with a hand on my arm.

"Ally, what is going on with you?" she hissed under her breath. "First you ditch out on dinner last night, then breakfast this morning, and now you're completely overreacting to everything I say. You still haven't even told me why you changed your mind and decided to come down."

I looked at my hands. That was not something I felt like trying to explain right now. Not with Cooper downstairs waiting on me.

"Clearly it had nothing to do with wanting to spend time with us," she added with a hint of sarcasm.

I looked into my mother's eyes. All my potential replies sounded petulant and childish. I wanted to tell her I didn't like it here, living in this house where you couldn't put your feet up and you had to dry off completely before stepping inside, where Gray got all tense if he found a crumb or a stain or a droplet of water. I wanted to tell her that all the rules made me tense, but that seeing her and Gray together one hundred percent of the time made me even tenser. Watching them touch hands grabbing for a morning bagel and letting their fingers linger. Seeing the way they looked at each other when I made a joke or Quinn said something silly. It all felt too much like a family, and it wasn't a family I wanted to be a part of. I wanted to be a part of *my* family. Me, her, and my dad.

But I couldn't say any of this. So instead I said, "Remember when you and dad renewed your vows?"

Her eyes instantly looked sad. She dropped her hand and turned away from me. "Ally—" She sounded fed up, at the end of her rope.

"Mom, I'm just asking. Do you even remember that? Because it wasn't *that* long ago," I said, following her toward the sliding glass doors that led to the deck outside my and Quinn's rooms. "You guys were really happy. I know Dad screwed up, but don't you even want to talk to him?"

"He didn't just screw up, Ally," she said, giving me a look that made me feel two inches tall.

"For the past two years you've been telling me that I have to find a way to forgive him. That he didn't mean to do what he did," I said tersely. "But now that he's back, you won't even talk to him. You're such a total hypocrite."

I'd never said anything that harsh to my mom in my life, and as soon as the words were out of my mouth, I wanted to take them back. But instead, I turned around and walked out of the room, trying to escape before she reacted.

"Ally, get back here," my mom said quietly.

I kept walking and jogged down the stairs. Cooper was waiting in the living room, the TV remote in his hand, a Wimbledon tennis match playing on the big screen.

"This TV is sick!" he said, his eyes bright.

I grabbed his wrist as I raced by. "Come on. Let's go."

Startled, Cooper dropped the remote. It clattered on the glass coffee table and an odd squeak escaped Gray's throat. We had just made it to the glass door that looked out over the main deck with the infinity pool, and the beach, when my mother reached the loft railing one story above.

"Ally!" she shouted. "This conversation isn't over. Not by a long shot. We're going to talk about this later."

I slipped outside and slammed the door as hard as I could. Every inch of me clenched in humiliation.

"Sorry about that," I told Cooper. Then I looked down at my hand around his arm, and released it, embarrassed.

"Don't worry about it." He held the ends of his towel with both hands. "My mom can be a bitch too."

"My mom's not a bitch," I said quickly.

He shot me this look like *whatever*, which somehow made me feel foolish. And also made me wonder what *his* mother was like.

"Well, thanks for giving me an excuse to escape," I said.

"No worries." He placed his hands on the railing and looked out at the empty beach below. It was low tide, and the waves were gently lapping the shore. "Damn. This is beautiful."

I stared at his profile. Suddenly I wished Jake could see me right then, standing out here, looking out over the ocean with this perfect beach boy. I bet he'd regret not apologizing then. He'd regret the fact that he'd yet to call.

"Yeah, but maybe we should walk up the beach a little," I said, glancing warily at the house.

He shrugged. "Works for me." For a second he leaned back, clinging to the railing with his feet planted, then looked at me mischievously. "Race ya."

And he was gone, jogging down the wide wooden stairs in his flip-flops with a teasing laugh.

"Cheater!"

I ran after him, letting the wind whisk away the last bits of my anger. I could deal with my mother later. For now—just this once—I was going to pretend it was actually summer.

Daily Field Journal of Annie Johnston
Friday, July 2

Position: Corner table at Jump.

Cover: In need of caffeine to aid in plowing through summer reading list.

Observations:

8:35 p.m.: Subject Jake Graydon stares out the window from behind counter. Uniform: black T-shirt, khaki cargo shorts, brown Jump apron. He pulls out his phone, checks it, puts it back.

8:40 p.m.: Subject Shannen Moore walks in. Uniform: patched denim cutoffs, deep red tank top, flip-flops, aviators. She stops dead in her tracks when she sees Subject Jake behind the counter. (Query: Is it possible that Shannen didn't know her BFF was working here?)

Shannen: Oh. Hey. You work here?

(Assessment: Guess so.)

Jake: Um, yeah.

Shannen: Oh.

Subject Shannen places her bag down on the counter.

Shannen: Let me get a latte.

Subject Jake grabs a cup. Drops it. Dives for it. Grabs it. Fumble recovered. Subject Shannen narrows her eyes.

Shannen: Actually . . . make that a vanilla soy latte. With whipped cream. And cinnamon.

Subject Jake doesn't move.

Shannen: Also a bialy. Everything. With low fat cream cheese. Unless you don't have everything, and then I just want plain, but with the cranberry cream cheese. But don't put too much on. And I don't see any chocolate chip muffins. Can you check in back and see if they have any? But I'll take that vanilla soy latte first.

Subject Jake looks at her over his shoulder. (Assessment: He's imagining a gruesome death scenario.)

Shannen: Please.

(Assessment: Someone is no longer someone's BFF.)

Jake

"What is the definition of the word . . . 'obsequious'?"

I stared out the bay window in my room. It looked out over the kidney-shaped pool in our backyard. The ancient woman next to me cleared her throat, then made this choking sound. She spit up something into her mouth, and swallowed it. I was about to vomit.

"Mr. Graydon? Obsequious."

The pink flash card fluttered in her spotted, gnarly fingers. I looked at the word. How did she print in such perfect block letters when every inch of her body was constantly shaking? She had all this excess skin under her chin and it hung so low it covered the collar of her flowered shirt.

"Um . . . annoying?" I guessed.

She sighed, and a mouthful of onion breath hovered over my room like a toxic cloud.

"It means dutiful . . . servile." She placed the flash card down on the pile of words I'd gotten wrong. It was a lot bigger than the ones I'd gotten right. But now I'd remember "obsequious." Because it was what I was being right now.

In my lap, my phone vibrated. Even though it was loud, she didn't notice. I glanced at the screen. It was a text from Hammond.

Where r u dude? Get ur ass down here already.
I texted back.

Can't. Stuck w Shale's SAT tutor.
Thought u were talking 2 ur mom.
I did. No dice.

119

The old lady lifted another card. I took a deep breath and held it. Then texted again.

Have u seen ally?

There was no response.

"What is the definition of . . ."—cough, phlegm rattle—"mendicant?"

I brightened slightly. I knew this one. "Begging . . . or a beggar."

She smiled. Her front two teeth were brown. "Good!"

The card went on my correct stack. My phone vibrated.

Not really. She's avoiding us.

I let out a frustrated sigh. I don't know what I'd been hoping for. That she was sitting around moping? Asking about me? Why would she be doing that when she'd basically told me she couldn't give a shit about me right before she left? I still couldn't figure out what I'd done so wrong that day. If she'd given me five more seconds, I would have explained everything. I would've told her why I kept the whole thing about her dad a secret. And maybe she would have forgiven me. She would've had to. Because I didn't really do anything wrong. It was all Shannen.

My teeth gnashed like they did every time I thought about Shannen lately. We'd been having the perfect night until she'd gone and effed it all up. Me and Ally were *this close* to being together like a real couple. I'd never even wanted that with anyone before, and the second I did? Gone.

The door to my room opened behind us and I quickly shoved my phone under my leg. The old lady tutor might have been hard of hearing, but my mom wasn't missing a thing lately with the mood she'd been in. The other day she'd called me out because I'd left my damn Xbox on pause overnight. Like we had any problems paying the electric bills. It was like she was looking for ways to get on my case.

"How's it going in here?" she asked.

I didn't acknowledge her, but tutor lady smiled as she turned haltingly in her seat. I could hear her bones creaking as she moved.

"Fine, fine. He's coming along," she said.

What? Seriously? Maybe she could only remember that I'd gotten the last one right. I sat up a little straighter.

"Good! I'm glad to hear it," my mother said. From the corner of my eye, I saw her smooth my bedspread. Guess Marta, our cleaning lady, hadn't done a good enough job that morning. "See, Jake? I knew you could do it if you just focused."

Right. Whatever you say. But I wasn't about to contradict her. I knew an opportunity when I saw it. And this was an opportunity to make a deal. To maybe get a chance to see Ally. I turned in my chair, hooking my arm over the back. My phone dug into my thigh as it slid toward the edge of the seat.

"Hey, Mom, I was thinking . . . since I'm doing so well . . . maybe I could go down the shore tonight? Just for the rest of the weekend," I added quickly.

She stood up straight and let her hands fall heavy at her side. "Jake, no."

"But Mom—"

"You have to work this weekend," my mother said. She picked up my sandals and tossed them into my closet.

I cursed the day I'd left my schedule on the kitchen counter. My mother had made a copy on the printer in the office and tacked it to the damn refrigerator.

"I can get someone to cover my shifts," I said. "Please. Mom! I'm missing everything."

"This is not about getting someone to cover for you," my mother said, closing the closet door with a bang. "You have responsibilities now, Jake. You need to learn to honor them."

My fingers clenched into fists. Suddenly my room felt insanely small. Like there was no air. Like the ceiling was slowly lowering above my head. Everyone I knew was down the shore—sleeping late, playing volleyball on the beach, eating Bay Village pizza every day, and wakeboarding while the sun went down. But me? I was trapped in my tiny cell, breathing in noxious onion fumes and learning words no sane twenty-first-century person ever used in actual conversation.

"This sucks," I said, slumping back in my chair. As I moved, my phone hit the floor. And vibrated loudly. I lunged for it, but my mother was too fast. She plucked it off the carpet and checked the screen. Her face went ashen.

"Your mom blows," she read.

My heart curled up and died. "He didn't mean—"

My mother's mouth was a very thin line. She turned the phone off and dropped it in the pocket of her white shorts. "You can have that back when we're done here. Meantime, I think I'll call Hammond's mom."

My face was on fire. "Mom, come on. Don't."

"I think she should know the kind of language her son is using, don't you?" she said.

I swear old lady tutor laughed. Or maybe she was just choking again.

"As for you, Jake, maybe we were unclear on what 'grounded for the summer' means," my mother continued. "The sooner you accept that this is your life for the next two months, the better off you'll be."

I bit my tongue to keep from pointing out that she'd let me go to the movies with Chloe. Maybe *she* was unclear about what "grounded for the summer" meant. I mean, she was the first one to blur the lines. I was just trying to make them blurrier. But if I said anything, she might go the other way. She might not let me go to the movies again, and then I'd really be screwed. So I just kept my mouth shut and slumped a little lower.

"I ordered sushi for dinner," my mother said. "When you're done here, you can go pick it up."

"Fine," I said through my teeth.

"Keep up the good work, Mrs. Tate!" my mother said as she walked out of the room.

When she closed the door behind her, I swear I heard the sound of prison bars clanging.

Ally

That night, after an awkward dinner, I lay on my stomach on my bed with the door of the deck open, listening to the waves and reading *Wuthering Heights*. It was the first of the four books I'd have to read off my summer reading list if I wanted to start off AP English on the right foot in the fall. I lazily turned the page, trying to stop my brain from going where it kept wanting to go.

To Cooper's tan, wet abs.

I shivered, giggled, and buried my face in the book for a second, inhaling that musty Orchard Hill library scent. Then I cleared my throat and straightened my face. I'd just pretend I was in class. That I had a teacher staring me down and I had to concentrate. That would keep me from—

Cooper's smile. His wet hair clinging to his forehead. His arm muscles flexing as he grabbed for me playfully in the water. God he was hot.

I pushed myself up onto my butt and was about to slide back into the pillows, when there was a quick, authoritative rap on my door. My heart caught.

"Come in?"

Gray opened the door wide and stood on the threshold. He wore a salmon polo, unbuttoned one button too many, and crisp, gray flat-front chinos. "Ally, I'd like to talk to you."

Oh. Great.

I swallowed hard. "I'm actually right in the middle of this chapter and it's an assignment for school, so—"

"This will only take a minute."

He stepped inside and half closed the door. Still, I felt trapped. I laid the book aside, lifted my chin, and waited.

"It's about your mother," he began, placing his palms together. "She's . . . very upset with you."

I felt a flash of anger. I knew how my mom was feeling. I'd known how my mom was feeling every day of my life from the day I could talk. I didn't need him to tell me.

"No. You know what? That's a cop-out," he said. "It's not just your mother; I'm very upset with you, too."

"Excuse me?" I blurted, pressing my hands into the mattress.

"Look, I realize you're going through a lot right now, with what happened at Shannen Moore's party and your dad coming back out of nowhere, but when I invited you and your mother down here for the summer, I was not expecting to be sharing my house with a sullen, rude teenager for two months."

My jaw dropped. I shoved myself up off the bed, standing on the far side—as far away from him as I could get. "Oh, well I'm sorry if I'm not living up to your high expectations!"

"That's not what I meant," he said. He took a second, squeezed his eyes closed, and scratched at his forehead. Apparently he'd never had to give Quinn a talking-to, perfect as she was. My very existence seemed to have stumped him. I crossed my arms over my chest and waited. "Look, what I meant to say is . . . this is just no way to behave . . . taking your disappointment and . . . and anger out on the rest of us. Now, I know that your mother isn't quite ready to talk about the situation with your dad, so if you need someone to talk to—"

"You?" I practically screeched, backing up a step. "Are you kidding me? You want me to talk to you?"

His face dropped a bit. "Is that so hard to imagine?"

"Uh, yeah!" I shouted. "You are not my father."

The words hung in the air for a long moment. I heard a creak down the hall and wondered where my mother and Quinn were, whether they were listening.

"I'm aware of that," he said tersely.

"Oh, are you? Because it doesn't seem that way, what with you coming in here for this little heart-to-heart," I said sarcastically. "I only came down here because I didn't want to be away from my mom and because I didn't want to deal with all that crap at home. I did *not* come down here because I want to have some kind of relationship with you."

His skin turned all blotchy. I'd never really seen Gray angry, but I had a feeling that I was about to get my first eyeful. "Well,

I'm sorry to tell you that I'm not going anywhere. And as long as your mother and I are together, you're going to have to have *some* kind of relationship with me."

"We'll see," I snapped.

He shook his head, fed up, and turned to go. His hand was on the side of the door when he looked over his shoulder at me, his expression condescending.

"You know, you didn't seem to mind me so much when I was introducing you to Rick Morris the other day," he said. "I think it's about time you take a look at your conduct and decide if this is the person you really want to be."

He closed the door behind him, having gotten in the last word, and I let out a frustrated screech. What did he expect me to do? Turn down an intro to the scout from one of my top schools? I wasn't a moron. I just didn't need another father. What a total asshole, trying to make me feel guilty.

Well, guess what, Gray? You lose. Because I don't feel guilty. Not at all. In fact, all you've just done is made me more determined than ever to get rid of you.

I grabbed my phone and speed-dialed my father. I got his voice mail.

"Dad? It's me. I was just wondering when this grand master plan of yours to win Mom back is going to kick in. Because whatever you need, I'm here. Call me back."

I hung up the phone and threw myself down on my bed, hands on my temples.

Just breathe, I told myself. *Just breathe. . . . Everything's going to be fine. Everything will be okay.*

Unfortunately, no matter how many times I repeated it, my heart refused to believe it.

Daily Field Journal of Annie Johnston
Saturday, July 3

Position: Newsstand at Garden State Parkway rest stop, exit 100.

Cover: Pretending to read <u>OK!</u> magazine. (Note: And wondering . . . who reads this crap? News flash: Salma Hayek has cellulite! Do I need to pay $3.99 for a picture of it?)

Observations:

12:43 p.m.: Subject Connor Shale and Subject Josh Schwartz hit the Burger King counter, along with a throng of tank-top-clad humanity. Subject Josh takes two bacon cheeseburgers from the warmer, plus fries and onion rings, but Subject Connor orders something special from the lady behind the counter. (Note: It's a parkway Burger King. What do you think you're getting? Filet mignon, grilled to order? Fresh seasonal prawns in garlic sauce? Grab a Whopper and be on your way, loser.)

12:50 p.m.: Subject Josh Schwartz merrily eating burger at table. Subject Connor Shale still waiting for something at counter. (Note: He's banging his hands against the metal top of the warmer. Assessment One: He's getting antsy. Assessment Two: He has no rhythm.)

12:55 p.m.: Subject Josh Schwartz has finished his food and rejoined Subject Connor Shale on line and is sucking on a chocolate shake. (Assessment Three: Josh has a stomach of steel; that took less than five minutes.) The two of them start to argue. (Assessment Four: Josh wants to get back on the road. Connor is not about to give up on his coq au vin special.)

1:01 p.m.: Subject Josh shoves his sunglasses on and storms out. Subject Connor shouts "Fuck this place" and flings a stack of trays over, which causes a toddler in SpongeBob swim shorts to burst into tears. As he follows Subject Josh, Subject Connor grabs a package of cookies off the counter next to me, throws a tenner on the counter, and walks out. (Note: He, of course, does not see me.)

1:02 p.m.: I tell the startled counter girl Connor was with me, pay for the cookies with his ten, and take the change. I just made a cool seven dollars and one cent. (Assessment: Cresties are good for the economy. Mine, anyway.)

Ally

"So who lives here?"

Cooper gestured at the huge shingled mansion a few houses up the beach from Gray's. It was Saturday morning, and he'd stopped by to keep me company while I waited for Annie to show up. As soon as he'd arrived, I'd dragged him out to the beach just to get away from my mom and Gray. When I'd come downstairs from my room and grabbed a bagel earlier, they'd both said good morning to me, and that was it. They were probably waiting for me to apologize. As if that was going to happen. I wasn't the one walking into people's rooms and ambushing them out of nowhere.

"That's Chloe's place," I said. "They're not coming down this summer."

The Appleby house had a wraparound deck overlooking the ocean and a winding staircase leading up to a widow's walk. The turret in the center of the widow's walk was kind of an open loft space where Chloe, Shannen, Faith, and I used to gather on rainy days to paint one another's nails, play snap, and talk about the boys. I could practically see us up there now in our short shorts and halter tops, lying on our stomachs, sucking on those jawbreakers they sold down at Bay Village.

Suddenly I felt very, very sad.

"No?" Cooper said, eyebrows raised. He flung one of the shells at the house. It bounced off a pylon and hit the sand.

I shook my head.

129

"Why? Not big enough for 'em?" he joked. But his eyes weren't laughing. He flung another shell and it clanged against a tin seagull sculpture on the Applebys' deck.

"Ha-ha," I said flatly, turning around to head back toward Gray's. We were already a few houses away and I didn't want to go too far, in case Annie arrived. As Cooper whipped another shell at Chloe's, I quickened my steps. "You really hate summer people, huh?"

Cooper smirked at me. "Not all of them."

I smiled and looked down at my feet. Then he turned to launch one final missile.

"So how'd things work out with your mom yesterday?" He flung a shell toward the water this time, so hard it looked like he almost threw his shoulder out.

"Not good. That wasn't about you, you know," I said as another shell hit the surf. "I mean . . . I don't want you to think she's, like, mad at you or something."

He paused and looked at me, confused. "What? Oh, this?" He held up the shells. "This isn't about your mother." He pulled back and threw the whole handful of them at the water. I saw a dozen tiny drops pop up where the shells fell. "This is about mine."

I paused, holding my hair back from my face as the wind shifted direction. "What's wrong with your mother?"

He scoffed, staring out at the water. "Interesting way to put it."

I blushed. "Sorry, I didn't mean—"

"No, no. It's okay. I just meant . . . the better question is, what *isn't* wrong with my mother?" he said wryly. But it was clear by the set of his jaw that he wasn't amused.

"Oh," I said, an uncomfortable twist in my gut.

He shook his head, moving his lower jaw around. "I don't know what you guys were fighting about, but I can tell you it's all fucking pointless," he said. "They never listen, and they don't care about anyone but themselves. I swear my mom just sees me and Jen as burdens keeping her from doing what she really wants to do." He paused and looked sidelong at me. "And from who she really wants to be with." I swallowed hard. Was that how my mother saw me right now? As a burden trying to keep her away from Gray? I *had* tried to convince her to ditch him and stay home with me. And I did want her to get back together with my dad. Was she up there in that big, sterile house right now resenting me for wishing my family could fix itself?

I hated how unsure I felt. I put my hand on Cooper's arm. "I'm really sorry. I—"

Cooper flinched. He looked at me and laughed. A sarcastic, almost condescending laugh. "Whatever. I'm just venting."

Then he casually strolled away from me up the beach. It took me a second to catch my breath. I felt like I'd overstepped my bounds somehow, and wasn't sure what to do about it. In front of Hammond's house, Cooper paused and tipped his head back, letting the breeze tug his hair off his face. I caught up to him and hugged my own arms, feeling conspicuous.

"I'm sorry." He tipped his head forward and squinted at me. "I'm an asshole."

"No, it's—"

"It's not." He dropped down onto the sand and looked up at me. "I didn't mean to . . . whatever. It's not your problem. Let's talk about something else."

I sat down next to him. Close, but not too close. "It's okay.

It's cool. I understand." And I did. Kind of. I'd had a couple of emotional freak-outs of my own lately.

"Thanks."

He looked sad, and somehow young, sitting, hugging his shins in the sand. My fingers itched to push his hair back from his face, but that seemed too intimate, so I didn't. He lifted his hands and his arm brushed mine. I got goose bumps everywhere. He rested his wrists on his knees, so his arms were straight, then placed his chin on his upper arm as he faced me. Suddenly I was very aware of how half-naked we both were— him in just a bathing suit, me in a tank top and shorts. I could smell the tangy scent of his sport sunscreen. There was a tiny grain of sand on his lower lip.

"I'm glad I bumped into you the other night," he said.

"Yeah?"

His face was so close I could see the bleached ends of his eyebrow hairs.

"Yeah."

He was going to kiss me. Did I want him to kiss me? If my pounding heart was any indication, I did. Jake's face flitted through my mind as my eyes fluttered closed. And then a whistle split the air. I looked over at Gray's house. Annie was waving both hands over her head on the deck, her backpack dropped on the floor next to her.

"Annie!" I jumped up, flinging sand all over Cooper's legs.

My skin buzzed, and my lips hummed from the aborted kiss, but I didn't look back.

"Hey!" she shouted, racing down the stairs.

We ran to each other across the beach, and she flung her arms out to hug me, making a big kissy face like we were long-lost lovers. She wore a black T-shirt that hung off one shoulder, cutoff denim shorts, and hot pink leggings over black Converse. Her short, dark hair was pushed back with black-and-white checkered sunglasses.

"Okay, you weren't kidding. That place is, like, a museum," she said.

"I know, right?"

Then she looked past me at Cooper. He was just rising up from the sand, dusting off his torso, and the sun bounced off his tan, making him look like something out of a surfing movie. Damn. I could've just kissed that.

"Is that the hottie?" Annie whispered.

"Um . . . yeah," I said.

She grinned proudly. "Hey!" she shouted to him. "I'm Annie. Ally's better half."

Cooper loped over. "Not possible for her to have a better half."

Now Annie was really impressed. "You got any brothers?" she joked.

"Nope. But I have a single dad who's kind of cool when you can actually find him," he replied.

My heart sank as Annie and I exchanged a look.

"God. Sorry. I've got some kind of disease today that only affects my speech." He rubbed his hands together and looked Annie up and down. "I *do* have a sister, though."

Annie smirked. "Normally I don't swing that way, but if she looks anything like you . . ."

"Annie!"

Cooper laughed. "Well, I guess I should let you guys . . . girl-bond or whatever. I'll see you two around later?"

"Most definitely," Annie replied.

Cooper lifted a hand as he walked up the beach toward the house and the driveway beyond, where he'd parked the truck he shared with his sister. Annie and I both watched until he was out of sight.

"All right, he is *way* hotter than—"

I lifted a hand. "Don't say it. Don't say his name. We are living in a *him*-free zone right now," I said.

"That's very Zen of you," Annie said, sliding her sunglasses down over her eyes.

"It's a whole new Ally Ryan," I replied.

"Does the new Ally Ryan eat? Cuz I'm starved and from the look of that house, I'm guessing there's nothing fried, processed, or chocolate anywhere in it."

"You got that right," I said, walking backward up the beach. "Come on. I'll take you to Pinky's."

"And tell me all about Cooper?" she asked.

"And tell you *all* about Cooper," I promised.

As we walked around to the driveway where the car she'd borrowed from her mom for the weekend was parked, Annie told me about the goings-on at home. How David had gotten a job with a landscaper and was making buckets of cash. How Marshall had started going out with Celia Linklater and now thought he was a player. How she'd seen both Shannen and Chloe lurking around town, shopping alone, never together. I wondered if that was the gossip she'd been texting about the other day, and thought it couldn't possibly be. She'd said she had big gossip, and solo shopping was not big. So *did* she have something big about Jake? Something she was just not telling me because I'd told her not to mention him?

"Okay. How do we get to this Pinky's?" Annie asked as she pulled out of the driveway.

"Just hit the Boulevard and make a left. We'll get there eventually."

"I like it. Very chill. Maybe I could get used to the vibe down here," she said.

I spent the entire drive obsessing about Jake, opening my mouth to ask her about him, then clamming up again and forcing myself to stay quiet. Yeah. That was my vibe all right. Very chill.

Daily Field Journal of Annie Johnston
Sunday, July 4

Location: Take a Dip ice cream, under the awning out back.

Cover: None. I came here to say hi to Ally and get some rum raisin, but what I just saw, I had to write down.

Observations:

4:55 p.m.: Subject Hammond Ross talking to Ally Ryan behind the counter at Take a Dip ice cream. Uniform: light blue Take a Dip T-shirt, baggy shorts, sneakers. Subject Hammond is talking. She's cracking up laughing. The phone rings. Ally goes to get it. Subject Hammond checks his hair in the reflective side of a napkin dispenser while her back is turned. She hangs up. Subject Hammond puts the napkin dispenser down and wipes his palms on the back of his shorts. He puts his smile back on. They turn to look at the door and I duck out of view, my back to the wall.

5:02 p.m.: I feel safe to look again. Ally is at the sink washing something. Subject Hammond LEANS IN TO SMELL HER!

(Assessment: Holy crap. Hammond is in love with Ally.)

Ally

"So then Todd is hanging . . . upside down, from the edge of the high dive and he's just screaming . . . 'I didn't want to go in head first! I didn't want to go in head first!' And I'm like"— Hammond cupped his hands around his mouth—"'You shoulda thought of that before you flipped over, dude!'"

I held my stomach as I laughed, practically doubled over behind the counter at Take a Dip. It was the Fourth of July, and it was pouring outside. Fat raindrops battered the plate-glass windows and every car that zipped by sprayed a wall of water on the roadside sign advertising two-for-one single cones. The fluorescent lights inside the shop made everything look dingy, from the unpolished chrome on the milk shake blenders to the film over the top of the dipping chocolate. We'd had one customer in the last hour, and our shift manager, Deb, had long since retired to the back room with her cell phone. When she'd gone, I had silently cursed her for leaving me alone with Hammond. But now . . . I was actually having fun.

"So what happened?" I asked.

"He fell," Hammond said matter-of-factly, toying with one of the ice-cream scoops in its bucket. "And he so didn't want to fall on his head, he flipped over and landed on his stomach. It was the belly flop heard round the world."

"Oh God. That must've hurt," I said, biting my bottom lip.

"His stomach was red for hours. We took a picture of it," Hammond confirmed with a nod. "I'm sure someone has it somewhere."

I smiled, feeling all fuzzy and nostalgic. It was kind of nice to hear the stories of things that had happened while I was off living with my grandmother in Baltimore. Nice, but also odd. I'd always known that life had gone on without me, but it was weird to hear how easily and normally it had gone on without me.

Hammond crossed his arms over his chest, his feet planted wide in that self-assured stance of his. He was so much better looking when he wasn't being a jerk. Already he'd gotten a tan, which made his blond hair look lighter, and he'd wisely chosen a light blue T-shirt that brought out the blue in his eyes. His had forty colorful scoops of ice cream on it, the flavor's name beneath each scoop, and read TRY 'EM ALL! across the top. We looked at each other for a long moment, as the refrigerator sputtered and roared into another cooling cycle behind him. Suddenly I had this vivid memory of him clutching the front of my T-shirt around my stomach right before we kissed that night a million years ago, because he didn't know what to do with his hands. I quickly turned away and leaned against the counter, blowing out a loud, theatrical sigh.

God I hoped he couldn't tell what I was thinking. I almost never thought about that night. So why was it coming up now?

"So are you gonna do Backslappers again in the fall? Because if you are, maybe you could be mine this time," Hammond said. He leaned down next to me, our elbows almost touching.

"I don't know." I'd only joined last year because I'd still been nursing that childish dream of getting back with my friends. But now everything was different. I'd had enough Crestie drama, and the soccer team and Backslappers were just littered with it.

"Well, Chloe is *not* an option, and I don't know what's up

with Shannen," Hammond said. "Maybe we could—"

His elbow nudged mine. I stood up straight and backed away, hands in the back pockets of my jeans.

"I don't know," I said quickly. "I might try out for the play instead."

His face screwed up as he turned to face me. "The play?"

"Yeah. I used to be into that stuff, remember?" I said. "In Baltimore I actually had a good role one year. I just—"

At that moment, the door to the shop opened, and my phone rang. It was like the powers that be were giving me a double save. A middle-aged guy shook the hood off his head as he ushered two little kids in colorful rain jackets through the door. I pulled my phone out and my heart skipped a nervous, excited beat.

"It's my dad."

Time to put the plan in motion.

Deb emerged from the back room. "Hi-eeee!" she said to the dad and his kids. She was one of those people who found any way possible to make most one-syllable words into two. "What can we get for you?"

My phone rang again.

"It's okay," Hammond said to me. "We got this."

"If you're going to take a call, please take it in ba-ack!" Deb sang, her blond curls bouncing around her head as she tilted it toward the door.

"Thanks, guys."

I ducked through the door into the dim stillness of the back room, which was so tiny I had to slide sideways to get between the stacked boxes of plastic bowls and the ripped vinyl back of the desk chair. I stood beneath the open window, leaned into the side of the ancient water fountain, and hit talk. I felt hot all over from the weirdness with Hammond, so I took a breath and told myself it was nothing. Just old feelings stirred up by boredom and the proximity of Hammond's body to mine.

"Hi, Dad."

"Hey, kiddo! How's it going? Is it raining as hard there as it is here?"

I looked up at the window and all I saw was gray. "Yeah. It's pretty bad. So . . . you got my message?"

"Sure did," he said. "Sorry I couldn't pick up. I had class last night."

"That's okay," I replied. I traced an arc on the concrete floor with the toe of my sneaker, thinking about Gray's parting comment the other night. "So . . . what's up? I mean, is there a plan or . . . ?"

"Yes! Yes," he said. "There *is* a plan. And there *is* something you can do."

I stood at attention. "Really? What?"

"Do you think you could get your mother to drive you into the city next Saturday afternoon?"

My brow knit. How the hell was I supposed to do that? "Um . . ."

"I was thinking you could tell her you want to meet up with friends or something," he said.

Was he not acquainted with my mother? She would never let me wander around New York City alone with friends for the day. Then an idea hit me and I blinked. Unless . . .

"Actually, I signed up for the humanities elective next year and they did strongly suggest we visit some museums this summer," I told him.

"Perfect!" he crowed. "Tell her you need to go to the MoMA. That's right in the neighborhood I need you to be."

"Why? What are you gonna do?" I asked, feeling breathless. I turned toward the back door, away from the shop, as if Hammond and Deb could possibly hear me through the steel door over the whir of the freezers and the banging of the rain.

"I'm going to re-create our first date," he said. "She's going to love it. There's no way she's going to be able to ignore me after this."

I grinned. Their first date. It was exactly the kind of romantic gesture my mother lived for. I felt proud of my dad for thinking of it. And kind of ridiculously happy. He did still know her. He did still love her. And he was willing to go the extra mile to show her.

"Okay. I'll tell her about the museum and let you know what she says," I told him.

"Thanks, bud. What would I do without you?"

My heart constricted and I bit my tongue to keep from blurting the first thing that came to mind. Namely, *You seemed to manage it just fine for the past couple of years.* Now was not the time to get all obnoxious on him. He had a plan. He was executing the plan. That was all that mattered.

I heard some muffled laughter through the door, and checked the grainy security screen on the desk. Cooper, Dex, Jenny, and another guy I recognized from the beach— nicknamed Stoner—had just come in. Dex was tearing through the T-shirt cabinet, unfolding all the shirts, holding them up against his chest and wagging his shoulders around as he modeled them. I rolled my eyes.

"Dad. I'm at work and I gotta go."

"Okay. I'll talk to you later. And Ally? Thanks for offering to help. It means a lot."

Weirdly, my heart sort of welled. "No problem, Dad."

I ended the call, pressed my hand into the cold metal door, and took in a breath. God I was emotional lately. And I hated it. It just wasn't me. I cleared my throat and shoved my way back into the shop. The rain-slicked father and his kids were gathered around one of the two café tables near the front.

"Hey! There she is!" Jenny shouted. She jumped up and landed butt-down on the counter, throwing her arms out to hug me. Deb shot me an irritated, but somehow still smiling, look so I quickly hugged Jenny back just to get her down again. She slid off and leaned her elbows on the counter. "So can we get, like, free ice cream for knowing you?"

Cooper laughed. "Jenny. Uncool." He shoved her aside with the full girth of his shoulders and she groused, but moved. "Hey," he said to me, pressing his hands into the counter so that his feet came off the ground. "I like the outfit. Minimum wage works on you."

I blushed and tucked my hair back under my Take a Dip baseball cap.

"You gonna order something?" Hammond asked gruffly.

Cooper's eyes grazed Hammond and his feet hit the ground. "Can I get a vanilla with a side of *ham?*"

Dex and the other two cackled. Deb did not look pleased.

"Creative," Hammond said. "You sure are pretty for a smart guy."

"And you sure are ugly for a rich guy," Cooper shot back.

"Okay, okay, we get it. You two don't like each other," I

said, holding up my hands. Jenny and the boys laughed their assent, loudly. "Deb, can I take my fifteen?"

"Sure." She gave me a wide-eyed, clenched-lipped look that I took to mean, *You can take your fifteen if you get these assholes out of he-ere!*

"I'll be in the back if you need me," she said to Hammond. "If you all aren't gonna order something, I'd appreciate you making way for other customers," she said to the rest of them.

"What other customers?" Dex asked, holding a balled up T-shirt in each hand as he gestured around the shop.

Deb rolled her eyes and shoved through to the back room.

"Come on," I said, walking around the counter. "Let's go outside."

"Are you kidding? It's like Armageddon out there," Cooper said.

I sighed, glancing past him at the pile of T-shirts Dex, Jenny, and Stoner had made on the vinyl bench that ran the length of the window. "You guys are gonna get me in trouble."

"All right, fine," Cooper said. "We just stopped by to tell you there's a party at Chum and Howie's tonight. They throw it every Fourth and its always a good time. You in?"

He reached out and tugged once on my belt loop. My heart tugged with it. A party with the locals. How very not-Crestie. I glanced at Hammond behind the counter. He was wiping a rag in a circular motion about two feet away, clearly listening in.

"Yeah. I'm in," I said. "But who are Chum and Howie?"

"Only the most awesomest dudes on the island," Stoner put in. He'd walked up behind Cooper with a green Take a Dip tee slung over one shoulder. His eyes were typically half-mast and his goatee was made up of straggly brown curls and non-specific crumbs.

"Dude. Put. The shirt. Back," Cooper said. Like he was directing his very own toddler.

Stoner groaned and tipped his head back, but did as he was told.

"These guys have a cottage down by the lighthouse," Cooper explained. "They're cool. You'll like 'em."

"Okay. But is it cool if Annie comes?" I asked.

"Of course," Cooper said.

"Who's this Annie person? She sounds hot," Dex said.

Cooper flicked his forehead and Dex moped away, rubbing the wound.

"What about our party?" Hammond blurted, no longer able to keep quiet.

I rolled my eyes at him. Like I had any plans of attending the Cresties' Fourth of July extravaganza. Had he not yet gotten the memo?

"What?" he asked, palms up.

Cooper smirked. "I'll come by to get you guys. Like, nine o'clock?"

"Sounds good," I told him. "I'll . . . see you then."

He reached out and gave my hand this sort of awkward squeeze. I couldn't help thinking that if I'd let him kiss me on the beach yesterday, he'd probably kiss me now. But he didn't. Instead he helped his friends shove all the T-shirts back in the cabinet, then gave me a nod as he ushered them out. But my lips were actually tingling as I watched him go.

Jake

I had thought, since it was raining like a mother-bitch, that no one would come out for coffee. But I was wrong. Everyone came out for coffee. Some people came with their dogs, even. And then, they all stayed *inside* the shop to drink their drinks. And to make annoying demands about Splenda and nutmeg and extra muffins because their stupid dog ate theirs when they weren't looking.

I hated this fucking job.

And then, Shannen came in. And I hated it more.

She was fourth or fifth on line. I couldn't tell because the lady with the cell phone kept pacing as she shouted into it. Behind her were a couple of guys from the soccer team. I wasn't sure if they were all together, but I could tell the guys had noticed me and were whispering about me. Losers.

I was still trying to figure out how *not* to be the one to take Shannen's order, when the office door slammed. Mr. Ryan came walking out, stepped in the big puddle of coffee that'd been there for the last hour, and slipped. His arms flung out and his eyes widened. He would've gone splat if I hadn't lunged for him and caught his arm.

"Are you okay?" I asked. I hoisted him to his feet. His Jump baseball cap was sideways and half off his head. His face was all red.

"What the hell was that?" he demanded.

I knew he was really pissed because he never cursed. Not even damn or hell.

"Oh, um . . . she . . ." I turned and started to point to this woman Keisha, who'd spilled the coffee, but she tensed at her register. She was an even bigger bitch than Leena, so I stopped myself. "I mean we . . . spilled a coffee," I said stupidly.

"Well, when you spill coffee, Jake, you mop it up," he blurted.

Half the people in the store stopped talking. Which was a noticeable difference in the loudness. He turned and grabbed the mop from the corner, shoving it at me. Which was so unfair, because I hadn't even spilled the damn coffee. And now the soccer dudes and Shannen were all laughing at me.

"Fuck this," I muttered under my breath. I mopped up the mess—did a pretty messy job of it—and tossed the mop into the bucket. "Fuck this stupid place."

Then Keisha was standing there, her hips taking up almost the whole aisle behind the counter.

"Take your half hour," she said.

My shoulders drooped in relief. "Yeah?"

"Yeah. You're not scheduled for another fifteen minutes, but I'll cover you."

I looked at her. She was thanking me for not ratting her out. Okay. So maybe she wasn't a bigger bitch than Leena.

"Thanks."

I tugged the plastic gloves off my hands, shoved them in the trash, and went out the back door. Not only did I not have to wait on Shannen and her friends, but I didn't even have to pass by them on my way out. The second the rain hit my face, I knew. I knew that I wasn't going back there. My shift wasn't over for another four hours, but there was no way I was spending the rest of July Fourth measuring out sugar for snotty customers and taking a beating from my boss.

I made it to my Jeep, yanked open the door, and started the engine before I even got it closed. It was only five fifteen. I could be at Hammond's house down the shore by eight. Seven thirty if I floored it. In less than three hours, I could be with Ally.

I peeled out of my space, and never looked back.

Ally

My heart pounded as I approached Gray's bedroom that night. He'd gone out to the deck a few minutes earlier and I knew my mom was still inside getting ready. Now was the best shot I had for putting my dad's plan into action. The door was open and my mom was at the vanity table, brushing out her hair, wearing her white cotton robe. I held my breath and knocked on the outer wall. She turned around.

"Hi!"

"Hey," I said, stepping inside. "Can I talk to you for a sec?"

Her eyebrows shot up in surprise. It was all I could do to keep from rolling my eyes. Like it was *so* out of the ordinary for me to come talk to her?

"Sure."

I'd only been inside Gray's room once since we'd been here, when he'd given us the grand tour on our first evening, showing us everything from the dusty attic to the garage where he kept an old BMW for use in "emergencies." He'd even shown me where the keys were hidden—in a drawer nearby—which I thought was pretty cool of him. Especially considering the only "emergency" I could imagine was me having to make an early-morning escape from him and his hospital corners. The walls of his bedroom were a super light gray-blue and framed black-and-white shore scenes had been hung here and there to set the mood. The bed was huge—it had to be even bigger than a king—and took up half the room. I tried not to look at it as I approached my mother.

"I was just wondering . . . could you drive me into the city next Saturday to meet Annie?" I asked.

My mother blinked and sort of scoffed. Clearly this was not what she was expecting. "To do what?"

"To go to the MoMA?" I asked, swallowing hard. "Mr. Hanson sent out an e-mail saying that anyone who brought in a receipt from a museum this summer would get extra credit in the fall. I still have the e-mail if you want to see it."

I pulled out my phone, but my hand was shaking. My mother stared at it.

"How much extra credit exactly?" she asked, leaning one hand into the bench at her side.

"I don't know. He just said extra credit," I said. "It won't take that long. We'll just check out a few of the galleries and then come home."

My mother looked up at me, her eyes narrowed, and I swear the seagulls outside could hear my pulse racing. She couldn't possibly know this was a plot. Could she?

"Okay, fine. I suppose it would be nice to go into the city for the day," she said. "But I get to pick our lunch spot."

"Done!" I said. I was so excited I threw my arms around her. She hugged me back tightly and I suddenly felt tears well up in my eyes. I couldn't remember the last time I'd hugged my mom.

But whatever. That hardly mattered right now. What mattered was I'd done it. I'd fooled her. And next Saturday, my dad was going to get the shot he needed to woo her back.

"So . . . is that what you're wearing to the party?" she asked as I pulled away.

I looked down at my white shorts, gray lace-trimmed T-shirt, and dark blue hoodie. "Yeah. Why?"

"I don't know. I thought everyone usually got a little more dressed up," she said, lifting one shoulder.

My stomach sank as she turned back toward the mirror and began fastening a diamond into one ear. I'd never seen those earrings before in my life. Guess Gray was out a few thousand this month.

"I'm not going to the Rosses'," I told her. "Cooper invited me and Annie to this party down by the lighthouse." I turned and started for the door, preferring to put an end to it there.

"Ally—"

Apparently she had other ideas.

"Mom, I've told you, like, a million times, I don't want to hang out with Hammond and those guys," I said, whirling to face her. "It's like you don't believe me."

She sighed and got up, sliding a clutch purse from the edge of the table. Shaking her head slowly, she dumped a lipstick and compact inside, then snapped it shut.

"I guess I just thought when we got down here . . . I don't know . . . that you'd relax that rule a little," she said with a small, hopeful smile.

"So when you said I wouldn't have to see them if we came down here, you were, what, lying? Manipulating me?" I said. "Real nice, Mom."

I strode out the door, fuming. My mother came after me as I jogged down the stairs to the second floor. Quinn stood outside the door of her room, her arms crossed over her chest, staring at me. Great. Just what I needed. An audience.

"Ally—"

I stopped on the landing and forced myself to breathe. *You just got her to say yes to the MoMA*, I reminded myself. *Don't mess this up.*

"Mom," I said as calmly as I could. "Annie hates those people. She drove all the way down here to see me, and I'm not gonna make her go to a party with a bunch of people she can't stand. She's already waiting for me in her car."

This was both true and a lie. Annie did hate the Cresties, but she would have killed to go to their party. Annie was working on some kind of exposé about our town's tonier half, and she jumped on any excuse to observe them in their natural habitat. She'd almost strangled me when I said we weren't going, and only backed down when I told her how much I wanted to hang out with Cooper.

My mother looked at the floor and nodded. "I get that. I do. But can't you split your time or something? Go to Hammond's first for an hour and then to this other party?"

No. I could not spend an hour at Hammond's. Because spending an hour at Hammond's meant spending an hour with Faith and her annoying clinginess. It meant spending an hour with Hammond and that freaky sexual tension from this afternoon possibly returning. If I could help it, I would not be standing within a three-foot radius of Hammond Ross again for the rest of my life.

At that moment, a horn honked in the driveway. Saved by Cooper.

"That's him, Mom. We're going to follow him to the thing. I gotta go."

For good measure I stood on my toes and gave her a kiss on the cheek.

"Fine! Have fun! But just so you know, Ally Ryan, you will be spending some time with your family this summer!"

I raced across the living room and out the door, gulping back a surge of bile at her insinuation that Gray and Quinn were my family. Little did she know that I would be spending some time with my family this summer. My real family. Starting next Saturday afternoon.

Ally

"So are you, like, in love with my brother?" Jenny shouted into my ear.

"What? No!" I replied.

I sucked half the punch from my cup. If there was alcohol in it, I couldn't taste it, so I had decided to pretend that there wasn't any. After the last few days and that "family time" comment from my mom, I deserved to let loose a little. Suddenly, a cheer went up from across the yard. Someone had built an elaborate catapult worthy of a physics fair blue ribbon, and half the party's attendees had spent most of the evening flinging various items at the wall of the abandoned house next door. From the looks of things, this catapult had been in use for months—the dilapidated structure on the other side of the fence was peppered with holes, cracks, and stains of various hues and sizes—and as Jenny and I looked on, Cooper and Dex were helping some other guys load it up with a huge, dimpled watermelon.

"Really?" Jenny was incredulous as she smacked my arm with the back of her hand, spilling half her beer over the rim of her cup and not noticing. Both of us wore hoodies with the hoods up to ward off the misty drizzle, and she pushed hers back slightly, as if to better see me. Her blue eyes were wide. "Everyone's in love with him."

I glanced over at Cooper, who was stepping back to yank the release on the catapult. There were quite a few girls eyeing him over their drinks. I wondered if he *knew* they were all in love with him.

Probably.

He let her rip. The watermelon surged through the air and exploded against the white-shingled wall of the house. Everyone within ten feet of the catapult was pelted with watermelon bits. The resulting cheer was the loudest yet.

"This is the coolest party ever!" Annie cried, bouncing over to us with an old crab-trap crate full of potential catapult items gathered from the vicinity. Inside I saw a lawn gnome, a rusty spade, and an actual crab, which I hoped was already dead.

"Agreed," I said. And the best part about it? No Cresties to be found.

Annie's expression drooped a little. "What's wrong? Are you upset that Cooper's not talking to you?"

"Annie!" I said through my teeth. Jenny snorted a laugh and held her hand to her nose.

"No. No, no, no." She dropped the crate of launchables at her feet and took hold of my arm. "You *made* me come here and miss a perfectly good Crestie party. I could be taking notes right now . . . watching Faith upchuck her meager lunch all over the Rosses' state-of-the-art automatic toilet bowl. I did not miss that so you could come here and *not* talk to him."

Cooper was slapping hands with Stoner, his biceps flexing under the sleeve of his clingy black T-shirt.

"He totally likes you," Jenny said, toying with her braid.

"He does?" I asked.

"Um, yeah!" She sucked down some more of her beer. "He mentions you at least three times a day. With my brother, that's like he may as well have bought a ring."

At that moment, Cooper looked over at me. He said something to Stoner, then walked across the overgrown grass, dodging revelers as he came.

"What're you, avoiding me?" he said with a smirk.

I blinked. "What? No! I—"

He took my hand and tugged me toward him. My knees bumped his and I blushed. Then he turned both my hands so that my palms were facing out, and matched his palms to mine for a second before lacing our fingers together. He had this way of throwing me off balance and then suddenly grounding me that made me feel like his own personal Ping-Pong ball.

"Wanna go somewhere?" he asked.

"Where?" The word was a squeak.

He looked over his shoulder, tilted his head, and pulled me away from my friends.

"Don't worry about me!" Annie shouted after us. "I'll just be here flinging gnomes!"

Cooper and I laughed as he walked me around the side of the house, helping me carefully step over a fallen section of the rotting picket fence, which had been lain flat by weather or time or some less-natural disaster. At the front of the house was a short wooden deck with a crooked railing. On the deck was an untrustworthy porch swing, with some gray-haired dude splayed across it, snoring. Cooper roused him, and the guy loped off into the night, toward the bay, where dozens of people were partying on a rickety dock, a cloud of smoke muting the twinkle lights strung above their heads.

The porch swing creaked loudly as we sat, but didn't crash to the ground like I expected. Cooper settled into the corner and put his arm out, like he expected me to cuddle into his side. I thought of Jake suddenly, and sat down on the opposite end.

Stupid, stupid, stupid. What was the matter with me? It wasn't like I'd be cheating or something. Jake and I had never even officially been together and we definitely weren't now. I wished I had taken Cooper up on the unspoken invitation, but it was too late. He cleared his throat and sat up.

"You hate this party, don't you?" he blurted.

My face scrunched. "What? No. I'm having fun." I turned my knees toward his. "Why would I hate this party?"

"I don't know. Because—" There was a huge crash, followed by a gasp, then a screaming cheer. We locked eyes for a second, then laughed. "Maybe it's not . . . sophisticated enough for you."

My insides went all squirmy. "Why? What do you mean?" He gave me this look. Like *duh*. And now I was offended. "Wait, you think because I'm a Crestie this isn't my type of party? Because I am *not* a Crestie, okay? I just currently live with one."

"Whoa, whoa, whoa." Cooper held up a hand, shaking

his head at the same time. "Back up. *Beep, beep, beep.*" He motioned like he was guiding a reversing truck into a parking space. "What's a Crestie?"

My face burned bright enough to replace the busted porch light. Overhead, the sky suddenly opened up again and the world filled with muffled screams and shouts and pounding feet as everyone crowded inside. The raindrops pinged and plinked off of the various discarded items—tapped kegs, an old tin fishing boat, a coiled garden hose—in the dirt patch that was the front yard.

"Right. Um, forget I said anything."

Cooper laughed. "No, no. There's no forgetting anything now." He inched closer to me and rested one arm on the back of the swing. "What's a Crestie?"

I blew out a sigh and rolled my eyes. "All right. Back home there's this crest and all the rich kids live on it. At some point, like, a million years ago, the kids on the other side of town nicknamed them the Cresties and they've been called that for so long that it's, like, who they are now. Sometimes they even use it to refer to themselves. Sarcastically of course. But I think they secretly like it."

Cooper gaped. "That might be the dumbest thing I've ever heard."

"I know. And I live it," I said. "So what does that make me?"

Cooper narrowed his eyes. One of the gutters on the porch overflowed, suddenly sprouting a gushing waterfall behind our heads. Little splatters peppered my arms. "So wait. I'm confused. You are a Crestie, or you're not a Crestie?"

I could have told him the whole story. How I used to be one, what had happened with my dad, why I was no longer one, how my mom was dating one. But suddenly, it all seemed too exhausting. And too silly to waste time explaining. I was here, with him. And the Cresties didn't matter. They didn't matter so much, he didn't even know who they were.

Suddenly, I'd never felt so free.

"I'm not," I said, sliding a little bit closer to him. Our knees touched, and when I laid my own arm along the back of the swing, our fingers touched too. "And you know what? I don't want to talk about them anymore. I'm just a normal girl who's loving this party. I swear."

Cooper looked into my eyes. His hand shifted and suddenly it was holding on to mine. "You are *not* what I expected."

Who ever is? I thought. Jake wasn't. My mom wasn't. My dad wasn't. Even Shannen, Hammond, Faith, and Chloe weren't exactly what they appeared.

"I'll take that as a compliment," I said.

"You should."

And then he grazed my bottom lip with his thumb. And then he kissed me.

Jake

It took way longer to get to LBI than usual. People can't drive for shit in the rain. There were all these accidents and people were, like, doing twenty-five whenever they came to a frickin' puddle. But whatever; I was there now. At Hammond's. And from the look of it, everyone else was too. There were cars parked everywhere—in the driveway, in the street, in front of

kieran scott

the neighbor's driveway—like everyone knew they were in for the night so it didn't matter if they blocked in everyone else. I took a deep breath and looked at myself in the mirror. My heart was pounding a mile a second.

Ally was inside. I was going to see Ally.

Probably should've used that four hour drive to figure out what to say to her.

Shit. Whatever. Let's get this over with.

I got out of the car, pulled my hood over my head, and ran through the rain. When I shoved the sliding glass door open, a bunch of adults turned to look. Like I was some homeless guy crashing their party. They were all wearing linen pants and sandals and jewelry, and there was me in my coffee-stained shorts and crappy kicks.

"Dude! You made it!"

Hammond came outta nowhere and slapped my hand. He had a cup full of beer in his other hand and he was wearing a pink polo shirt. Where the hell does he get these clothes?

"Hey. Yeah." I glanced around the room. Ally's mom and Dr. Nathanson were over by the bar, and I saw Faith's mom and the Idiot Twins' parents, and Quinn and her friends, but no Ally.

"Jake!" Faith practically screamed. She wove through the crowd with her cup of punch over her head and air-kissed me. "What are you doing here?"

"Did your mom unground you?" Hammond asked. "Thank God. It's been boring as shit down here."

Faith slurped her drink and nodded. "So boring."

"Not exactly," I said. I moved a little farther into the house and scanned the room, like I was looking for somewhere to put my sweatshirt. There were a bunch of graduated seniors in the kitchen. I nodded at them. No Ally.

"If you're looking for the keg, it's out back," Hammond said. "Dad's cool with us drinking as long as everyone crashes here."

"No. I'm good."

"I know what he's looking for," Faith said in a teasing voice. She rocked up onto her toes, and scanned the room. "But you're not going to find her here."

I chose not to argue. I was too tense to play games. "Where is she?"

"Where's who?" Hammond said stupidly.

"Ally!" Faith squealed. Because the people in the cheap seats wanted to hear.

"Oh. Right. Yeah. She's not here," Hammond said, taking a slug of beer.

"Do you know where she is?"

Hammond sucked the foam off his lips. He didn't look at me. "Nope."

Something inside me flipped. "Yeah you do. Come on, dude, where is she?"

"You sound like her mother. She's been asking me every ten minutes if I know where this party is Ally went to." He chugged the rest of his beer, crushed the cup, and tossed it toward the kitchen, where it hit some girl in the leg. "Fuck her. She doesn't want to hang out with us, she doesn't have to."

He started across the room toward the stairs, but I grabbed his arm.

"Well, who's she hanging out with?" I asked.

Hammond took a deep breath and blew it out, like he was losing patience. "Some local dude. I don't know."

"What local dude?" Faith and I said at the same time.

"He said they were having a party at Chum and Howie's, whoever they are," Hammond said. "Some huge rager up by the lighthouse."

My teeth pressed together. Who was this local dude and why was he taking my girlfriend . . . ?

She's not your girlfriend. She is *not* your girlfriend.

"So let's go," Faith said.

My eyebrows popped up. Best. Idea. Ever. "Yeah. Let's go."

Hammond appeared interested. "But I don't even know where it is."

"There aren't *that* many houses by the lighthouse," Faith said, raising her palm.

"Yeah. So we'll drive around until we find it," I added.

Never before had Faith and I been on the same page. She grinned. Apparently she was enjoying it. I smiled back.

Hammond looked around. His parents were yucking it up over by the fireplace with some other coiffed adults.

"Shit. This party sucks anyway. Let's go."

It took fifteen minutes to drive to the lighthouse. Another fifteen to find the "rager." There were people dancing on the roof in the rain. From the look of the shack and its weather-beaten wallboards, I was shocked they were still alive. I slammed the door of Hammond's car and started toward the house, but I was still two steps from the door when I froze. All the blood in my body rushed to my head, and I suddenly saw myself driving my fist into the wall.

Because sitting—no, practically *lying*—on the porch swing, with her tongue down some blond surf dude's throat, was my not-girlfriend.

Ally

"Jake!"

The word exploded from my mouth before I fully registered that he was actually there. He held his right hand in his left. Both were shaking.

"Ow! Son of a bitch!"

He whirled away, flinging his hand out, cursing under his breath. Then Hammond came jogging up the steps.

"Dude! Did you really just punch the wall?"

For me. Jake Graydon had just punched a wall for me. I felt this euphoric rush and then Cooper stood up next to me, and suddenly Faith was there also, wrinkling her nose at the house and cringing away from the rotted porch railing. And the rush crashed spectacularly.

What the hell were they all doing here?

"You're bleeding!" Faith exclaimed with another nose wrinkle.

Blood ran in a trickle from Jake's knuckle and splattered the floorboards between his feet. Jake just stared at me. At my lips. Which still tasted like Cooper's ChapStick. Suddenly, and for no apparent reason, I felt like a cheating slut. But Jake was not my boyfriend. He was *not*.

He was just the guy who'd punched a wall over me.

"You should really get some ice for that, man," Cooper said.

"Who the fuck are you?" Jake spat.

Cooper tilted his head quizzically. Like he had just been faced with some exotic and heretofore unidentified breed of asshole. "I'm the guy who was invited here. Who the fuck are you?"

Jake took a menacing step forward, so Cooper did the same. Hammond's hand instantly shot out, pressing against Cooper's chest. This was going nowhere good, and it was going there fast.

"Back off, loser," Hammond spat.

"These are them, aren't they?" Cooper said with a laugh.

"Them, who?" Jake said, his eyes darting to me.

"The Cresties." Cooper did air quotes. He was cackling now.

"What the fuck do you know about it?" Hammond asked, shifting so his entire forearm was against Cooper's chest now. Cooper jostled back, then shoved himself forward. Their feet scuffled against the floor. My heart throbbed behind my eyes.

"Guys!" I shouted, putting my hands up. They froze. "We're not going to do this."

"Do what?" all three of them said in unison.

Like they didn't know.

"Ally, why don't you just come back with us?" Faith said plaintively. "We could all hang out! Maybe we could go to Café Bacci and—"

"Just stop, all right?" I blurted. "I don't want to hang out with you. Not any of you! Take the hint already."

Faith's face sort of crumpled and Cooper laughed. But I couldn't stand there and try to make her feel better. I'd finally told her the actual truth. I took Jake's wrist and pulled him down the steps. It was just drizzling now, and the water cooled my adrenaline-flushed face.

"What are you doing here?" I asked through my teeth.

"I came down to . . . I don't know . . . to talk to you," he said, looking past me with venom in his eyes, I can only assume at Cooper. "And then I find you . . ." He gritted his teeth and shook his head. "What the hell is up, Ally? Are you, like, *with* that guy?"

"I don't know . . . maybe," I said.

His jaw dropped and he took a step back. "Are you kidding me?"

"Me? What about you? I haven't heard two words from you since I left. . . . No wait, since Shannen's party . . . and then you come down here . . . what? Expecting me to, like, fall at your feet or something?" I demanded.

"What did you want me to do? You basically told me at Shannen's that you never wanted to talk to me again. And then . . . when I tried to, like, explain it to you . . . you told me you didn't give a shit about me," he rambled. "God! Why am I even here?"

"You never tried to explain anything!" I shouted back. "You just wanted to act like none of it ever happened."

This look crossed his face. Like, yes, that's what I wanted. Like, what would be so bad about that? He didn't get it. He was never going to get it.

"I don't get you," he said.

"Fine. Then maybe you should just go."

"Yeah. Maybe I should."

Neither one of us moved. He looked past me again and his eyes clouded over.

"I . . . I thought . . ."

My heart welled pathetically inside my chest. It was still waiting. Waiting for him to say the right thing. The one thing that would make it all better. But at that point, I had a feeling there was nothing he could say that would do that. Then his mouth snapped shut.

"You should come with us," he said. "Your mother's worried about you."

The exact *wrong* thing.

I snorted a laugh. "Oh, really? Is my dad worried too? Are my parents your best friends now? Why don't you get them both on conference call and maybe the three of you can figure out where I'm supposed to be for the rest of the summer at all times. When you've got a plan, gimme a call. I'll be right here."

Then I turned my back on him, stomped up the steps, and grabbed Cooper's hand. Annie stood in the doorway and I nearly leveled her as I barreled by. I slammed the door so hard, a shower of paint shards fluttered to the floor of the living room.

"Wow," Annie said.

I was shaking from head to toe as I breathed in. "That's one word for it."

Ally

"You sure you're okay to drive?" Cooper asked.

He assumed I'd been drinking, like everyone else around here, but I hadn't. At least not since that first cup of punch last night. Though maybe I'd been acting a little buzzed. My body had been on high alert ever since Jake and his entourage had sped off into the night. It was even tenser now that it was time to say good night to Cooper. We hadn't kissed again since the porch, but whenever he was near me he seemed to find excuses to touch me—a hand on the small of my back to steer me out of

the way of staggering partyers, a brush of my arm as he reached
behind me for a cup. Kissing him had been . . . odd. I'd never
kissed anyone I barely knew before. I'd been so self-conscious
from the moment our lips touched—trying to figure out where
my hands, my knees, and my tongue should go—that I hadn't
really registered how it felt. But I was willing to try again.

"I'm fine," I told him.

"Best. Party. Ever." Annie said, hooking her arm around my
neck from behind. She rested her chin on my shoulder, which
was hard for her to do considering she was a foot shorter than
me. She kind of got on her toes, tilted her head back, and bent
me forward to do it.

"She, however, is not," I laughed.

"Whoo hoo!" Annie shouted, throwing her arms up and
releasing her joy toward the bay. We were standing just outside
the side door of the small house, on what was once probably
a pretty patio, but was now a kind of sunken, overgrown rock
garden. All over the yard, the party stragglers hung on by a
thread, trying to extend the night into dawn. A couple of guys
played beer pong on a dilapidated Ping-Pong tabletop balanced
atop a precarious pile of laundry baskets, fish crates, and beer
cases. A girl in a cowboy hat leaned back on an inflatable
chair, braiding the hair of the chick sprawled across her lap.
Closer to the makeshift bar, half a dozen bikini top/miniskirt-
wearing chicas danced and occasionally cheered, while a pair
of dudes too drunk to rouse themselves looked on and nodded
appreciatively.

"Have I mentioned I like her?" Cooper asked, pointing.

I laughed. "She's a keeper. Don't worry. I'm gonna drive her
car back."

"Okay." He didn't look worried. "So . . ." He took a step toward me. His hand ran up and down my bare arm. Goose bump city. "I'll see you later?"

"Yeah. Definitely."

He leaned down to kiss me, closed-mouthed but lingering; his soft lips offered the promise of more. Then he stepped back again.

"Bye," he said.

"Bye."

He dropped his head forward as he loped back toward the house over the uneven paving stones of the patio. I bit my bottom lip, but felt like my grin would break off my face.

That was not odd.

"So, I guess we're over Jake," Annie said, standing stiller than she had in hours.

I lifted my shoulders, even as a twist of guilt took me by surprise. "I tried to tell you."

"But you have to admit, it *was* pretty romantic," Annie said. "Him running up the steps, slamming his hand into the wall . . ."

Together we headed for the broken gate in the white fence that surrounded the property. Annie stepped over a pile of beer cans and kicked aside a half-inflated kiddie pool, nearly tripping herself. I put out a hand to steady her.

"Yeah." It was. It was really romantic. And also humiliating. And exciting. And confusing. And annoying. And all-consuming. All I'd thought about for the rest of the night was Jake . . . and whether or not Cooper wanted to kiss me again. How could I possibly be all-consumed by one guy and feeling tingly about another?

As we made it to the gate, a very tall, very thin guy was coming through with a pastry bag. He had a short beard and shaggy black hair. The sun was just starting to come up over the far side of the house, lighting his face and making him squint. I gave him a glance and kept walking, but something in his eyes made me stop dead in my tracks.

It was fear.

And I knew him.

I turned around.

"Charlie!?"

He ducked his chin and looked up at me, almost sheepish. "Whatsup, Al?"

Annie raised one eyebrow as he turned around.

"Charlie! Oh my God! What are you doing here?"

I didn't know what to do with my hands. Should I hug him? No. I'd never hugged him before, so why start now? But I was so surprised to see him. And he looked so very different. When he'd left Orchard Hill, he'd been clean-cut and athletic, bulky even. The guy standing in front of me now with his shorts hanging just south of his hip bones was lean, lanky, and possibly stoned. He swayed a bit on his feet and placed the pastry bag down on a weathered Adirondack chair just outside the gate, as if its weight was throwing off his equilibrium.

"Don't tell anyone, okay?" he said.

"Don't tell anyone what?" I asked.

He sighed and took a couple of steps toward me. When he looked up, he narrowed one eye. "That you saw me?"

Now Annie was intrigued. She stood right next to me and looked into his face like she was trying to place him. He shot her a kind of wary look and held his hand above his eyes to shield them from the brightening sun.

"No. Of course not," I said. "But . . . why? I mean, what are you doing here?" I asked again.

"I live here." He gestured lazily over his shoulder. "This is my place."

I narrowed my eyes. My brain, apparently, was tired after a full night of partying and drama. I'd met Howie, a slightly chubby, self-proclaimed hacker extraordinaire with Coke-bottle glasses. Which could mean only one thing. "You're Chum?"

His head bobbed. "Short for Chuck Moore."

"Shut up!" Annie had finally caught on. "You're Charlie Moore? Shannen's brother?"

He reared his head back, showing us the underside of his chin. I shot Annie a *just chill* look.

"I thought you were in Arizona," I said.

"She told you that, huh?" He sat down sideways on the edge of the Adirondack chair and ran his hand over his hair. "I was . . . for a while. But it just wasn't my scene. I moved back here last year and got a job with a security company. You know . . . one of those places all our parents hire to check on the houses during the year?"

I nodded. My parents used to employ one of those. I'd never forget that one December night they'd called at two a.m. to tell my dad an alarm had gone off at the shore house. He was out the door in ten minutes and called us two and a half hours later to tell us a wood plank had shattered a window in a windstorm. He'd fired the company the next day for not actually checking the house before calling him.

"So you're not in school?" I asked. The very idea of Charlie

Moore—über-popular, three-varsity-letter-athlete, everyone-wants-me-as-a-prom-date Charlie Moore—not being in school simply made no sense.

"I'm taking classes at Monmouth," he said.

"Oh. Cool."

He should've been at Yale, debating politics in some elite study group. He should have been at Michigan scoring winning goals in Big Ten soccer games. He should have been at UCLA, surfing and making all the girls swoon.

"Anyway, you can't tell Shannen you saw me, okay?" He stood up again and ran his hands down the backside of his plaid shorts. "She thinks I'm this big thing at Arizona State."

"I promise, I won't say anything," I told him. "We're not currently speaking, so it shouldn't be too difficult."

"What?" He looked baffled. Like imagining me and Shannen not being friends was as hard to picture as him being a stoner at Monmouth State. "Why?"

"It's a loooong story," Annie said. He eyed her warily. "For another time," she added.

"I don't live on the crest anymore," I said. "We've kind of . . . grown apart."

I wasn't about to tell him his adorably mischievous little sister had grown into an evil troll.

"Oh." He nodded as if this made perfect sense as an explanation.

"But I don't get it," I said. "Why come here of all places? All our friends spend their summers down here. Did you really think you could go without seeing them?"

He lifted his shoulders. "Figured if I hung with the locals, I'd never bump into anyone. And I never did . . . till now."

We both smiled.

"Well . . . I guess we should go," I said, edging away. "I guess I'll . . ."

"See you around?" Charlie said. "Cool."

I nodded and Annie and I headed for her car. She grabbed my arm as she made her way over the uneven gravel.

"Charlie Moore!" she squealed under her breath. "Do you realize what this means?"

I realized exactly what it meant. It meant I had a secret to keep from Shannen. Just like the one she'd kept from me. And I wasn't entirely sure how I felt about that.

Suddenly, my phone rang. I looked at Annie, confused. My mother had stopped calling around two a.m. when I texted her that I was fine and was going to crash at a friend's with Annie. She'd texted back that we were going to have a "long talk today"—a promise that made my stomach clench every time I remembered it—and my phone hadn't made a peep since. "What time is it?"

She checked her watch. "Five fifteen."

I fumbled my phone from my pocket. The call was coming from Jump. What the hell was my father doing calling me at five a.m.? Had my mother called him to tattle on me? Was I in trouble? Seemed unlikely, since they weren't speaking, but I couldn't think of another reason. I decided to bite the bullet and answer it.

"Hello?"

"Ally, good morning," my father said. He was frazzled. He always sounded formal when he was frazzled. "Sorry to call so early, but have you seen Jake?"

I shook my head slightly, trying to make sense of my dad

asking that question, via phone, at dawn. For some reason, I instantly knew I had to lie.

"Um . . . no," I replied. "Why?"

He muttered something I didn't understand. "He ditched in the middle of his shift last night; went on his break and just didn't come back. It was mayhem here. Just mayhem. I don't know what he was thinking."

I was stunned. Jake had bailed on my dad to come down here? I didn't know whether to be pissed off or flattered.

"I called his mother and she had no idea where he was. We thought he might have gone down there."

I pressed my lips together and stayed silent.

"Well, if you see him, please tell him to call me," my father said.

"Sure, Dad," I said.

"Okay. Thanks, kiddo. Go back to sleep."

I closed my eyes as a seagull cawed overhead. "Okay. Bye, Dad."

"What was that?" Annie asked as I hung up.

"That was just me lying to my dad to protect Jake," I said matter-of-factly.

Annie laughed. "This just gets better and better."

"Yeah," I said sarcastically. "Can I ask you something?"

She shrugged, and almost knocked herself over doing it. "A'course."

"The other day, when you said you had Crestie dirt, was it about Jake?" I asked.

She blew out her lips. "No."

"I don't believe you."

"Okay, yes."

She turned and clomped toward her car.

"What was it? Annie!" I jogged after her. She yanked on the passenger side door, but it was locked. My heart hammered against my ribs. "Is he going out with someone? You have to tell me."

"It's nothing," Annie said. Then she looked at me, all defeated. "Can you please open my door?"

I tossed the keys up and grabbed them in front of her face. "Only if you tell me."

She rolled her eyes hugely. "Okaaaay!" She gave me this hesitant sort of look. "He came into the store looking for you."

"He did?" I asked.

"Yeah. He went up and down all the aisles and everything, then bought some mints and left them there."

I considered this. "Did he ask about me?"

"No. But it was obvious why he was there." She turned back toward the car and pulled on the handle with both hands. "Can we go now?" she whined.

"In a minute." I leaned back against the door and studied her face. She refused to make eye contact. "That's it? That's *all* you have to tell me?" I wheedled.

She nodded. "Yup. That's it."

"Swear?"

"Swear." Then she glanced at my newish sandals. "Can we go now before I barf on your feet?"

I stuck my tongue between my teeth. "Ish. Fine."

But as I trudged across the uneven dirt to the driver's side of the car, I didn't entirely believe her. Something else had happened. I was kind of dying to know what, but I took comfort in the fact that she'd tell me at some point. Eventually my little gossip-hound best friend always cracked.

Jake

All night I couldn't stop thinking about that guy Ally was with. His cocky face. That toolbox hair. He'd had his hands on her back, right above her waistband. That was the thing that kept coming back to me, and it made me feel sick every time it did. He didn't get to touch her like that. No one got to touch her like that.

I knew I had to get home and deal with the fallout. My mom had called me forty-two times the night before. Finally, once the party was over, she'd gotten through to Hammond's mom, who'd come into Ham's room still holding the phone at, like, one a.m. She'd told me my mom was too angry to talk to me, but that she didn't want me driving home in the middle of the night. I was supposed to be back at my house by ten this morning. It was already nine fifteen as I walked down the beach toward Dr. Nathanson's house. So yeah. That wasn't going to happen.

I stopped on the sand and flexed my hand, wincing as it throbbed through the gauze Faith had wrapped around my knuckles. Clenching my teeth, I looked up at the house. Ally was in there somewhere, probably still sleeping. I knew what Hammond would say if he saw me.

Why was I going back for round two? How far up my ass was my head?

But I knew why. It was that thing Ally had said about how I never explained. It had been driving me nuts all night. Because she was right. That day outside Jump, I avoided it. I had hoped we'd never have to go there, that we could just pretend like nothing had happened. And she'd called me on it. She'd called me on my bullshit. So now I had to explain. Just to prove to her that I wasn't the jackass she thought I was.

And there was something else, too. I could've sworn, when she'd first seen me, for just a second, she was happy I was there. There was a split second, when my hand was pulsating and my blood was rushing in my ears, that I thought she was going to throw her arms around me. I hadn't imagined it. It was real. I just had to get her to look at me like that again.

I blew out a breath and walked slowly up the stairs to the deck. I was halfway there, when a sliding glass door opened overhead. Ally stepped out onto a smaller deck. She was wearing her Orchard Hill High soccer T-shirt. The one she got for being a backslapper—my backslapper. Was that a good sign?

"What are you doing here?" she snapped.

Okay. Maybe not a good sign.

"Can I talk to you?"

She glanced over her shoulder and groaned. "I'll be right down."

She was gone for about thirty seconds. I didn't understand how she could make it seem like it was such a chore just to fucking talk to me, when all I wanted to do was talk to her. Then the door to the big deck opened and she came out. I walked up the last few steps. She looked tired, but it didn't matter. She was still beautiful. Maybe I should say *that*. Maybe then she wouldn't hate me.

I opened my mouth to talk.

"So, you ditched out on my dad last night, huh?"

My tongue turned to dust. "What?"

"He called this morning looking for you," she said.

Fuck. "What did you tell him?"

She rolled her eyes. Already this was not going as planned. "I told him I hadn't seen you."

I sank down on the nearest lounge chair and put my head in my hands. I was kind of surprised by how sick and guilty I felt. The gauze on my right hand grazed my temple. "Thank you."

"Thank you? That's it? I lied to my father for you," she said, hovering over me.

I lifted a shoulder and leaned back on my hands. "So? Payback's a bitch."

She looked stunned. Like I'd just slapped her. "So . . . what? Because he left us for two years I should punish him by lying to him?"

"No. That's not what I meant. Just . . . he lied to you, so . . ." I realized, suddenly, that this was not the right conversation. "Forget it. I don't know what I meant." I stood up again and blew out another breath. I kneaded my brow with my fist, trying to get my thoughts in order. "This was not how this was supposed to go."

"Then maybe you should just leave."

She turned and started for the door, and suddenly, I was pissed. How many times did I have to try with her?

"What's the matter with you?" I blurted.

"What?" She whirled around.

"I said, what's the matter with you?" I repeated. "What the hell did I do that was so bad? So I knew where your dad was. What did you expect me to do? How was I supposed to tell you that? It was none of my business. And you . . . I . . . we were just starting to . . . you know . . ."

I groaned, frustrated. Why couldn't I just say what I was thinking? We were just starting to hook up. I was just starting to like her. I was just starting to think that I maybe wanted her to be my girlfriend. And I was supposed to do . . . what? Deliver her the most awful fucking news of her life?

"So what you did was better?" she demanded. "Keeping the secret? Laughing at me behind my back with all your little friends?"

I shook my head. "No one was laughing at you."

And if they had I would've beat their ass.

Her hands dropped to her sides. "Oh, come on, Jake! You were there! At Shannen's party? Everyone was laughing at me. If you had just told me . . . if I had known . . . I never would've gone there. That whole night never had to happen."

"So I fucked up," I said, lifting my shoulders. I had this desperate feeling inside my chest. Like I just wanted to grab her and shake her, or grab her and kiss her. Whatever it took to make her stop talking and go back to liking me. "What am I supposed to do about it now?"

"Nothing," she replied. She had this condescending smirk on. It made me feel like shit. "You're not supposed to do anything, Jake. You're just . . . you're not the person I thought you were."

Ow. Ow. That literally effing hurt.

"What does that mean?" I asked. "I'm not good enough for you now?"

She shook her head slowly and looked at the ground. Her hand was on the door handle and all I could think was, *I have to stop her from sliding that door open. If she slides that door open, it's over.*

"No, it's not that," she said to the wooden slats under her feet. "It's just . . . this year sucked. I mean it really, *really* sucked. But you . . . you were the one thing that just . . . didn't."

Okay. That sounded good. So why with the gut pain?

She looked up at me, one hand around her waist, the other sort of thrown out, like she was begging for money on the streets. That's how she looked. That desperate.

"You were there for me through all this crap, and I trusted you, but then, when it really mattered, you kept this *huge* secret from me," she said. Her eyes were so wet they were drowning.

"So I make this one little mistake and all the other stuff—all the being-there-for-you stuff—that doesn't matter anymore?" I asked.

A tear fell and plopped on her shirt. "It wasn't some *little* mistake!" She turned away, shaking her head like I was just too stupid to live. "I can't do this. I'm out, Jake. I'm done."

I swallowed hard. This could not be happening. Didn't she get it? I wanted her. Only her. I'd never wanted only one girl before in my life. And I'd had her. We'd had each other. Why didn't she give a shit about that?

"I don't understand."

"When I get back home, I think we should just stay away from each other," she said, looking at me now. "You stay on your side of town, and I'll stay on mine."

"So that's it?" I said.

She yanked on the door. It slid open wide. My heart fell out of my chest. "That's it."

Jake

Fuck her. No seriously. Fuck. Her. After all that crap . . . all that sneaking around . . . the fact that I came to warn her that night at the pool and got my ass thrown in detention, the awesome frickin' birthday present I got her, losing my best freaking friend over her . . . None of that mattered? What the hell does that even mean, "You're not the person I thought you were?" Screw you. Maybe you're not the person I thought you were, hooking up with random local losers after what? Like, a week of being away.

Fuck. Her.

I pulled into my driveway at top speed. Had to slam on the brakes to keep from taking out my mother's beloved lawn jockey. Another fucking reminder of Ally Ryan and all the bullshit I did for her. I gave the Jeep door a good slam and started for the house. Three hours on the road and I was still fuming. I needed to punch something. Again.

My mother came out the front door. Her hand was stretched out flat, palm up. Her eyes were so wide it was like someone was pulling the lids back with little strings.

"Keys."

"What?"

"Keys!" she said. "Now, Jake. Give me your keys."

I stopped. I would've cursed, but she probably would've taken some gardening tool to my tires. I dropped the keys in her hand.

"That's it. For the rest of the summer, you are not leaving this house unless it's to go to work or to class," she spat.

She turned on her gold heel and walked over to the door. Then she stood next to it and waited for me to go inside. I wanted to bail. To walk to Shannen's. But I wasn't talking to her. Or go to Hammond's. But he wasn't there. I gritted my teeth and slunk inside.

"What. The Hell. Were you thinking?" She followed me into the kitchen. I took the pitcher of iced tea out of the fridge and poured myself a glass, but I was wound so tight that half of it splashed on the counter and soaked the gauze on my hand. I sat down on one of the stools at the island.

"Mom—"

"Don't Mom me," she spat, throwing my keys in the junk drawer and slamming it closed. "How do you think I felt when I got a call from your manager telling me you'd never come back from break? You don't answer your phone. You don't tell anyone where you are. And you'll be lucky if you don't lose that job!"

"Yeah. Lucky," I said under my breath. Because it was *so* much fun over there.

"Yes. Lucky," she shouted, walking around the kitchen island. "Because if you lose that job, you're getting another one. I don't care if it's mucking stalls over at the riding academy or cleaning bathrooms at the club. You *will* be working this summer."

"I'm sorry, all right? I'll apologize to Mr. Ryan," I said.

The name tasted sour in my mouth. Like I'd just upchucked.

"Yes. You will. And just so you know, your first practice-test scores were abysmal." She grabbed a sheet of paper out of another drawer and tossed it in my direction. The gesture fell kind of flat when it fluttered toward my feet and hit the floor on its face. "You're not going anywhere for the rest of the summer."

"You said that already," I said.

Her face turned so red so fast I thought I was going to have to call 9-1-1.

"You can go to your room now."

I huffed a sigh and got up. For a second I thought about picking up the paper and checking out my scores. I was kind of curious. But I didn't want to give her the idea that I cared. So instead, I took the steps two at a time, being careful not to spill any of the tea on the pale rug, and retreated to my room. The whole place smelled of carpet powder, which meant Marta had been there this morning. She'd left all the windows open to air the place out, so it was warmish inside, but I didn't care. I flung myself down on my bed and breathed.

Fresh air, actually, was a good thing.

Fuck Ally. Fuck my Mom. I'd just play video games all summer and in the fall I'd hook up with every freshman who blinked at me. They could both go to hell.

Except I couldn't stop thinking about the way Ally had looked at me when she first saw me last night. That half a second when she was glad I was there. What the hell happened to that?

Once I started breathing normal again, a pair of voices caught my attention.

". . . matter to you . . ."

". . . sorry . . . they just don't . . ."

I sat up straight. That was Chloe and some guy. Some guy was yelling at Chloe. I walked slowly over to the front windows. They were standing near the end of the driveway. Chloe and Will Halloran. He was gesturing like he was angry. She was standing there, toying with her sunglasses.

WTF? Was he, like, threatening her or something? I felt this surge of adrenaline. Maybe there *was* something around here to punch. I went for the door, but then Will turned and got in his truck. I heard the door pop and then he peeled out. Chloe speed walked inside, and it was over.

But still. I don't know. Something was up. I pulled my cell phone out and called her. It took five rings, but she answered.

"Hey, Jake." She sounded fine. Totally up.

"Hey. What was that all about with Halloran?" I asked, glancing out the window again.

"Oh, you saw that?" She laughed. "That was nothing. I guess my parents owe them some money and he came to get it, but they weren't here."

"So he decided to take it out on you?" I said.

She laughed again. "It was no big deal. I handled it."

I turned away from the window and leaned back against the sill, scanned the room for something else to punch. But my knuckles stung angrily from the iced tea soaking slowly into the wounds. My adrenaline started to die off.

"Yeah, well. If he gives you any trouble, just call me."

There was a long pause. I almost said her name to see if she was still there.

"Thanks, Jake," she said quietly. "That's really sweet of you."

I sat up straighter. See? I wasn't such a bad person. Chloe Appleby thought I was sweet. Too bad Ally Ryan wasn't around to hear it.

Daily Field Journal of Annie Johnston
Monday, July 5

Location: Beach outside Gray Nathanson's House.

Cover: Reading the Sandpiper newspaper; Ally is napping next to me.

Observations:

5:35 p.m.: Subject Gray Nathanson returns from driving his daughter, Subject Quinn Nathanson, to theater for rehearsal. Uniform: white shorts, light blue T-shirt, sunglasses. Subject whistles and twirls his keys as he walks up the stairs. Subject Mrs. Ryan opens the door with a huge smile. Uniform: one-piece bathing suit, linen cover-up, no makeup. Subject encircles Mrs. Ryan in hug. The two go at it like a couple of teenagers. (Note: Sickening.) They glance over at the beach, see no one's watching. (Note: Ha!) He picks her up and carries her inside. They kiss all the way up the stairs to the bedroom, where he slams the door with his foot. (Note: Shudder.) (Assessment: Dr. Nathanson and Mrs. Ryan are in deep. Also, it's a good thing Ally snored through that.)

5:47 p.m.: Subject Hammond Ross appears on the beach. Uniform: plaid bathing suit, white T-shirt, visor. He starts walking toward us. Sees me. Pauses. Turns. Takes a few steps toward us. Pauses. Takes his visor off. Scratches at his hair. Puts his visor back on. Turns around. Lopes back in the direction from which he came. (Assessment: My very presence makes Hammond Ross nervous. Score.)

Jake

I had to work at noon on Tuesday and I got there at exactly 11:59. I figured if I had to get right on "the floor," as everyone called it, Mr. Ryan wouldn't have time to yell at me. I was wrong.

"Jake."

His voice sounded just like Coach's when he's fed up over the team's lack of effort.

"Hey," I said, turning around. He stood in the doorway to the back room, holding the door open with his foot. I tried to look him in the eye, but he was seriously pissed, and I ended up looking at the blinking smoke alarm over his head.

"May I see you a moment, please?"

He was talking without totally opening his mouth. Something else Coach did.

"Uh." I looked over my shoulder for an out. "Don't you need me to—"

"Now."

I swallowed. "Okay."

As I walked past him into the back room, I ducked my head away from him. My palms were sweating, so I wiped them on my shorts. He let the door slam, which was something he told all of us never to do. Something about startling already caffeine-jittery customers.

"Have a seat."

I sat in the metal chair next to his desk, which creaked and leaned sideways. My stomach swooped and I pressed my toes firmly into the tile floor to keep from going over. On his desk was an open notebook with equations scribbled all over it, and a study guide with the words "Securities Training Corporation" across the top.

"I'm not even going to ask for an explanation," he began. He stood in front of me with his arms crossed over his chest. His eyes skimmed the cuts on my knuckles, and I stuffed my hands under my arms. "Because there is no explanation for what you did. Leaving here in the middle of your shift is unacceptable, do you understand me?"

I nodded. "Yes, sir."

"Because of what you did, Keisha had to work out your shift, which meant she had to call in a sitter to take care of her son last minute," he continued, not moving a muscle. Unless you counted that scary throbbing vein off the corner of his left eye. "That's money out of her pocket so that you can act like an irresponsible jerk. Do you think that's fair, Jake?"

I stared at him. Did he really want me to answer?

"Do you?"

Guess so.

"Um, no?"

"You don't sound entirely certain about that," he said. "So let me make this clear for you. If you intend to continue working here, I need you to be entirely certain about it. So. Was what you did fair to your coworkers?"

My face was burning like I'd gone out front and laid it down on the espresso machine. I stared at the emergency exit behind his head.

"No," I said.

"No. I didn't think so." He turned around and walked toward the far wall, where he'd hung up all these inspirational posters.

The one he was standing in front of was red with white letters and said, YOUR WORK REFLECTS ON YOU. TAKE PRIDE IN YOURSELF.

"I know you kids hate to hear this, but you're almost an adult now," he said quietly. He looked half over his shoulder at me. "So you really need to ask yourself one question. Is this the person you really want to be?"

I've had stingers in my calf before, and they kill. They just knock me over right where I'm running. But that was the first time I got a stinger in my chest. Between this, and what Ally had said to me yesterday . . . I mean, I'd always thought I was just fine the way I was. Actually, I'd never really thought about it at all. So why the fuck did people suddenly feel the need to make me think about it?

"I'm really sorry, Mr. Ryan. It won't happen again."

This was what my mother had told me to say. When I'd left the house, I told myself I'd never say it. But now, I actually meant it.

"Thank you for that," he said. He turned fully around now, and looked at the floor. He looked sad all of a sudden. Had I actually made a grown man sad? "Just think before you act, Jake. That's all you need to do. Believe me. I know. One impetuous decision . . . and your whole life goes off the track."

All right. Enough was enough. It was one half of one shift. And who the hell was he to tell me how to live? He'd left his whole family and not looked back.

"I get that, sir," I said, my voice all tense. "But it's just a part-time job. How is messing up once going to screw up my whole life?"

He glowered at me. I'd heard that word before, but never really knew what it meant. It meant someone's eyebrows came together and their forehead got all scrunched, and their eyes got all narrow and their face was both yellow and red at once. Basically, it meant he looked like he wanted to kill me.

"Well, it's at least going to screw up your week," he said. He went to the broom closet and yanked out this gross mop with gray strands of curled rope dangling heavily toward the floor. "Because as of right now, you're on janitor duty." He threw the mop at me. I stood up and caught it, but it still almost took off my ear. "Go clean the bathroom. And when you're done with that, there are about ten bags of garbage that need hauling out to the back."

When he stormed out, he let the door slam. Again.

I took out my phone. Thinking about Ally, about the way he'd left them, about how small she used to look whenever I talked about him . . . I didn't want her to look that way when she thought of me too.

I opened up my messenger and hit her name. My thumbs hovered over the keyboard. I held my breath, and typed.

I rly am sry. Just wanted u 2 kno.

Then I hesitated for a second and added one word.

Friends?

I closed my eyes and hit send before I could rethink it.

Daily Field Journal of Annie Johnston
Friday, July 9

Position: Across the street from Shannen Moore's house.

Cover: Pretending the chain came off my bike—I'm on my knees, fiddling with the wheel. As if I have a clue.

Observations:

9:05 a.m.: Subject Shannen Moore and her mother come out the front door shouting at each other. Which is, of course, why I stopped here. Shannen's uniform: plaid boxers, gray tank top, no bra, messy hair. Mom's uniform: sensible jeans, sensible shoes, sensible T-shirt, Louis Vuitton luggage.

Mom: I told you last night to be up by eight. It's not my fault you don't listen.

Shannen: I thought you were kidding! We cannot stay with them!

Mom throws her very expensive bags into the back of her car and slams the door.

Mom: Shannen, please. I'm exhausted.

Shannen: I'm not going.

Mom: Yes. You are.

Shannen: No. I'm not.

Mom: Yes. You are.

Shannen: No. I. Am. Not.

(Personal note: Is Shannen FIVE?)

Mom (so loud it scares two squirrels out of the nearby tree): YES YOU ARE!

Subject Shannen is so startled I'm about ninety-nine percent sure she starts to tear up. (Personal Note: The bitch can cry???)

Mom (more calmly): You have exactly five minutes to throw as much as you can into a bag and get back down here. I'll be waiting in the car.

Subject Shannen looks away. Her leg bounces. She opens her mouth, closes it, moves her jaw around. Her mother gets in the car and closes the door. Subject Shannen groans. More squirrels flee. She goes inside and slams the door. Mrs. Moore adjusts her rearview mirror and spots me. I casually get on my bike and ride up the hill, where I hide behind one of the Cornwallaces' massive rhododendrons.

9:13 a.m.: Mrs. Moore pulls out of the driveway.

Subject Shannen is in the passenger seat. Sulking.

9:15 a.m.: I come out of hiding. As I pass by the Moores' house, a curtain in one of the windows flutters closed.

(Assessment: Mrs. Moore and Shannen just left Mr. Moore. And he did zilch to stop them.)

Ally

I didn't have to work on Friday, so I slept as late as humanly possible, hoping by the time I got up my mom and Gray would be out at some farmers' market or art show or something. When I finally made myself sit up, I slid my phone off the bedside table and checked the texts. It was still there. The text from Jake. So I hadn't imagined it.

I rly am sry. Just wanted u 2 kno. Friends?

I had yet to reply. Did he really want to be friends? Was that even possible? Did it even matter?

I groaned and pulled a hoodie on over my tank top and shorts, then shoved the phone into the pocket. As I trudged downstairs, I realized I was out of luck in hoping my mother wasn't home. I heard her laugh mix with someone else's and closed my eyes. My head felt so heavy I thought it was going to drop off and roll across the floor. Sometimes sleeping late just makes me feel more tired than usual. What was up with that?

At the bottom of the stairs, I stopped in my tracks. Shannen and her mother were sitting across the island from my mom. Well, Shannen's mom was sitting. Shannen was more slumping so far down on her stool she was about to slide to the floor like a piece of overcooked spaghetti.

"Ally! There you are!" My mother's voice was all happy, but her smile was strained. Silent message: *Don't be a pill right now.* Shannen, meanwhile, tried to bore a hole through the marble countertop with a concentrated glare. "Look who's come down to visit for the weekend."

I glanced from Shannen, who would have been dead on sight if I had a gun or a bow and arrow or even a sizable spitball, to her mother, who had always been nice to me. Shannen's mom had a short, black bob, dark eyes, and a perpetual good attitude. How she could have spawned Satan was beyond me. Except that her DNA had mixed with Shannen's dad's. *He* definitely had some Beelzebub in him.

Of course, right now all I could think about in her presence was that her son—her pride and joy, the guy she hadn't seen in more than two years—was living just fifteen minutes away. And I was the only one in the room who knew it. And it was really unfair. To both of us.

"Hi, Mrs. Moore," I said.

"Hi, Ally." Her tone was apologetic. Was she apologizing for surprising me, or for bringing my worst enemy with her? "Listen, we came down here in part because your mother and I think that it's about time you two girls talk to each other."

I looked at my mother, who confirmed this with her hopeful expression. They had to be kidding. Why, in the name of all shattered high school friendships everywhere, would I ever speak to Shannen Moore again?

"I'm sure that Shannen has a very good explanation for what she did." Here, Mrs. Moore paused and looked at her daughter, who may as well have been a wax statue. "Although she's yet to share that reason with me. But I *know* she's sorry."

Yeah. She looked sorry. Really sorry.

"Mom, I can't do this right now," I said.

She opened her mouth, and suddenly my phone rang. I fumbled it from my pocket and saw Cooper's name on the screen. My heart seized up, bringing a blush to my cheeks. I turned away from the kitchen.

"Hello?"

"Hey, it's Cooper."

His voice sent a pleasant warmth zipping through me.

"I'm downstairs in the truck and I'm thinking pizza. Wanna come?"

I had never wanted to do anything more. Ever.

"Yes! I'll be down in two seconds." I turned the phone off. "I gotta go."

"Ally," my mother said.

I was already halfway across the living room when I turned to walk backward. "Oh, hey! We're still on for tomorrow, right? The city thing?"

My mother hesitated at the topic change. "Yes. We're still on, but Allyson . . ."

I grabbed my wallet, which I'd thankfully left on the glass table next to the door.

"Allyson Lauren Ryan."

Ugh. I stopped. I *hated* it when she used my middle name.

"You cannot leave this house right now," she said, storming toward me.

"Mom! I can't believe you did this," I whispered furtively. "She's, like, . . . I mean, she's evil, mom. Pretty much everything bad that happened to me this year? It was her fault. This summer already sucks and now I get Shannen Moore shoved in my face?"

My mother exhaled through her nose and crossed her arms over her chest. "I know it's no excuse, but her family is going through a rough time. I'd really like you to talk to her."

"So her dad sucks. We all know this," I said, glancing toward the open entryway to the kitchen. "That doesn't mean she can be such a bit—"

My mom's eyes widened and I stopped. My face turned pink.

"Well, you know she is," I said, looking at the bamboo floor.

"Ally, her parents are getting a divorce," my mother said. "That's why they're here."

My heart lurched. Suddenly I felt bad for Shannen. I saw her get up and walk toward the fridge, checking her phone for texts.

"They are?" I asked.

"Yes. And they may be staying here for longer than a few days while things get . . . sorted out."

And the sympathy was gone. "What? Mom! Come on!"

I brought my hand to my forehead, feeling desperate and angry and very trapped. Shannen was going to be living here? The person who had left our old lawn jockey on our front stoop, tricked me into breaking into the school pool and gotten me two weeks' detention, and—oh yeah—showed the world a video of my wayward father working behind the counter at a deli while getting humiliated by a bunch of kids? That girl was going to be living down the hall from me? Who knew what she could get up to with such easy access to my room, my stuff, my life? Then a horn honked outside and I remembered. I wasn't trapped. I had an escape vehicle right outside.

"I gotta go," I said, yanking the door open.

"Ally," my mother said, fed up.

"Mom," I replied, matching her tone.

I bolted out the door and slammed right into Hammond's broad, polo-shirted chest.

"Hey," he said. He cleared his throat, but didn't move. Didn't back up or move to the side or anything. "I came over to see Shannen. Bummer about her parents, huh?"

"Yeah. Bummer," I said flatly. "So, what? Faith's not with you?"

He looked confused. "No. Actually, I've barely seen her since last weekend. She might've gone home. I think you kind of crushed her, you know."

I felt a pang of guilt, remembering the look on her face at Charlie's party, but quickly pushed it aside. Faith had been a psychotic bitch to me all year. I couldn't feel guilty for blowing her off. And now I'd gotten what I wanted—one less person stalking me. Of course I'd be exchanging Faith for Shannen and I was definitely not sure about the merits of that deal.

"Okay. Well. See ya!" I said with false enthusiasm. I stepped past him and jogged down the steps.

"Wait, Ally!"

"What?" I demanded, whirling on him.

He walked down a few steps, standing over me, and shot Cooper a look. "What're you so pissed about?"

I rolled my eyes. "You know what, Hammond? If you don't know, then I can't help you."

Cooper waited with one hand on the wheel and one on the stick shift. I got in the truck, slammed the door with the telltale creak of a car that has lived its life in the salt air, and sighed.

"That guy so wants to get in your pants," he said by way of greeting.

I did a double take. For a moment my thoughts fell on my phone and Jake's text, but that made no sense. And Hammond was still watching us from the steps.

"Who? Hammond?" I choked a laugh. "No."

But my face was purple. Cooper noticed this, and chuckled.

"Yeah. Real convincing."

"Can we just go?" I asked.

"Your wish is my command, Crestie Girl."

We lurched forward into a three-point turn, and I bit back a retort at his awful choice of nickname. He was, after all, driving the getaway car. But hadn't he heard what I'd said that night? I was not a Crestie. I didn't want anyone thinking I was. Especially not the guy who was supposed to be helping me forget them.

Jake

"Keisha?"

She hadn't talked to me or even looked at me our entire shift. It was almost midnight, Friday about to become Saturday, and Chase was putting away all the sugars and nutmeg and cinnamon, signaling to the stragglers that it was time to move on. Keisha was cleaning out the pastry case, bagging up the old stuff for the soup kitchen van that came every night. She kept her shoulder to me and said nothing, but I knew she'd heard me. My heart started to pound.

"Look, I just wanted to thank you," I said defensively. "But if you're not interested—"

She huffed a sigh and stood up straight. She put her plastic-gloved hand, which was clutching tongs, on her hip and looked me up and down. Her ten million braids were pulled back in a sanitary ponytail and she wore the tightest jeans known to man.

197

She had a small waist and round hips and would've been hot, if she was, like, ten years younger.

"Thank me for what?"

Like she didn't know. She was just messing with me. Which was so exactly what I needed after a five hour shift of wiping down tables after half the kids from school.

"For the other night," I said. "For bailing. I heard you took my shift so . . . thanks."

She nodded slowly. "Right. Pay me back for the babysitter, and we're square."

She plucked a blueberry muffin off the yellow wax paper and shoved it in the bag.

"What?" I said.

"Sixty bucks," she said. Pluck, dump. Pluck, dump. "You got it?"

"Um . . ." I laughed, uncomfortable. "Didn't you make overtime covering my shift?"

She shoved another pastry into the bag and stood up straight. "You got some nerve, kid."

Chase was holding the door open for a twenty-something couple and they all stopped to look back at us. She was that loud.

"So I should take that money and put it toward the sitter I shouldn't have had to pay? Then I worked for five extra hours for next to nothing. What kind of idiot are you?"

Someone over by the door snorted a laugh. Then it closed.

"I—"

"And what about the fact that my kid had to go to bed without me?" she demanded. "He hates going to bed without me. And you know what happens? He wakes up in the middle of the night five times screaming for me 'cause he's all confused. So not only did I cover your ass, but I didn't sleep that night, and my kid didn't sleep that night."

"I'm . . . I'm sorry," I said.

Chase laughed and shook his head. He was on his phone texting, so I couldn't tell if he was laughing about me or the text. Or maybe texting about me and laughing about it.

"Sorry." Keisha blew out her lips and closed the empty case. "Some of us actually need the money we make here to pay bills. Some of us have actual responsibilities and people who count on us."

She walked past me, tossed the tongs into the sink with a clang, and snapped the gloves off.

"Sixty bucks and we're square," she said, looking me up and down again.

I swallowed hard. "I don't have it on me."

I swear I thought she was going to punch me right in the face.

"They've got an ATM across the street and I'm here another hour, rich boy," she said.

I pretended not to hear Chase snickering behind me as he locked the door.

Daily Field Journal of Annie Johnston
Saturday, July 10

Location: Scoops Ice Cream (with David).

Cover: Splitting a five-scoop sundae for lunch.

Observations:

1:25 p.m.: Will Halloran walks in. Uniform: hooded sweatshirt, cargo shorts. (Note: I don't usually record the uniform of Norms, but this is odd, considering it's ninety-two degrees outside.)

Will (to David): S'up man?

David: S'up.

Will goes to the counter and buys a water, a bag of M&M's, and a bag of Gummy Bears. Walks by again on his way to the door.

Will (to David): Later.

David: Later.

(Assessment One: Boys are Neanderthals.
Assessment Two: I'm invisible to Norms, too, now?)

1:28 p.m.: Will Halloran crosses the street and stops a few doors down from the movie theater. He shoves the water and snacks into his various pockets, then casually buys a ticket and walks inside. (Note: Ah. Now it all makes sense.)

1:31 p.m.: David eats the last of the Reese's Pieces from the sundae. I fling a spoonful of fudge at his shirt. He retaliates with a projectile cherry. Sheer madness ensues.

1:35 p.m.: We're just cleaning up from the food fight when I see Subject Chloe Appleby approach the theater across the street. Uniform: huge sunglasses, white sundress, espadrilles, date-hair. She buys a ticket and ducks inside. (Assessment: Chloe's been spending a lot of time at the movies this summer. Conclusion: That's what you do when all your friends ditch you for the shore.)

Ally

"Where did Annie say she'd meet you?" my mother asked, checking out the crowded sidewalk as she edged the Land Rover along Fifty-third Street.

"Um . . . right in front of the museum," I told her.

That was where my father was supposed to be standing, anyway. My mom's plan was to drop me off with Annie, find a place to park the car, and then come back to meet us. We'd spend an hour or two in the museum and then go grab a late lunch. My father's plan was to take my mother out for a meal at the swank restaurant where they'd had their first date, and then go for a carriage ride through Central Park.

"It's not original, I know," he'd told me. "But I was young and stupid in love."

I didn't care what they did, as long as it worked. As long as they started to patch things up.

"Do you see her?" my mom asked as a yellow cab zoomed around us and cut us off.

"No . . . I—"

And then I finally spotted my father. He was wearing a tan summer suit and a blue shirt, and carrying a huge bouquet of red roses. My heart all but stopped and I glanced at my mother's profile. Two seconds later, she saw him, too. And her face went gray.

"What's *he* doing here?"

He smiled and lifted his hand in a wave. My mother looked at me, her eyes wide. "Ally, did you know that your father was—"

But I guess the answer was written all over my face. Her jaw set and her cheeks flooded with color. She cut the wheel so fast she almost took out a bike messenger, who let out a string of angry curses. Suddenly she was throwing the car in park in front of a huge red sign that read NO STOPPING OR STANDING. She was so furious, it took her a good thirty seconds to get the seat belt undone.

This was not a good sign.

"I can't believe you would do this," she said angrily.

"Mom, please! Just give him a chance!" I begged.

But she was already out of the car and striding toward him, the full skirt of her red sundress fluttering around her legs. I tumbled out on the other side, nearly falling into traffic, and chased after her.

"Of all the pathetic attempts to impress me!" my mother said as I approached. "Using our daughter to set up a surprise date? Getting her to lie to me? Do you really think that's how you're going to win back my trust?"

I stood by, eyeing the pedestrians who were taking in the scene, trying to swallow and breathe and not burst into tears. It was about ninety-five degrees out, and the air was so thick with humidity it was pressing in on me from all sides. The entire world smelled like stale pretzels and sour milk and exhaust.

"Mel, please," my father said, holding the flowers down at his side now. "You won't call me back. You won't answer my e-mails. What else was I supposed to do?"

"How about take the hint?" my mother asked. "I don't want to see you."

"Mom, he just wants to talk to you," I begged under my breath. "Please . . . for me . . . just . . . can't you at least hear him out?"

My mother clicked her teeth together and shook her head, looking toward the tip top of the buildings around us, as if praying for guidance. Then she groaned and walked over to the car, leaning back against it.

"All right, fine," she said, her arms crossed over her chest. "You have five minutes. Go ahead. Talk."

My father laughed lightheartedly. "Five minutes? That's all I get after twenty years of marriage?"

Bad move. I swear I actually saw steam come out my mother's ears. "Let's just say I docked you five minutes for each of the years you were MIA, how's that?"

For the first time, my father seemed to grasp the severity of the situation. Clearly he wasn't going to get my mother laughing about this anytime soon. He licked his lips and his Adam's apple bobbed up and down. Suddenly, I was holding the roses and he clutched his hands together in front of his mouth.

"Melanie . . . I'm sorry. I don't know what else to say except I'm sorry," he began. "When I left, I thought I'd be gone for two weeks. I needed time to clear my head . . . to regroup . . . to figure out what my next move was."

"And you couldn't figure that out with me," my mother said. "The person who stood by your side through everything. The person who fielded the dozens of angry phone calls from our friends after they lost their life savings."

My father's jaw clenched and unclenched. "No . . . I didn't think I could. I was ashamed." He glanced at me quickly and I felt suddenly nauseous. He didn't want me to see him like this. *I* didn't want to see him like this. "I wanted . . . I wanted to come back to you with a new job and a plan and a future. But it . . . it didn't work out that way."

My mother stared at him and for the first time I saw the smallest, tiniest hint of softness in her eyes. "You could have called me. You could have told me all this. You could have told me where you were, for God's sake, Chris. Do you know the nightmares I had? Do you know what you put Ally through?"

I looked away, across the street, my eyes stinging. There was a guy selling fake designer purses, shoving them in ladies' faces as they walked by. I stared at him until his back was so blurry I could only see color.

"I'm sorry. I just couldn't face you. And the longer I waited, the more impossible it felt," he said.

There was a long moment of silence, aside from the whistles and shouts and car-horn honks. A rivulet of sweat made its way down the center of my back and the cellophane around the flowers cut into my palms.

"But now . . . I have a plan," my dad continued, his voice far more hopeful. "Charlie is going to give me a job as soon as I pass my Series Seven. I'm going to get it all back, Mel. Everything can go back to the way it used to be, except this time . . . no mistakes."

He reached for her hands and I blinked. She actually let him hold them. For a good ten seconds, they stood there, holding hands, looking into each other's eyes. Then, slowly, my mother pulled her hands away. When I saw the look on my father's face, my heart died.

"Not everything," she said.

"Mom—"

"Ally, get in the car," she said, reaching for the door handle.

"What? Melanie, please. Just talk to me. Shout at me. Hit

me. I don't care," my father said, reaching for her. "But we have to talk about this. We have to figure it out."

"Why?" my mother said. "Give me one good reason why I should figure it out with you. Why I should trust you again."

"Because," he said. "Because I love you."

I held my breath. And held it. And held it some more.

"I have to go," my mother said. "Ally. Car. Now."

I started to move, finally, still clutching the roses. My mother yanked open her door as my butt hit the leather seat, which was already scalding from sitting in the sun.

"So, what? It's Gray Nathanson, is it?" my dad said, his voice bitter. "You're gonna tell me you're in love with *him* now? Go ahead. Go ahead and shack up with him, then. We'll see how that works out for you."

I heard the slap before I even realized what my mom was doing. I gasped and my hand flew up to cover my mouth. I could see the red marks on his cheek, left behind by her fingers. I stared through the windshield at my father, sorrow welling up inside of me. Why had we ever thought this would work? What were we thinking? My dad was so stunned he didn't even move. For the first time in my life, he looked small. Broken. Old. And then we were peeling out into traffic, lurching toward and through a yellow light. Just like that, it was over. The day that I'd been looking forward to, the day that was supposed to save my family—obliterated.

My mother's breath was so ragged I thought she might faint. I slowly put the flowers on the floor, the cellophane crackling loudly, and leaned back in my seat. My heart and stomach felt hollow, like they weren't there at all. Carefully, I reached for my seat belt and clicked it, feeling as though any sudden movement might set her off. When I finally hazarded a look at my mother, she was leaned forward over the wheel, as if she could somehow make the car go faster by throwing her weight behind it.

"Mom?"

"Don't."

"But I—"

"Don't, Ally."

I swallowed hard and blinked back tears. She didn't say one word to me for the entire drive back to the shore.

Ally

"Have you ever been inside this one?"

Jenny and I paused in the middle of the beach that night as she pointed up at the darkened Appleby house. My feet were buried in the cold sand and the wind whipped around us like it was trying to kill something. The reeds at the top of the beach were flattened against the dunes, and the clouds overhead moved so fast against the cobalt blue sky, it was making me dizzy. My face already stung from spending hours in my room alone, thinking about the look on my dad's face that afternoon, and crying my eyes out. Now I was so tense my arms were permanently wrapped around myself. My mother still wouldn't talk to me, and when I'd come down for dinner, Gray had given me a look that could have killed a charging elephant, then dropped a folder of take-out menus on the counter and walked out with Quinn for destinations unknown. I was officially *persona non grata* in the world of my pseudo-family. All I felt like doing was curling up in a ball and dying, but the last place I wanted to be was inside that house. Thankfully, Cooper had called to tell me he and his friends were going to be partying a little ways up the beach. So here I was.

"Cuz I looooove this one," Jenny added.

I blinked, returning to the now. What was with the Lane family's jones for Chloe's house?

"Yeah, actually. One of my friends lives there."

It seemed easier than saying *former* friends and then explaining the whole sordid idiocy.

"Really? Does she keep any clothes in there?" Jenny asked, taking a couple of steps toward the deck. "I bet she has awesome clothes."

"All right, all right. Let's go before you get yourself into trouble," I joked, putting a hand on her shoulder.

Jenny shot me a wide-eyed, innocent look. "What? I was just asking."

We started up the beach together and she shook her head, glancing back over her shoulder. "How do you have a house like that and not even use it?"

I took a deep breath and looked out at the ocean, not about to explain why Chloe hadn't come down. There were whitecaps on the water as far as the eye could see, and the surf was so loud we had to raise our voices to be heard. Thinking about Chloe made me feel sad all over again. I'd recently seen her get devastated, just like my dad had been devastated that afternoon. And both were sorta kinda my fault.

"Come on, let's go back to the fire. It's freaking freezing out here."

There was a whoop and a shout down the beach, and I saw

Charlie's shadow loping toward the others, which gave me more of an excuse to get back there.

"Chum's here," I said.

"Oh! I *love* Chum! He always brings beef jerky!" Jenny gave a little jump, tugged her red-and-white-striped hood over her braids, and jogged ahead of me. Her heels kicked up so much sand, I had to slow down and shield my eyes.

"Hey, Ally," Charlie said, lifting his chin.

My shoulders felt heavy as I said "hi." Because I suddenly remembered that there was something I had to tell him. Something I figured he'd want to know. God. Could this day get any more depressing?

"Can I talk to you for a sec?" I asked.

Cooper looked back and forth at the two of us with a suspicious, possibly jealous, expression. I managed to feel flattered for a second, before the weight of what I was about to do flattened it like a two-hundred-pound dumbbell to the pinky toe.

"Sure. What's up?" Charlie asked.

He walked over to me, hands in the pockets of his blue sweatshirt, head bowed. I moved a few steps away from the fire and he followed.

"Uh oh. This seems serious," he joked, and laughed. But when he looked at my face, he stopped smiling. "What is it? Did something happen to my mom? Did he—"

"No. Your mom's fine," I said quietly. The fire crackled and sparked behind us, the wind blasting our faces with smoke. "She's . . . here."

Charlie actually looked over his shoulder.

"No, not *here* here, but down the shore. She's staying with us. And so is Shannen," I said.

"Shit. You didn't tell them, did you?" he asked.

"No, but . . . here's the thing. . . . My mom says your parents are getting a divorce," I said.

Charlie's head popped up. His eyebrows, too. He looked, suddenly, like the Charlie I used to know. All happy and alive inside.

"She's leaving him? Shut the eff up." He smiled and nodded a few times as he looked at our feet. "Go, Mom."

Okay. So maybe this wasn't a bad piece of news. All of a sudden, I sensed a disturbance in the force. Everything went quiet, except for the crackling of the fire and the whistling of the wind and the crashing of the surf. Before I could even look over at Cooper for an explanation, she was there.

"Hey! What're we drinking?" Shannen asked, slapping her hands together.

Charlie ducked behind me. As much as a lanky giant can duck behind a girl like myself. He grabbed my elbows from behind and pressed his head into the small of my back.

"Shit. Shit, shit, shit."

"What?" Shannen said as the locals just stared. She lifted her chin in my direction. "I'm with her."

You are so not with me, I thought. And would have said were it not for the fact that her brother's long-ass toenails were cutting into my heels. Only Shannen would feel like it was okay to crash a party with my friends mere weeks after completely destroying me. She really did live in her own little world where everyone else revolved around her.

"Chum? What the hell are you doing back there?" Dex asked.

"Fuuuuuuck," Charlie said to the ground. Then, ever so

slowly, he released me and stood up. Shannen's face fell so fast it made a dent in the sand at her feet. "Hey, Shan."

"Charlie!?"

It was like that scene in *Grease* in the parking lot when Danny and Sandy first see each other after their summer of love and Rizzo's the only one who knows what the heck is going on. I was Rizzo. Shannen threw herself at Charlie and they hugged. He picked her up off the ground and her legs kicked up.

"What the hell are you doing here?" Shannen demanded as her feet hit the sand again.

"Slumming, you know," Charlie lifted his shoulders.

"Hey! Watch it," Cooper joked, but he sounded serious.

"Come on," Shannen said, shoving his arm so hard he turned sideways. "I thought you were in Arizona."

"Yeah, that's kind of a long story," Charlie said, hanging his head. What was with all this head hanging? Back in the day this kid wore his chin higher than anyone I knew. "Don't be mad at Ally, though. I made her promise not to tell you."

Shannen's eyes flashed as she looked up at me. "You knew?"

I bit down so hard on my tongue my taste buds filled with blood. *Don't kill her. Do not kill her. There are too many witnesses.*

"Yes," I said slowly, loudly. "I *knew* where your *brother* was and I didn't *tell* you." I spoke like she was a tourist in from Greece who knew zero English. Very slowly. Very succinctly. Determined to get my point across.

Shannen sort of flinched. She tucked her hair behind her ear, which was something she always used to do when she didn't know what to say. I hadn't seen her do it once since I'd been back in Orchard Hill.

"Let's go somewhere," she said to Charlie.

"Like where?" he said.

"I don't know. Anywhere. We need to talk," she said. "There's a *lot* going on."

Charlie glanced at me, but didn't say that he already knew. Instead he nodded, lifted a hand at the crowd, and trudged off with Shannen by his side. From behind, it was amazing how much they looked like each other. Same long legs, same dark hair, same hunched shoulders. They'd always been the perfect pair. The brother and sister who made only children like me wish for a sibling. He shouldn't have been exiled, and she shouldn't have turned into a bitch.

"Damn," Jenny said, stepping up next to me.

"What?" I asked. In the sullen mood I found myself in, I expected her to say something deep and meaningful. Something that would make sense of all this contradictory crap spinning in my head.

"He took the jerky with him."

I scoffed a laugh. For some people, it was all just about the jerky. Must have been nice when life was so simple. Over her shoulder, a light flickered to life a little ways off in the distance. The deck light at Gray's house. My heart skipped a tense beat as my mom walked out to the railing and leaned into it. The wind tugged her hair back from her face as she scanned the beach, and I realized with a surge of hope that she was looking for me. Of course she was looking for me. I hadn't told anyone where I was going. Maybe she was ready to talk about this afternoon. And for the first time all summer, I was more than ready to listen.

I took one step toward the house, and then Gray came out behind my mom and slipped his arms around her waist. She turned to face him and he held her in his arms and the two of them started kissing like they were auditioning for some awful, middle-aged porn movie.

So, she wasn't looking for me at all. Apparently she didn't give a crap where I was, who I was with, or what I was doing. Maybe Cooper had been right all along. Maybe all I was to my mother was the person keeping her from the people she really wanted to be with.

Suddenly I felt very small. And stupid and angry and naïve.

"Hey, Crestie Girl. Want a beer?"

I looked up at Cooper. He held a can of something with the word "Lite" splashed across it. Ice dripped from the can and hit my feet, sending shivers up and down my legs.

"Sure," I said, taking it from him. "Why not?"

And while Gray slid his hands under my mom's T-shirt in the distance, I chugged a beer for the very first time.

Daily Field Journal of Annie Johnston
Sunday, July 11

Position: Gourmet salad bar at Dickson's Farm (favorite Crestie summer lunch spot).

Cover: Deciding between Kalamata or regular, martini-type olives.

Observations:

12:34 p.m.: The Halloran Electrical van pulls up outside. Brakes squeal. Music is cut dead. Will, who's much more of a Wendy's guy than a salad guy, gets out from behind the wheel, walks around the front, and opens the passenger-side door. A pink espadrille searches for the ground. I recognize it before I see the person it's attached to. Subject Chloe Appleby. (Note: THIS is interesting.)

12:36 p.m.: Will and Subject Chloe walk to the salad bar, pick up plastic trays, and go about making their salads. They talk, laugh. Subject Chloe makes suggestions.

12:37 p.m.: Will's hand touches Subject Chloe's back. She doesn't flinch away. It doesn't linger long.

12:43 p.m.: On their way to have their salads weighed,

they grab a basket and fill it with eight premade wraps and a bunch of sodas.

12:48 p.m.: There's some kind of debate at the register as Subject Chloe and Will both try to pay. Not sure who wins. The Weight Watchers crowd has just arrived and is blocking my view.

12:50 p.m.: Subject Chloe and Will walk out. He opens the car door for her. She smiles as she gets in. They speed away. (Innocent Assessment: They were just buying lunch for the crew working on her house. Not-So-Innocent Assessment: They're totally doing it.)

Jake

There was a circle on the page in front of me, with a big "$x=?$" over the diameter line. Or was that the radius? Which one went straight across? I used to know this. I had a feeling that if it was gray and raining and less than sixty degrees outside, I *would* know this. But today? With the sun in my face and the pool shining out there and knowing that every single person on the planet was having more fun than me? I didn't know what the hell that frickin' line was and I didn't care.

Why hadn't Ally texted me back? Was she so pissed at me that she couldn't even be text buddies? Or was it because I'd asked her to be friends? Maybe she still wanted to be more than friends, so when I'd asked to be friends, she'd been offended. Couldn't she just write something back? Let me know she'd gotten the text? Was it so hard to type yes, no, or maybe into a damn phone?

I took out my cell, deciding to call her out with another text. Something that struck the exact balance between caring and not caring. What was the word? Aloof. I needed to find the aloofness.

Ten minutes later, I was trying to think of something good to say. Maybe I *should* be paying more attention in English class.

Suddenly, Chloe appeared in my yard. She just walked out from behind the bushes and I almost had a heart attack. She squinted up at the house, like she was looking for something. I stood up and waved, shoving my phone back into my pocket. She smiled and waved back. Then she motioned for me to come downstairs.

This was the benefit of having the biggest house in town. My mom was in it somewhere, but clearly nowhere with a window on the backyard. I walked to the door of my room, opened it silently, and peeked my head out. Nothing. I ran downstairs on my tiptoes and cut through the dining room—which we use about four times a year—to get to the backyard. Mom was more likely to visit the kitchen than the dining room. Like, ninety-nine percent more likely. If they made SAT questions about how to avoid my family members, I'd be going to Harvard.

"Hey!" Chloe said as I slid open the glass door to the back patio.

I lifted a finger to my mouth to shush her, then pulled her around the corner. No windows. Awning overhead. Unless you were in the pool, you couldn't see us.

"What's wrong?" she whispered.

She was wearing a pink bikini under her white tank dress and I could see about seventy-five percent of her breasts from my angle. I cleared my throat and looked away. I'd also be going to Harvard if the questions were about how best to sneak a glance at cleavage. But Chloe was my friend, and still Hammond's girl in my mind, so I'd have to control myself.

"I'm still grounded. Seriously grounded."

"Oh, sorry." She pulled her lips down and back for a second. "Faith told me she saw you down the shore over the weekend, so . . ."

"Yeah. Big mistake," I said.

"Oh." She tilted her head and ran her fingertips along the wrought iron edge of our smaller patio table. "So, did you see anyone?"

I bit my lip. I hated it when girls dug for info. I wasn't good at knowing what they wanted to hear and what they didn't. "Well, I saw Faith." She looked at me like *I knew that already*. "And Hammond and Ally," I admitted.

"Were they, like, hooking up?" she asked.

"What? No." I shoved my hands in my pockets. "Ally doesn't like him."

Her eyebrows shot up. "So you think he likes Ally."

Crap. Was that what that sounded like? "No. No, of course not," I said. "Chloe, they weren't even at the same party. Ally's, like, hanging with some local crowd. Hammond said he's barely even seen her."

Her expression brightened. "Yeah?"

I suddenly recalled, vividly, the sight of Ally on top of that local dude, and felt sick to my stomach. But she didn't need to hear about that. I'd made her feel better already.

"Yeah."

"So if you're grounded, I guess that means you can't hang out," she said.

"I wish."

She groaned and leaned back against the pillar behind her. I breathed out, relieved. Looking down at her cleavage accidentally was no longer an issue. "I'm so bored!" she said.

"At least you don't have to take some dumb-ass class this afternoon," I said, rolling my head around to crack my neck.

"What class?" she asked.

"English Literature," I said in a low voice, trying for a British accent. "My mom's making me take it."

She stood up straight and frowned. She wasn't interested, was she? That would be insane.

"When's it meet?" she asked.

"Mondays, Wednesdays, and Fridays for, like, six weeks," I said. "It's two o'clock at Bergen."

"Okay. I'm in."

"What?" I laughed. "Are you serious?"

She shrugged. "It sounds like fun."

I reached forward and put my hand on her forehead, which I'd seen Shannen do a hundred times. Chloe rolled her eyes and smiled as she batted my hand away.

"Just making sure you're feeling okay," I said.

"I know. I get it," she said. "I like to read." She walked a few steps past me and took her sunglasses off her head, folding them in front of her. "Besides, if I join the class, then we can hang out and study together. Your mom can't ground you from studying."

She made a good point. "I don't know. The class might be full. I mean, studying stuffy, dead English dudes for the summer? That's, like, a major draw."

Chloe laughed and put her sunglasses on. "I'll pick you up at one thirty."

Then she twiddled her fingers and walked away. I felt energized all of a sudden. It was good, making somebody feel happy for once. Having someone be glad to have me around. I went back inside to study and put the new mood to use before it went away.

Daily Field Journal of Annie Johnston
Monday, July 12

Position: Cream of the Crop denim boutique, Orchard Avenue.

Cover: Shopping for jeans. (Personal Note: Do people actually spend $258 on one pair of jeans? I can buy everything in Old Navy for that price.)

Observations:

1:27 p.m.: Subject Faith Kirkpatrick walks in. Uniform: green off-the-shoulder minidress, sky-high wedge sandals, sleek ponytail. (Query: What's she doing home from the shore?) I skirt the clearance rack so she doesn't see me, get distracted by a cute pair of rolled, cropped jeans. Hmmm . . . these are actually—

The dressing room curtain snaps shut. Subject Faith's already inside and I didn't see what she picked out. Damn you, Lucky Brand sale jeans!

1:32 p.m.: Still considering jeans when Subject Chloe Appleby pulls up to stoplight outside in her white convertible. Uniform: puffed-sleeved, pink button-down. Subject Jake Graydon is in the passenger seat. Uniform: light blue T-shirt, Ray-Bans. Subject Jake says something. Subject Chloe laughs. The light turns green, and they zip off. (Assessment: Subject Chloe's really sowing those wild oats now that Hammond's out of the picture. Personal Query: Do I tell Ally?)

1:35 p.m.: I buy the jeans. On sale, it still takes half my paycheck.

1:42 p.m.: (Location: Scoops.) Experiencing extreme buyer's remorse. Have enough cash left for ice cream, but can't stomach it. This is a personal first.

1:45 p.m.: (Location: Cream of the Crop.) No returns on clearance merchandise! Damn you, Lucky Brand sale jeans! Damn you to Hades!

2:30 p.m.: (Location: My room, in front of the mirror.) Okay. They're actually pretty cute.

Ally

I was scooping out strawberry ice cream for an adorable towheaded kid on Monday afternoon when Hammond walked in, ducked behind the counter, and sauntered up to me, all smiles. I already had a headache from being out too late with Cooper, Dex, and Jenny yet again, and had this awful sour taste in my mouth I just could not get rid of. I was definitely in no mood to deal with the likes of Hammond Ross.

"Hey, Crestie Girl."

"Don't call me that."

I let the freezer door slam, handed the cone to the kid, and rang it up. His dad paid me three dollars and told me to keep the change.

"Thanks." I tossed the money in the tip jar, on which the handwritten sign read send us to college! tnx! I wasn't entirely sure people were going to want to send us to college if we couldn't even spell out the words "Thank You," but the tip jar was not my domain. I grabbed a sleeve of napkins and started to restock the dispensers on the counter.

"Why not?" Hammond said, leaning into my shoulder slightly. "You let that local loser call you that."

"How do you even *know* that?" I said through my teeth.

"I heard him say it the other day when—"

"Well don't," I snapped. I dropped a dispenser on the counter with a clatter. "I hate it when he says it, so it's even worse when you do."

He raised his hands in mock surrender. "Sorry! God. You

know, all I did was go to a party. What's the big frickin' deal?"

"A party you weren't invited to," I said, shoving the napkins so far into another holder the ones on the other side popped out. "And you brought Jake *and* Faith."

"It's a free country!" Hammond blurted.

He walked past me, his hip bumping mine, and shoved through to the back room. The door hadn't even closed when he was back again.

"What's up your ass this summer anyway?" he asked.

I dropped the napkin holder on the counter. "What's up my ass is that you people can't seem to get the hint," I said. "I don't want to be friends with you anymore. I'm not a Crestie. So stop following me around."

"That is such bullshit!" Hammond said.

"This is a happy place, people!" Mitch called out from the back.

Hammond rolled his eyes and let the door close. Out of the corner of my eye, I saw some customers approaching—vacationers of all shapes and sizes, wearing colorful T-shirts and with deeply red skin.

"What's such bullshit?" I demanded.

"Just because you moved away doesn't mean anyone stopped caring about you!" he spat.

He was breathing really hard. I could see the outline of his chest muscles heaving up and down. I looked up into his eyes and he didn't flinch. He stared back into mine. I felt a shiver go through me. He inched closer. And then, the door opened.

"There's my Crestie girl!"

My face turned beet red. It was Cooper, of course. Hammond cocked his head in a sarcastic way and took a step back. Cold air rushed in all over my hot skin. As I glanced at Hammond's pink cheeks, I felt guilty all of a sudden. And confused. And very, very warm. He hadn't really been about to kiss me, right? That was just inconceivable.

"You're such a working stiff," Cooper said. He leaned both forearms into the counter and smiled. "How late are you here?"

I held my breath as Hammond slid past me to help the sunburned family, who had come in behind Cooper. The shrieks of the kids bounced off the linoleum and echoed against the plate-glass windows. They pressed their noses against the glass, leaving smears I was going to have to clean up later.

"Ally?"

Suddenly I couldn't remember what day it was, let alone what time it was or when my shift ended. Luckily the Day-Glo, ice-cream-cone-shaped clock above his head told me we were well into the afternoon.

"Um . . . till six," I said, vaguely recalling the numbers scrawled on the schedule.

"Cool. We're hitting the Fishery after." He fiddled with the tip jar, holding his hand over the top as a seal and turning it upside down and back, upside down and back. "Dex said they got in a whole boatload of fresh clams this morning. I'll pick you up."

I hesitated. I knew that going to the Fishery with Cooper and his friends didn't just mean fried clams for dinner. It meant another late night of partying on the beach, drinking the beer I still didn't understand how they procured, making out in the cold sand with Cooper, and getting windburn around a roaring fire. Only some of which was pleasurable (the making out part). All I really wanted to do right then was take a long shower, cuddle up in some sweats, and watch TV. But my mother had only barely thawed toward me, and Gray and Quinn were avoiding me like I was covered in slime. Plus, every time I was inside the house, I was walking on eggshells waiting for Shannen to pull something or Gray to try for another heart-to-heart or my mom to suddenly decide to berate me about my dad. She hadn't even asked me where I'd been the past couple of nights. It was like she hadn't even noticed I'd been gone.

But still . . .

"I don't know. I think I should maybe try to have dinner with my mom," I said.

"You mean the bitch who keeps choosing her smarmy boyfriend over you?" Cooper said, pulling a face. "That makes sense."

Hammond shoved an ice-cream scoop into the coffee chip with serious violence.

"She's not a bitch. And I—"

"Dude. You hang out with your mother all year," Cooper said. "It's summer, for fuck's sake." He threw his arms out, palms up, like he'd just made the argument to end all arguments. He didn't even notice the death glares he was getting from the mom at the far end of the counter. "Besides, I'm way hotter than your mom, right?"

I laughed and felt myself relax. He had me there. And besides, what was one more night of avoidance? I actually felt relieved, all of a sudden, letting myself be persuaded. "All right, all right. I'll come with you. But I can't stay late."

"Yes. I win." Cooper casually pumped a fist. Which made me feel momentarily annoyed. Why was he making it a contest?

He leaned in for a kiss, and I let him have one because I

wasn't sure whether I was overreacting. Then he grabbed one of the wooden taster spoons and stuffed it inside his cheek like a lollipop. His flip-flops snapped as he walked out, and he nudged the mom of the singed brood with his elbow.

"You don't wanna go through him. He sneezes on the ice cream." He tilted his head in my direction. "Tip her. She's the goods."

Hammond's fingers clenched around the sugar cone and scoop he held in his hands. Cooper grinned happily and walked out into the LBI sun.

I groaned and leaned my tired body into the counter, wondering how he could be so awake and chipper when he drank way more and stayed out way later than I did. Whatever happened, I was not staying out past midnight tonight. I had to put my foot down. No matter what.

Jake

"In theess classss weee weeeeel deeetermeeen who are . . . theee consummate authors of theee . . . twenteeee-*ith* ceentureee."

I pressed my lips together. I couldn't laugh. I would not laugh. Because if I started laughing, it would be all over. Then Chloe, who was barely holding it together, would laugh, and we would not stop. Ever.

But this dude was making it so effing hard! Not only did he have the weirdest accent I'd ever heard, but he looked, no joke, like a frog-human hybrid. His lips were flat and protruding, and he licked them about once every five seconds. His face was wide, sitting on his neck like a watermelon. And he was balding. With only a little hair above his ears and then one, black curl right in the center of his forehead. His eyes bulged so much it was like when he turned sideways, you could see the outline of the whole ball under his eyelids. Plus, he was wearing green.

"Does aneewonnn have anee . . . authors they think should beeee added to theees lissst?"

A few hands shot up. He turned toward the board and lifted his arm. There was a huge circle of sweat staining his shirt. I snorted. I couldn't help it. Chloe looked at me wide-eyed, and slapped her hand over her mouth. I shook my head and shifted in my seat.

The thing was, this was so not Chloe. Usually, especially in class, she was a total prude. She followed the rules. She listened to every word our teachers said. She wrote most of those words down. And she shot dirty looks at anyone who stepped out of line.

Kind of like that dude in the front row with the striped shirt was doing to us now. I turned my attention to the board. The professor was writing down names as people called them out. Names like Hemingway, Fitzgerald, Forster. Names I'd heard, but had no interest in knowing more about.

"Goot. Goot."

Chloe and I looked at each other. "What the hell does *goot* mean?" she whispered, ducking her head and turning it sideways. When she did this, her hair covered her face, which I thought was lucky. Guys don't have a built-in defense like that.

"I think he's trying to say 'good,'" I replied.

Chloe pulled a face. "What kind of accent *is* that? Franish? Polczech? What?"

Another snort escaped my nose. Now three people turned around to stare. Chloe blushed and slumped down in her seat slightly. Something else I'd never seen her do.

"Now weee weeel deestreebuooot thee seeleebusss . . ."

A fly zoomed in through the open window and banged itself against the fluorescent light over his head. The teacher stopped abruptly. His eyes darted around the room, following every single movement of the fly. I thought my cheeks would explode, trying to hold in the laugh. But when he licked his lips, I couldn't do it anymore. I doubled over and so did Chloe.

Everyone in the room now looked at us, but we couldn't stop. Chloe was completely red and her eyes were filled with tears. I'd never seen her laugh like that ever.

"Eees theeere a probleeem?" the teacher asked, walking our way.

Chloe faced forward, breathing hard, but couldn't seem to look at him. I covered my mouth with my hand for a second and got myself together. When I looked up at him, I convulsed silently once, but that was it.

"No," I said. "We're goot."

After that, Chloe had to excuse herself to the bathroom.

Daily Field Journal of Annie Johnston
Wednesday, July 14

Position: Aisle two at the Apothecary.

Cover: Looking through after-sun creams. (I somehow got a sunburn on my right arm. It's roughly the shape of Argentina. How did I miss that spot?)

Observations:

3:05 p.m.: Subject Mrs. Appleby and Subject Mrs. Graydon walk in together. They are each talking on their cell phone.

Mrs. Graydon: No you may not drive down to Seaside Heights. (Pause.) I don't care who else is going! I—

Mrs. Appleby: . . . because it's a cesspool. (Pause to roll eyes at Mrs. Appleby.) Chloe, I've told you a hundred times. If you'd like to go down to the Island, I will have Marissa go over and open up the house. (Pause.) Well that's not my problem, now, is it?

Mrs. Graydon: How many times do I have to tell you you're grounded?

Mrs. Appleby: . . . may not hang out on that boardwalk without adult supervision!

They both snap their phones closed, huff identical sighs, then laugh.

Mrs. Appleby: Kids. We had them why?

Mrs. Graydon: I know! What were we thinking?

Subject Mrs. Appleby and Subject Mrs. Graydon dissolve into giggles. (Personal Note: I'm going to go home and hug my mom now.)

Ally

"Hold it like this," I instructed, showing Quinn the basic, and I thought obvious, positioning for her hands on the basketball. "You shoot with your right, but guide it with your left."

Quinn tucked her blond hair behind her ears, squinted from behind her designer sunglasses, and shot the ball. It arced perfectly, swiped against the underside of the basket, and slammed into the pole.

"Ugh!" She slumped her whole body dramatically. "Why are we doing this? It's, like, ten thousand degrees out here!"

"Hey, you're the one who said you wanted to hang out," I said as I retrieved the ball.

She trudged, arms hanging like a simian, to the metal bench at the edge of the bayside court. A few yards away was a sand-bottomed playground where a troop of toddlers shrieked and chased each other down slides, their parents reapplying sunscreen every so often and checking their BlackBerrys.

"Yeah, but I thought we would go shopping or something," Quinn said, checking her arms for sunburn. "Isn't it, like, dangerous to exercise in weather like this?"

I gave a sarcastic laugh and joined her on the bench, letting the ball slam against it with a clang. I took a long swig from my water bottle and dragged my arm across my lips. "If you wanna go home, go home. No one's stopping you."

Quinn gave me an incredulous look, then shook her head. She pulled a bottle of water out of her Kate Spade bag and popped the top. "What happened to you?" she asked suddenly.

The hairs on the back of my neck stood on end. "What do you mean what happened to me?"

"You used to be semi-cool, but ever since we got down here, you've been acting like a complete bitch." She sipped her water then closed the top. "No offense."

My already warm face burned. "None taken," I said facetiously. I got up, dribbled toward the basket, and slammed the ball against the backboard. It didn't go through the net.

"You've really hurt my dad's feelings, you know," she said, undeterred. "Not to mention your mom's."

"What do you know about my mom?" I demanded, whirling on her.

Quinn blinked. For a second I thought she was going to back off, but instead she stood up, crossing her arms over her chest. "I know that she doesn't get why you can be so mad at her, and not even the littlest bit pissed at your dad when he's the one who left you guys," she shouted. "Which I don't get either, by the way. If my dad did that to me, I'd hate him."

I do hate him, I thought. *Or I did. Do I still?*

"He's my dad, okay? Wouldn't you want your parents to get back together if you could?" I blurted.

Quinn pressed her lips together. If I could have seen her eyes behind those ridiculously huge sunglasses, I was sure I would have seen tears. "That's different."

"Why?" I asked.

"Because my mom is *dead,* you idiot! She didn't leave me by choice!"

Now tears streamed down her face and I did feel like a total idiot. She was right, of course. The two situations weren't comparable at all. I took a step toward her.

"Quinn, I'm—"

"You know what? Forget it." She shakily shouldered her bag and turned away. "I don't know why I even bothered." Then she looked up at the parking lot. "Looks like you've got company anyway."

She jogged across the court to her bike and took off. I wanted to yell after her—to say something that would make her come back so I could apologize, but I couldn't think of a thing. Then a car door popped and I glanced over at the lot. Shannen Moore was just unfolding her long legs from her mom's car.

Great. Just what I needed. More confrontation. Wasn't this exactly the thing I wanted to avoid this summer?

Shannen was dressed to play ball. Nike shorts, battered kicks, white T-shirt. Her long bangs were held back with a slim headband and the rest of her hair was pulled into a high ponytail. I was surprised to see her out of her usual uniform of a tank top and worn pajama pants. Since arriving at Gray's house, Shannen had rarely been seen off the couch. Unless she was out secretly meeting with Charlie, she was watching reality TV. Everything from *16 and Pregnant* to *The Next Food Network Star* to *Dangerous Jobs*. Her slovenly habit of leaving crinkled-up junk-food bags stuffed between couch cushions had sent Gray into an apoplectic fit last night. It was kind of funny to watch, actually.

Shannen strode over to the court and tossed her keys on their lanyard in the grass. "You up for some one on one?" she asked me.

"Why are you here?" I demanded.

"Why are you being such a bitch?" she shot back.

I choked a laugh. If one more person called me that . . . "You can't be serious."

I slammed the ball into the ground so hard that she only had enough time to throw her arms up defensively before it hit her chest. I was still residually upset about the episode with Quinn, but I was even more pissed at Shannen. If she wanted to bury the hatchet, she'd picked a bad time to show up.

"What the hell?"

"Go away, Shannen." I turned and grabbed my water bottle off the bench.

"Will you just chill?" she said. "I know you hate me, but you don't have to try to kill me."

She popped the ball off the ground with her toe and grabbed it out of the air.

"It sucked, okay?" she said tersely. "What I did at my party. It sucked. I don't know what I was thinking."

I almost choked on a mouthful of water. She started to dribble the ball from hand to hand in a perfect V, watching its rhythmic path.

"That's crap. I knew what I was thinking." She shook her head at the basketball. "I thought I was losing Jake. I was trying to get rid of you."

I felt like an air-conditioning vent had just snapped on at full blast directly above my head. My skin tingled and my hair stood on end. There was a loud car horn and a bunch of male voices shouted in our direction. All I could make out were the words "hot" and "baby."

"I thought you and Jake were just friends," I said, my mouth dry.

"We are." She stopped dribbling and crooked her arms

behind her head, holding the ball against her neck. "We were. I don't know. He might never talk to me again."

She hurtled the ball at me. I dropped my water bottle, which bounced on the grass and rolled under the bench, and caught the ball.

"So, you wanted to be . . . *with* Jake."

"Kind of." She hooked her thumbs into the back of her elastic waistband and looked out at the glittering water of the bay.

"So you were torturing me because he wanted to be with me," I said.

"I guess."

"Are you kidding me?" I pulled the ball back with one hand and let it fly as hard as I possibly could, flinging it toward the backboard. It slammed against the metal with a resounding clang and bounced away. Shannen flinched. "Why didn't you just *tell* me you liked him? Why can't you ever just *talk* to anyone?"

"I'm talking to you now!" she blurted.

"Right. Like, a month too late!"

I walked over to retrieve the ball, biting down on my bottom lip as I turned my back on her. I thought of that night, how I'd stood there in front of all those people after that video of my father had played. How I felt like I'd been punched in the stomach repeatedly. How alone and exposed I'd felt. Everyone seeing my family's dirty laundry, our faults, our weaknesses, our secrets. All so she could have Jake.

"You shouldn't have attacked my family," I said, my voice wet. I picked up the ball and pressed it between my palms as hard as I possibly could.

"I know. I get it."

"No, you don't get it," I said, whirling on her. "When we

were little, the pranks you used to pull . . . they were funny sometimes and we all went along with them because we all thought you were so cool. But somewhere in there, you started crossing the line. This kind of crap? It's not funny. Do you even realize what you did to me? To my mom? Not to mention Chloe and Hammond and Jake and my dad and even Gray. I mean, what the hell were you thinking?"

"I'm sorry! I don't know!" She turned her palms up. "If it makes you feel any better, my mom's making me go see some shrink about it. She thinks I'm deranged, apparently. Like staying with some asshole who treats you and your kids like shit for twenty years isn't deranged. If only she would've—"

"Shannen!" I shouted, cutting her off. Anger radiated off of me in tight, jagged waves. "This isn't about you right now."

She scowled, but then sort of deflated. "I know. You're right. I . . . I stepped over a line. I'm sorry." She covered her face with both hands, ran them up into her hair, and took the headband off so that her bangs fell into her eyes. Then she tipped her head back and groaned at the sky. "God! I hate this. Look, according to my mom, we're gonna be here the rest of the summer, so I just thought . . . if we could maybe call a truce . . ."

I exhaled a laugh. I'd heard that one before. Shakily, I dribbled the ball toward the net and hit an easy layup. Considering how pissed off I was, I was shocked it went in, but pleased. Let her think this conversation wasn't affecting me.

"That's not gonna happen."

Her face fell. She looked suddenly like her waify kindergarten self, standing outside the school waiting for her mother to pick her up—late, as always, because there was some issue with her father. "Okay. Well, I just want you to know that . . . if Jake comes down to visit you, I won't bother you guys. I swear. I won't even—"

"Yeah, that's not gonna happen either," I said, shooting another basket.

"Why not?"

"Jake and I are not together," I said blithely. I turned around and tried a hook shot, but it missed. "You can have him if you want him so badly. We're done."

Shannen's mouth screwed up on one side. A look I'd known since we were kids. A look that said, *You're a moron.*

"He doesn't want me," she said. "He wants you."

My heart flipped inside out, but I ignored it. I picked up the ball and tossed it at the net. "Then he shouldn't have lied."

Shannen considered this. She sighed and sat down on the bench, her shoulders curled forward.

"Is it just me, or does everything suck?" she said.

I jogged for the ball and picked it up. All of a sudden, I felt the blistering heat. I walked slowly toward the bench and sat down on the end, ball between my feet, forearms on my thighs. Squinting against the sun, I looked at her over my shoulder.

"It's not just you."

Daily Field Journal of Annie Johnston
Saturday, July 17

Position: Corner table at Jump, Java, and Wail!

Cover: Reading <u>Beautiful Creatures</u> with my headphones on (no music, natch).

Observations:

12:59 p.m.: Subject Jake Graydon walks in. Uniform: wrinkled cargo shorts, black T-shirt, battered sneakers. (Assessment: He looks more disheveled at work than anywhere else.) He sees me and stops dead in his tracks. Looks like he's going to say something. (Personal Note: I'm kind of dying to know what it is.) Then he ducks his head and goes to the back room. (Personal Note: Damn.)

1:01 p.m.: Subject Jake Graydon is behind the counter, ready to work. I'm the only one here other than that weird old dude on his laptop who's apparently writing either a slasher film or a heated political blog, considering how intense he is.

1:05 p.m.: Subject Jake Graydon looks in my direction, looks away.

1:06 p.m.: Subject Jake Graydon looks in my direction, looks away.

1:08 p.m.: Subject Jake Graydon looks in my direction, looks away.

1:09 p.m.: Subject Jake Graydon looks in my direction, looks away.

(Personal Note: I'm trying really hard to keep a straight face at this point.)

1:10 p.m.: Subject Jake Graydon looks in my direction. I briefly consider flashing him just to see what he does. I don't. He looks away.

(Assessment: Somebody wants to know what Ally Ryan is up to.)

Jake

"Pretty dead around here, for a Saturday."

Mr. Ryan leaned in to the counter next to where I was already leaning. I stood up straight, feeling like I'd been caught snoozing. One of his favorite things to say was that there was always something to be done, even when it looked like there was nothing to be done. I looked around. There were exactly two people in the store. One was the gray-haired dude who was *always* here during the day, pounding on his laptop keys like they'd offended him somehow. The other was Ally's friend Annie. She sat in the far corner reading some book with a black cover and drinking her coffee. I kept waiting for her to come over and talk to me. Tell me something about how Ally was doing, or whether she'd said anything about me. Maybe I should go talk to her. But I didn't want to look desperate. And besides, I was pretty sure that wasn't something I should be doing, even when it looked like there was nothing to be done.

Mr. Ryan was looking at me and I realized I hadn't said anything.

"Yeah." I pushed one hand into my back pocket. Lifted my shoulder. "Everyone's down the shore."

Also, it was, like, one hundred degrees outside. Who wants coffee in that weather? Even iced? Mr. Ryan nodded absently and looked into space. Guess he wasn't in much of a *do something* mood either.

"Including my family," he said.

Uncomfortable.

"Did you see them? When you were down there."

I went over to the cappuccino maker and hit some buttons. "Um . . . yeah."

"I figured. She said you didn't, but . . ."

He paused and shook his head. My hands froze on the steam lever. Wait. Ally and her dad had talked about me? When? Why? What had she said?

"How'd they . . . I mean, how was Ally?" he asked.

Like always, I immediately saw Ally on top of that beach bum jackass. This was so not right. Was this guy really grilling me, a kid, for details about his wife and his daughter? I hit another button, and steam shot out the side of the machine. Mr. Ryan jumped forward and made it stop. I took a shaky step back.

"She was good." I paused. "I think she has a boyfriend down there."

As soon as I said it, I regretted it. Because why? Why did I feel the need to tell him that? From the corner of my eye, I saw Annie shift. There was no way she could hear me from all the way over there, right? She had her earbuds in.

"Really? She hasn't mentioned anyone."

Which I guess was good. But then she hadn't mentioned me to him either, which made me and beach bum jackass kind of even. Which didn't sit well. I leaned back against the counter.

"Do you talk to her a lot?" I asked, fishing for info. Blatantly.

"Yeah, of course." He looked at me sideways, then shook his head and leaned in to the counter again. "No. Not really." He took off his visor and ran a hand over his hair. He stared out the front window, where Orchard Avenue was deader than the campus of Orchard Hill High right now. "She's angry. They both are. And they have every right to be."

He had no idea how much right. Or did he? Had Ally or her mom told him what happened at Shannen's party?

"You like her, don't you?" he asked suddenly. "My daughter."

I looked at Annie. She was staring right at me, but looked away. I turned sideways so she couldn't read my lips or something. "Yeah. Yes, sir. I do."

"So what's the deal?" he asked. "She doesn't like you?"

"Um . . . no. Not at the moment," I said.

"Oh. Why?"

I shoved both hands into my back pockets. "It's a long story. Kind of a misunderstanding, I guess."

He nodded. "I've got a lot of experience with those. Especially when it comes to women."

"Yeah? So what do you do about them?" I said. "The misunderstandings? I mean, if you have so much experience."

Mr. Ryan shook his head slowly, his eyes sort of unfocused and staring. "If I knew that, believe me kid, I wouldn't be here talking to you right now."

Daily Field Journal of Annie Johnston
Monday, July 19

Position: Across the street from Shannen Moore's house.

Cover: Tying my "walking shoes." I'm pretending to be a power walker, although every old lady with a Pomeranian has lapped me.

Observations:

12:05 p.m.: There's a moving truck in the driveway. Subject Mr. Moore is arguing with two guys wheeling a standing piano through the front door. All I can make out is "told you jerk-offs" and "back inside!"

12:07 p.m.: The movers wheel the piano back inside. They take out a big chunk of the door frame in the process.

12:08 p.m.: Subject Mr. Moore turns a color of purple formerly unknown in this quadrant of the universe. The screaming that ensues is frightening in pitch and chock-full of tasty expletives.

12:15 p.m.: The movers have unloaded a whole mess of furniture onto the front lawn.

12:17 p.m.: The moving truck speeds off.

12:28 p.m.: Subject Mr. Moore slams the front door, sits down on the front step, and hangs his head between his knees.

(Assessment One: Mr. Moore is moving out.
Assessment Two: Not today, though.)

Ally

"So, where's Cooper?"

I looked at Jenny, who sat behind the wheel of her and Cooper's pickup. We were parked on a random side street off the Boulevard and the engine was on. She kept glancing in the side-view mirror like she was nervous about something.

"He said he'd meet us here," Jenny said, her hands on the steering wheel. "He's just getting out of work."

"So why don't we just drive around and park in front of the store?"

Cooper worked at Faria's, one of the surf shops on the main Boulevard in Beach Haven. I'd been there to visit him a couple of times and kind of loved seeing him in his element, advising people about surfboards and body suits and whatnot. Plus, every girl who walked in there drooled over him, so it was always fun when he kissed me hello in front of them. I wouldn't have minded catching him at the end of his shift today.

"Because we can't," Jenny said through her teeth. "Just—" She sat forward suddenly. "Here they come."

"They?"

I turned around to find Cooper and Dex barreling toward the car toting two huge cases of beer. They were both laughing as they tumbled into the open bed in back, even though Dex's head collided with the wall.

"Go! Go! Go!" Cooper shouted, slamming the back door.

Jenny yanked the wheel and the truck lurched onto the road, then into a wide, screeching turn. My heart hit my throat as we almost hit an ice-cream truck head-on.

"What happened?" Jenny shouted through the open cab window. "I thought you had it all set."

"We did. There were . . . complications," Cooper said. He and Dex laughed and slapped hands. "But we're all good now. I don't think anyone saw us."

There was this awful, hard rock of fear settling in the center of my chest. I clutched the bottom of the open window and turned to look at Cooper.

"Did you guys just *steal* that beer?" I asked.

"Steal is such an ugly word," Dex said with a straight face as we bounced over a speed bump.

"What's the big deal?" Cooper asked. "Where did you think we got it?"

I swallowed hard. I was basically an accessory to a theft. I was riding in a getaway car. "I don't know. I . . . I figured you got an older friend to buy it for you or something."

"Occasionally we do. When we have the money," Cooper said with a nod. "But we don't always have the money."

"It's no big thing," Dex said, lifting a palm. "My dad's in the restaurant biz and I happen to know they budget for unexpected loss of product."

"Besides, they overcharge you bennies for everything down here, so they can afford to give back to the local community," Cooper said with a laugh.

I rolled my eyes. Like their twisted logic made it okay. Suddenly I felt jittery and tense. I had to get out of this car. Like, now.

"Come on, Crestie Girl," Cooper said, putting his head through the little square window like a puppy dog. "If we didn't do this every once in a while, we wouldn't be able to throw all those parties you've been enjoying so much."

"Yeah. I never heard you offer to pay for anything," Dex groused.

My face was on fire. Were they really trying to make me feel guilty for this?

"Jen?" I said, staring straight ahead through the windshield. "Can you drop me at the next corner?"

"What?" Jenny said, her blond braid grazing her thigh as she looked at me. "Why? Are you, like, mad at us or something?"

"No. She's just a goody-goody who's never had to worry about money in her life," Cooper said with a laugh, dropping back into the bed of the truck again.

My face flushed red. He was my boyfriend, kind of. Shouldn't he be defending me rather than mocking me?

"I worry about money all the time," I snapped back at him. "But I've never stolen anything."

Cooper raised his hands in surrender and widened his eyes like I was overreacting. "Fine. Whatever. Bail if you want to."

"Here's fine," I told Jenny as we came to a stop sign.

She eased to a stop and I jumped out of the truck, slamming the door as hard as I could.

"Call us later when you unclench!" Dex shouted at me.

Jenny gave me an apologetic look and seemed like she was about to say something, but then the car behind her honked and they were gone. I looked Cooper in the eye as they slowly rolled past and he held my gaze the whole time, his expression unreadable.

And now, I was stranded. No bike, no car, and miles from Gray's house. I turned around and looked at the light pink cottage I'd been left in front of. Clearly, I was going to have to call someone to come pick me up. But who? My mom? Gray? Asking either of them for help right now didn't appeal. But neither did the alternatives of Hammond, Shannen, or Faith.

I took a deep breath, blew it out, and started walking back toward the Boulevard. Maybe I would do some window-shopping before swallowing my pride.

The sun beat down on the back of my neck as I made my way along the pebble driveways and around the cars parked along the side of the road. What had just happened? I'd thought I was meeting up with my boyfriend and his sister for chowder and skee ball, and instead I'd witnessed a beer theft, been dissed by my maybe-boyfriend, and ended up alone.

As I reached the Boulevard I stopped and stared across the street at the red stop hand telling me not to cross. Cars full of beachgoers, shoppers, boaters, and nature-seekers zoomed by, heading merrily to their destinations, and suddenly I felt completely exhausted. And not just because of the sun. Or the hustle and bustle, which was steadily climbing toward that midsummer crescendo. I felt exhausted by all the thinking. All the feeling. All the everything.

Maybe Dex and Cooper did kind of have a point. I hadn't ever asked where the beer came from, and I'd never offered to help pay. Was it possible that I'd kind of known in the back of my mind that there was something not quite right about the whole thing? Had I just been so wrapped up in my own crap lately that I chose not to think about it?

The light turned green. I crossed the street and headed up the wood plank steps into Schooner's Wharf, arguably the "downtown" area of LBI with its many shops and restaurants.

My stomach grumbled as the scent of grilled burgers hit my nostrils, and I turned my steps toward the Gazebo. If I wasn't going to be getting chowder with my friends, I might as well drown my sorrows in a burger and a milk shake.

I was just about to walk into the restaurant when Shannen and Faith came out of the T-shirt shop nearby. Faith had a small shopping bag—the kind that comes with jewelry—and Shannen was texting on her phone. Faith and I both stopped walking, but Shannen bumped right into me.

"Hey! Watch where you're—"

She saw it was me and tucked the phone into the pocket of her short plaid shorts. "Oh. Hey. Sorry."

"It's okay," I said automatically.

For a long moment, we all just stood there. Faith pointedly looked away from me. Shannen struck a kind of defiant pose, one knee cocked, fingers hooked into the waistband of her shorts.

These people used to be my best friends. We'd told each other everything. Now I couldn't even look them in the eye.

"What're you up to?" Shannen asked finally.

Breaking the law, I thought, but didn't say.

"I was just going to get some food," I said, gesturing over my shoulder at the open-air tables outside the restaurant.

"We were going to the candy store," Faith said, looking past me.

Shannen squinted as the screen door to the candy shop squealed open and banged shut. "Remember those swirled lollipop things we used to be addicted to?"

Faith looked at her shoes. "You guys liked those. They made me sick."

I smirked. "Remember when you barfed on Mrs. Appleby's life-size carousel horse?"

"That thing deserved to be barfed on," Shannen joked.

"I had actual nightmares about that horse," Faith said. "Remember its—"

"Red eyes!" Shannen and I said at the same time.

And we all laughed.

I sighed and looked down at the uneven bricks beneath my feet. My heart felt like it was pushing against cling wrap, tugging it, twisting it, trying to break free.

You hate these people, my brain said. But that stupid heart again . . . it was telling me I didn't.

"I guess one lollipop couldn't hurt," I said.

"Believe me, it could," Faith replied, sticking her tongue out.

"So we'll get you a pretzel," Shannen said, grabbing her arm and dragging her toward the store. "Let's go."

I followed them slowly, part of me still wanting to bolt, still screaming that it was a bad idea to hang out with them—to trust them. But then, who in my life could I really trust right now? And besides, I was going to need a ride home at some point. As Shannen pushed open the swinging screen door and the familiar, sugary scent hit me full force, I decided not to think about anything for the next fifteen minutes. It was just one lollipop, after all. I could worry about what it meant later.

Daily Field Journal of Annie Johnston
Wednesday, July 21

Location: Orchard Hill Country Club pool.

Cover: Pretending I lost my iPod when I was here last week as a guest of Misty Carlton's. (I've never spoken to Misty Carlton.) I told the guy behind the welcome desk, then snuck out here while he went to retrieve the lost and found box.

Observations:

1:05 p.m.: There's practically no one here. And the few people here are parents. Can't believe I used that excuse for this epic fail.

1:07 p.m.: A security guy steps out the back door, his eyes scanning the area. I duck behind the laundry cart full of freshly cleaned OHCC towels. He strides by. As I step out, bent on escape, I notice Subject Mrs. Graydon at the poolside bar, sipping an ice water with Subject Mrs. Stein. This could be something. I move closer.

1:08 p.m.: I sit on an empty stool two seats away from Subject Mrs. Graydon and start to casually snack. (Note: These peanuts are AWESOME.)

Mrs. Graydon: . . . think it really was the best thing

for him this summer. I can't believe the way he's applied himself.

Mrs. Stein: I'd ground my kids if I could. It never takes.

Mrs. Graydon: What does that mean, it never takes?

Mrs. Stein (takes a slug of her white wine): You could lock those two in a steel vault and they'd find a way out. Anything to see their little friends.

Mrs. Graydon (looks disturbed for a moment): Yes, well, the only friend Jake has seen this summer is Chloe Appleby. And that's one connection I don't mind making an exception for.

Mrs. Stein (eyes wide): Do you think they're . . .

Mrs. Graydon: (Smiles like a sly cat and lifts one shoulder.)

Mrs. Stein: Huh. We all thought Chloe and Hammond were going to end up married.

Mrs. Graydon: Yes, well. Things change.

1:10 p.m.: I fall off my stool from leaning too far to the side. (Note: It's difficult to hear over peanuts crunching in your mouth.) Am summarily escorted from the premises.

Jake

It was a Friday afternoon smack in the middle of summer. The sun was out. The skateboarders were skateboarding. And I was sitting on the grass in Veterans' Park, studying.

Something was seriously wrong with this picture. At least anyone who passed by would see I had a hot girl by my side. That was something.

"I actually really liked this book," Chloe said, stretching out on her stomach on the blanket she'd brought. She propped up on her elbows, with *This Side of Paradise* open in front of her face. "I've never read anything like it. Have you?"

She looked back at me, her hair sliding down over her bare shoulder. Bare because of the skinny-strapped sundress she was wearing. I raised my eyebrows. She couldn't be serious.

"Oh, right. You don't read," she said.

"Unless you count cereal boxes," I replied. I picked up my own book and crossed my legs. "And I'm usually half-asleep when I read those, so the words don't really sink in."

Chloe laughed and sat up again, rolling one shoulder back. "But you did read this. I mean, you answered all my study questions with no problem."

That's what we'd been doing for the last hour. Going over the study questions she'd searched for on the Internet and printed out. Girl knew some tricks when it came to studying.

"Yeah," I said. "It wasn't bad."

"Goot," she said with a nod and smile.

"Goot," I joked back.

She sighed and reached into her canvas bag for a granola bar. She offered one to me and I took it, keeping to my policy of never turning down food. A breeze rustled her notebook and she put her bag on top of it. She broke off a tiny corner of her bar and popped it into her mouth.

"Are you and Shannen talking?" she asked suddenly.

I clicked my teeth together. "Not really. Are you and Shannen talking?"

She shrugged. "Nope."

We both stared across the park as some scruffy-looking kids jumped their skateboards over the steps.

"What're we going to do when we get back to school?" she asked. "Everything's so screwed up."

"I don't know."

I hadn't really thought about it, but she was right. With her and Hammond not together anymore, and her and Shannen not together anymore, her only real friends would be Faith and me and the Idiot Twins. But she and I had never really been friends. And I had a feeling she just kind of tolerated the twins. Like they were little brothers you couldn't ditch. I didn't really have a big interest in hanging with Faith, so that left me with Hammond and the twins, and no Shannen *or* Ally.

God. This sucked.

"Let's talk about something else," I said.

"Yes. Let's." Chloe gave a quick nod and had another bit of her granola bar. "Summer is no time for heavy thoughts."

"It's no time for studying, either, but—" I lifted my book.

"You're right."

She grabbed it out of my hand and threw it on the grass about five feet away, along with her own. Then she lay down on her back on the blanket and tipped her chin up, letting out a sigh as she gazed up at the sky. She looked beautiful like that, her hair all splayed out around her. My heart did this weird skip thing. If I were anyone else, or she were anyone else, I would have kissed her right then. Because how could I not?

"Come on. Let's look at the clouds."

She put her hand on my arm, and I felt a stirring of attraction. I swallowed hard and lay down next to her, but kept a good distance between us. This was normal, right? I mean, she was gorgeous. Didn't mean I had to do anything about it.

"You're different this summer," I said.

She shielded her eyes with her hand and looked at me. "I am?"

I nodded and folded my hands on my stomach. "More . . . chill."

"And, what? I'm usually uptight and lame?" she asked with a laugh.

"No! Not . . . I just—"

"I'm kidding. I get it." She went back to looking at the sky. "I don't know what it is, but I just *feel* more relaxed this summer."

"It's kinda nice," I said, moving my head around on the ground until I found a comfortable spot.

Out of the corner of my eye, I saw Chloe grin. "Thanks. I think so too."

Ally

My fingers were sticky with ice cream and there was a smear of fudge across the front of my Take a Dip shirt that looked

like something far less sweet. Large clumps of my hair had
hardened due to an unexpected whipped cream explosion, and
I was pretty sure there was chocolate on the back of my neck.
As I walked across the great room at Gray's house, I just prayed
he was down at the beach, because if he saw me looking like
this, he was going to throw on a hazmat suit and spray me down
with bleach.

I heard a voice as my foot hit the bottom stair, and I froze.
My mom was out on the deck and the door was open, but the
screen door was closed. I glanced over my shoulder. She was on
the phone. And I'd swear I just heard her say the name Chris.

A quick glance and a listen told me no one was around.
Holding my breath, I tiptoed toward the door, making sure to
stay out of view behind the thick, open curtains.

". . . don't think you realize what it was like for me," my
mother said, her voice carried in by the ocean breeze. "I never
stopped loving you, Christopher."

My hand flew up to cover my heart. My mom was actually
talking to my dad! She'd just told him she loved him!

"Of course," she said. "Of course I did. Why do you think I
was so mad?"

I heard a squeak and knew she'd sat down on one of the
lounge chairs. I took an instinctive step back, but couldn't get
myself to move away. If something important was going to be
said here, I wanted to be around to hear it.

"All I wanted was for you to come back," my mother said
quietly. "For the longest time . . . that was all I wanted."

I bit my lip giddily and did a happy little dance. This was
so awesome! I wondered if she'd called him or if she'd finally
picked up one of his calls. What had sparked her change of

heart? Had she finally softened after seeing him that day in the city? Actually, who even cared? My parents were talking again. And from the sound of things, it was going well.

The clanging of the doorbell scared the crap out of me. My mom stopped talking and I sprinted for the kitchen and opened the fridge, trying to make it look like I'd been in there all along.

"I'll get it!" I shouted as my mom stuck her head through the door.

"Oh. Ally. I didn't even realize you were home," she said.

"Hi!" I shouted, running across the living room and trying as hard as I could not to sound too giddy. I yanked the door open as my mom returned to the deck. Cooper was standing on the front step. My heart caught at the sight of him. We hadn't spoken since the beer theft debacle. He pushed his hands into the pockets of his cargo shorts and gave me a sheepish look.

"Hey," he said.

I crossed my arms over my chest, wishing I didn't look as if an ice-cream shop had combusted all over me. "Hey."

"Look, I just stopped by to say I'm sorry," he told me. "We should have at least told you what we were doing there."

"Yeah," I whispered, glancing over my shoulder toward the deck. "You should've."

"But it's not like we were gonna get caught," Cooper implored. "We never have before."

"Yeah, well. You could have," I said.

"But we didn't," he said, lowering his chin.

"But you *could have*," I replied, feeling exasperated.

Cooper blew out a sigh and stared at his feet. "Can we just, like, agree to disagree?" He looked up at me through his blond bangs and bit his lip. Damn. Why did he have to be so adorable?

261

"Fine," I said. "As long as you never take me along again."

Cooper grinned slowly. "Come on. You can't tell me you didn't get *something* out of it. Just a teeny adrenaline rush?"

I stared at him, but found I couldn't keep a straight face, more because I was psyched about my parents than anything else, but still.

"I knew it!" he crowed.

"Shut up!" I slapped his chest with the back of my hand. "I didn't. Seriously. I don't want to get arrested. It's the last thing I need."

"Fine," he agreed. "You will be kept in the dark from now on. And I'm sorry about that crack I made about money. I know you're not one of *them*. It's just . . . it's easy to forget." He looked around the spacious, million-dollar living room and lifted his palms.

"Yeah. I guess I could see that." I took a step back. "You wanna come in? I was just gonna take a shower, but then we could go down to the beach if you want."

"Cool." Cooper stepped inside, rubbing his hands together. "Just so we're clear, are you inviting me into the shower or just to the beach?" he joked.

I guffawed. "Shhh! My mom's right outside."

"Oh." He cringed. "Oops. Maybe I'll just watch TV then."

"Yeah. Good idea," I said laughingly. I shoved him toward the couch, not even bothering to tell him to take his shoes off, and jogged for the stairs. Who cared about Gray's stupid rules anyway? Before long, he was going to be out of my life for good. As I went by the screen door, I trained my ears for the sound of my mom's voice, but this time I didn't catch any of her conversation.

But I did hear her laugh. And that could only be a good sign.

Jake

Mr. Ferguson (aka Mr. Froggy) walked into class with a pile of white paper under his arm. My blood pressure instantly skyrocketed. This always happened at the sight of tests. I was never nervous until I saw with my own eyes that it was actually going to happen.

He put the pile down on his desk and the rotating fan in the corner blew them toward the door. A girl in the front row jumped up to help pick them up. He thanked her, then clutched them as he looked at the five rows full of students.

"Thees test comprises tweentee multiple choice queeestions eend one eeessay," he told us. I cracked a smile, but didn't laugh. I was getting used to the accent. Also, I felt like I was going to pee my pants. He started to hand out the papers. "Theee multiple choice eees deesigned to eeeelucidate your understanding of theee mateeeriell. Thee eeesay will reeequire some . . . original thought."

He placed a test down on my desk, the final test in the final row. "Goot luck."

As he walked away, I looked at Chloe. "Goot luck," she whispered.

I tried to smile—it didn't work—and I looked at the page.

I knew the first answer. And the second. I also knew the third. My heart started to pound for a new and unfamiliar reason. I knew the answers. I didn't even have to think about it. I just knew. I grinned. I went through the multiple choice in ten minutes. Then I turned the page over to make sure I wasn't missing something. I wasn't. All that was left was the essay.

I looked around. Waited for the punch line. This was like a reverse nightmare. A couple of rows over, a girl chewed on her nails. I could see she'd only answered three questions.

Don't be a dick, I told myself. *Check it over. There must be something wrong.*

I went back and read the questions again, slowly, like my SAT tutor was always telling me. But all my answers were right. I was sure of it.

Chloe shot me a concerned look. I guess she read all my fidgeting as a bad sign, but it wasn't. I lifted my shoulders and glanced at the clock. I had forty minutes to write the essay. Usually I had to scribble out answers in huge handwriting with the clock ticking away the last five minutes of class, mocking me with every click.

This. Was. Awesome.

Daily Field Journal of Annie Johnston
Friday, July 23

Position: Corner of Orchard Avenue and Walnut Street.

Cover: None. I'm on my bike. Ready to go.

Observations:

(Note: I'm stationed here waiting for Subject Chloe Appleby and Subject Jake Graydon to return from the thrice-weekly jaunt to wherever the hell they're jaunting. They have to drive by here to get to the crest, and when they do, I'll follow them to wherever they go next. I owe it to Ally to find out what's going on. And to my future literary career.)

2:45 p.m.: Eureka! The white convertible approaches. I lean over the handlebars, ready to follow.

2:46 p.m.: Subject Chloe Appleby stops the car right in front of me, parallel parks like a pro (Note: Of course. Is there NOTHING she's bad at?), and checks her hair in the rearview. I fall off my bike trying to get away before they notice me. Knee officially skinned.

2:48 p.m.: Subject Chloe and Subject Jake Graydon walk to the corner. I scoot my back against the wall around the corner from them, clutching my knee to my chest.

Jake: . . . no idea it was going to be that easy.

Chloe: It wasn't THAT easy.

Jake: Not the essay, but the multiple choice, psssh, come on.

Chloe: Okay! Stop rubbing it in, genius! Have you started the next book yet?

Jake: No. But I'm starting it tonight. I bet I got at least a B on that test! My mom will die if I get a B.

Chloe: Maybe she'll unground you!

2:49 p.m.: Traffic lets up and they jog across the street and into Scoops. I stare, baffled. (Query: Studying? They've been STUDYING?)

Ally

Saturday afternoon, I was lying out on the beach in front of Faith's house with Shannen, Faith, Quinn, and Quinn's friend Lindsey, thinking that if Cooper could see me now, he'd probably break up with me for my complete hypocrisy. But when Faith had called that morning and included Quinn in the invite, Quinn had actually fallen on her knees begging me to say yes, obsessed as she was with the elder Cresties. I'd been so stunned by the sight of her down on the floor, and still affected by my residual guilt over the whole "my mom's dead, you idiot" thing, I hadn't realized I'd agreed until I hung up the phone.

But whatever. I'd been feeling a lot better ever since I'd heard my mom and dad talking. A lot less tense and pissed at the world. Might as well let others benefit from my new attitude.

I was just starting to doze to the sound of the waves when Faith's phone rang. She reached down from her striped beach chair, fished it out of her Kate Spade beach bag—exactly like Quinn's, but with green trim instead of pink—and checked the display. Her rattan sun hat was so huge it cast enough of a shadow for her to actually see the screen in all this blazing sunlight.

"It's my mom." She rolled her eyes and got up, inching away from us as she talked.

"What's that about?" I asked as we all watched Faith gesture with her free hand, scaring off a seagull that had gamely wandered close to our little camp.

"Her mom's being a beyotch about the guest list for the

end-of-summer party," Shannen said with a yawn, turning her face to lie on her left cheek. She'd been splayed on her stomach for the last half hour, the straps of her black bathing suit pulled down her shoulders to avoid tan lines. There were deep creases pressed into her cheek from her eye to her ear. "Apparently they're scaling back this year."

Quinn and Lindsey exchanged a startled look, probably worried they wouldn't be invited. The Kirkpatricks' end-of-summer parties were legendary in Crestie circles. Everyone who was anyone was there, so if you weren't invited, well, ergo you were no one.

"Ugh!" Faith tossed her phone at her bag and plopped back into her beach chair.

"What happened?" Shannen asked.

"She's holding me to fifty guests. Fifty!" Faith took out a brush and yanked it through her damp hair. "I'm going to have to cut Tori and all the other seniors."

"Who cares? They're out of here anyway," Shannen said, sounding bored.

Faith's jaw sort of dropped, but then she paused, brush still in hair, and considered. "Right. They are out of here. . . ."

"I think it's far more important that you invite the people who are sticking around," Lindsey piped up, looking up from her *Star* magazine. She wore a light pink bikini that showed off her dark skin and how she was way too endowed for a soon-to-be sophomore. In the past half hour I'd spied men of all ages doing double takes on her as they walked by. "You know, the underclassmen who are going to go see all your plays . . ."

"And who are going to vote for school officers," Quinn added, catching on.

"Huh. I never thought of it that way," Faith said, staring across the ocean. "They're not seniors anymore. *We* are."

"So screw 'em," Shannen said.

Faith smirked and sat back in her chair. "Yeah. Screw 'em."

Lindsey and Quinn surreptitiously high-fived. Crises averted.

"When *is* the end-of-summer party, anyway?" I asked, pushing myself up onto my elbows. The surf was surprisingly close to our little camp. In the time that I'd been lying on my back, the tide had started coming in.

"August seventh," Quinn said, before Faith could answer.

Faith shot her a perturbed look, and Quinn's already-pink face darkened. "I already have it in my iPhone."

"August seventh. Not exactly the end of summer," Shannen said with a yawn.

"It's the guys. They all have to get home for their 'soccer mini-camp' that week," Faith said with air quotes. "If we want an acceptable guy to girl ratio, it has to be that weekend."

August seventh was the next weekend Annie was coming down. Normally I wouldn't even consider attending the Kirkpatricks' all-Crestie bash, but Annie would kill to go. The hook ups alone would have her burning up the keyboard on her laptop. And I'd already forced her to miss the July Fourth party. But Faith detested Annie. And now, with the smaller guest list . . . But still, I had to ask. I mean, Annie's head would explode if I didn't at least try.

"Faith?" I said.

"Yeah?"

"I was kind of hoping to bring a guest," I said casually.

"Oh, don't worry." Faith waved a hand as she put her brush away. "You can totally bring your local boy toy."

I blinked. That thought hadn't even crossed my mind. Going to a Crestie party was probably the last thing he'd ever want to do. "Actually, I was sort of thinking I'd bring Annie."

Faith's lips flattened. "Um, no."

I sat up straight now, all the blood rushing to my face. "Faith—"

"Ally, she's a total freak! And this party is for us. The last party of the summer. The—"

"Omigod, Faith, just let the girl come," Shannen groaned, propping herself up on her forearms. "What's the big deal?"

We both looked at Shannen, stunned.

"Didn't you used to be friends with her or something?" Shannen asked, pulling her hair around to check it for split ends.

Faith and I exchanged a surprised look over Shannen's prone back. The very idea that Shannen (a) noticed anything about Faith's life that didn't directly pertain to her and (b) remembered it even after two years was kind of astonishing. "Yeah," Faith said.

"So let her come," Shannen replied, flicking her hair back again and shrugging one shoulder. "It's probably the last one you're ever gonna have anyway. Might as well go out with a bang."

"The last one?" Quinn said. "Why?"

Faith pursed her lips, like she'd just popped a lemon lollipop into her mouth. She looked down at her perfectly tan thigh and shooed a fly away. "My parents are getting divorced and they can't decide who's getting the house, so they might sell it."

"What?" I blurted.

Faith sighed. She gave me a *don't go there* look that made

me feel, all over again, that her parents' impending split was somehow my fault.

"Don't worry. I plan to talk them out of it," Faith said. She lifted her sunglasses from atop her head and placed them over her eyes, then leaned back again. "All right. Your little friend may come. But bring Cooper, too. He's hot."

"Gee, thanks," I shot back, wondering why I'd ever even opened this can of worms. Annie so owed me one.

"Isn't it so weird?" Shannen said, smoothing out the sand in front of her towel with the palm of her hand. "I mean, did you ever think that all our parents would be getting divorced?"

A hot stone burned to life in the center of my stomach.

"I know. Especially yours, Ally," Faith said, her face tilted casually toward the sky. Like she was discussing the weather and not my parents' marriage. "I always thought they were the perfect couple." She glanced sideways at Quinn. "No offense."

Quinn didn't reply, nor did she look at me. She was, in fact, looking pointedly away at her iPhone, scrolling through iTunes endlessly.

"Wait, what are you talking about? Did you hear something?" I asked, leaving my pride buried in the sand.

Faith looked at Shannen, who looked at me. "No. Not exactly. We just assumed . . ."

"Assumed what?" I asked, even though I knew.

"Well, your dad came back and your mom still came down the shore to play house with Dr. Nathanson," Shannen said. She glanced at Quinn. "No offense."

Quinn looked at Lindsey. Clearly she was starting to have second thoughts about the attractiveness of hanging out with her elders. "I think I'm gonna go in. Wanna come?"

"Definitely," Lindsey replied, dropping the mag.

"Wait."

Quinn was dusting the sand off the bottom of her flowered bikini, and froze.

"Have *you* heard something?" I asked.

She turned and looked at me with an apologetic sort of smile as she backed away toward the water. "I really don't want to be a part of this conversation."

But wait. No. My parents had been talking on the phone. She was laughing. She said she *loved* him. This couldn't be right. My heart pounded so hard it was making it difficult to breathe.

"Quinn. If you know something—"

"Come on, Lindsey," she said, grabbing her friend's hand.

The two of them ran into the surf, hair bouncing, sun gleaming off their skin, screeching happily like some Coppertone commercial as their calves hit the water. Shannen turned over and sat up. She rested her wrists across her knees.

"It's pretty clear they're breaking up, Al," she said. "For real."

The pitying look she gave me made me hate her more in that moment than I had at her party. Much more.

"You don't know what you're talking about," I blurted, gathering my things. I yanked my denim shorts on over my bathing suit and stood up. "My parents are talking again. They're going to get back together."

"Ally—"

"I have to go," I said.

Neither one of them tried to stop me as I threw my towel over my shoulders and stormed off. They were wrong about this. They had to be. They just had to be.

Ally

"Mom!" I shouted at the top of my lungs, closing the screen door with a bang. "Mom! Are you home!?"

She and Gray both came racing onto the landing outside their bedroom and leaned over the wooden railing to look down at me.

"Ally! What's wrong? Why are you shouting?" my mother asked.

I threw my wet, sandy towel on the back of the couch and saw Gray flinch. If he'd been in front of me at that moment, I seriously might have tackled him to the floor.

"I need to talk to you," I said shakily.

"What is it?" She jogged down the stairs, eyeing me with concern. Clearly she could tell this was of dire importance, because she'd barely spoken to me, let alone looked at me in a motherly way, in well over a week. She hit the first floor, Gray hot on her heels, and crossed over to me. "Honey, what's wrong?"

Her hands were on my shoulders. I glared at Gray and his floppy blond hair and his inappropriately unbuttoned plaid shirt. I wanted more than anything to tell him to go away, but I knew that was a waste of time. If he had to be here for this, then fine. I looked my mother in the eye, and my chin quivered.

"Are you and dad getting a divorce?" I asked, clutching my elbows.

Gray looked at the floor. My mother blinked. "What?"

"I was just down on the beach and Shannen and Faith said you guys were getting divorced," I told her, my voice wet. "So are you?"

Gray moved past me, slipped my towel from the couch, and draped it over his arm. "I think I should go."

My mom just sort of looked sideways at him as he made his way out to the deck and closed the glass door behind him. She reached up and touched my face, tilting her head as she looked at me.

"Oh, Ally—"

I pulled away from her, doubling over at the waist. "Oh my God, you are! Who knows about this? Does Quinn know? Do all the Cresties know? Have you even told Dad?"

"No decisions have been made," she said, holding her hands out flat.

"But you were talking to him on the phone! You said you loved him!"

My mother shook her head. "How did you—"

"How can you do this so fast? You're not even going to give him a chance?" I blurted.

"Ally, he was gone for almost three years," my mother said. "What's so fast about that?"

"That's not what I meant!" I cried. Everything around me swam. The modern wood sculptures, the glass dining table, the striped curtains. I felt like I couldn't focus on anything. Like the whole world was blurring out of my control.

"Ally, all I can tell you is your dad and I still have some talking to do," my mother said gently. "And Gray as well. He's a part of this too."

"Why?" I screeched, clutching my stomach. "Why should he be a part of *anything*?"

"Because I love him, Ally," my mother said simply.

My throat completely closed over and I felt like I was going to throw up. "You don't love him. You can't. You love Dad."

My mother sighed and looked past me out the window. "It's complicated."

"Well, what about me?" I blurted.

"What?"

"You said Gray is a part of this. What about me? Don't I get a say in who I want to be my father?" I asked.

"Your father will always be your father, Ally," she said. "He still loves you. That hasn't changed. We both do."

"Yeah, well. You could have fooled me."

I strode by her, grabbing a hooded sweatshirt off the hook by the door as I ran out.

"Where're you going?" my mother shouted after me. "I hope you're not going out with that Cooper kid!"

"Why not?" I blurted, whirling on her.

"Because I don't like the person you are when you're around him," she replied, walking toward me. "Don't think I haven't noticed how late you've been coming home, Ally. Don't think I don't know what's going on."

"Like you even care," I spat. "At least Cooper *wants* me around!"

Her jaw dropped and I fled, slamming the door as hard as I could.

Ally

"You know what pisses me off?" I said, one foot crossing over the other as Cooper and I navigated the crowded sidewalk in front of Fantasy Island, the family amusement park in the middle of Beach Haven. "All these families."

I swung my arm wide and almost knocked over a scrawny kid flying by on a skateboard.

"I mean, look at them! Look at *that* guy!" I pointed in the general direction of a beefy dad with two kids hanging on his arms as he tried to check his BlackBerry. His skinny, tan wife walked ahead of him, chatting on her phone, while one kid whined that he had to pee and the other begged for ice cream. "I mean, why are you even here? It's like they're *pretending* to be a happy family cuz it's, like, something they're supposed to do, but if you're just gonna be on your freaking phone all night, why not just *stay home*?!" I shouted as the dad passed us by. He glanced over his shoulder at me with an irritated look, but didn't seem to think I was talking specifically about him. He probably thought I was just some random, drunk teenager. Which, let's face it, I was. "Your kids would be happier in front of the TV than screaming to get your attention!"

"Okay, okay, that's enough with the public service announcement," Cooper said, stopping me and pinning my arms to my sides. He looked me in the eye. "Man. Who knew you were going to turn out to be a mean drunk?"

"I'm not," I pouted. "Just honest."

Some woman wearing her sunglasses and straw hat at night sideswiped me with her huge Michael Kors purse and I bristled. "Why are we here again? I liked the beach. Let's go back to the beach."

"We're here because you had a sudden craving for funnel cake, remember?" Cooper said, turning me toward the elaborate Fantasy Island gates with the carousel horse at the top, smiling down at us.

"Oh yeah. Right." I slung my arm around his shoulder as we walked by the security dude at the entrance. He gave me the stink eye and I tried to look casual and sober. "And you brought me here because you're the best boyfriend ever."

"That's me," Cooper said.

He held me around the waist as we skirted clumps of screaming children and a huge puddle of melting ice cream. There was a line in front of the funnel cake stand, so Cooper deposited me on a bench, told me not to move, and walked up to the window. He, of course, knew the girl behind the counter. As he waited for the food, ignoring the grousing of the other people on line, my phone beeped. I didn't even look at it. I knew it was my mother. She'd been calling and texting for the past three hours. Like she was worried about me. Yeah, sure. Just another parent pretending to give a crap about her kid.

"Here we go!" Cooper said, offering me a funnel cake on a flimsy paper plate. He tore off one end and popped it into his mouth. "You wanna eat it here or . . ."

"Let's go someplace else," I said as the kids on the Tilt-A-Whirl screamed. All the flashing lights, swirling rides, and wailing voices were making me dizzy. "Someplace alone."

Cooper nodded and tugged me up with one hand. "I know a spot."

I leaned my head into his shoulder as we walked out the back exit of the park and through the parking lot toward the bay. There was a playground in the sand near the edge of the water with a plastic climbing wall and a cave beneath it.

Cooper ducked inside, then stuck his head out.

"You coming?"

"Uh, sure." I dropped to my knees. The sand was cold and rough. When I crawled inside, I realized the cave was the perfect size for two people. We sat with our backs against the wall and our legs stretched out across the sand. Cooper tore off another bite of funnel cake and held it in front of my lips. I smiled and snatched it with my teeth, showering powdered sugar everywhere.

"Thanks," I said, leaning my head on his shoulder again. "I like you."

He laughed. "I like you, too."

He took a breath and a bite, then fed me another one. The sounds of the amusement park were muted inside our little cave, and it felt suddenly as if we were the only people in the world.

And then my phone beeped again. I groaned, pulled it from my pocket, and threw it at the wall. It thudded against the plastic then fell into the sand.

"Well. You showed that phone."

My eyes suddenly filled with tears. I was so sick of feeling like crap. So sick of worrying and stressing and being sad. Why couldn't my mother just leave me alone? She didn't care about how I felt. She'd promised I didn't have to hang out with the Cresties, then shoved them in my face all summer. She hadn't asked me what I thought about her and Dad getting divorced. She'd decided she didn't like Cooper without ever even having a conversation with him. Did she even care that he'd been there for me this entire summer while she was off making out with her doctor boyfriend? The guy barely knew me, but he'd listened to me when I complained about the Cresties and my parents and everything. He actually wanted to know how I felt.

"Cooper?" I said, leaning back.

"Yeah," he said, touching my hair with sugar-covered fingertips.

"My mom doesn't like you."

He smirked. "That's not surprising."

"But I do," I said. "A lot."

"Yeah?" He put the funnel cake aside and turned his knees toward me. Then his lips were on my neck and my eyes fluttered closed. "How much?" he whispered.

"Like, *a lot* a lot," I said.

"That's a lot," he said, his lips moving up my jawline toward my mouth. His hand slipped around my waist and under my shirt, sending tingles all over my skin.

"Let's just stay here for a while," I said, hooking my finger over the collar of his T-shirt. I looked into his eyes and bit my lip. Cooper grinned.

"I have no problem with that."

Then his lips came down on mine. Our tongues met and before I knew it we were lying down in the sand, doing things that should never be done on a playground.

Daily Field Journal of Annie Johnston
Monday, July 26

Position: Stanzione's Pizza.

Cover: Grabbing dinner with David, Marshall, and Celia.

Observations:

6:55 p.m.: Subject Chloe Appleby pulls up outside. She checks her face in the mirror before getting out and walking inside. Uniform: pink sundress, white sandals, pink-and-white headband. Will Halloran, who's behind the counter taking calls and looking far too happy considering he has to work two jobs, eyes her as she approaches.

Chloe: I'd like to order a large pie with broccoli.

(Personal Note: Way to ruin a perfectly good pizza.)

Will: Is that all?

Chloe: I'd like to have it delivered.

Will (shoots a look at our table): Are you sure you don't just want to wait?

Subject Chloe glances over her shoulder. I'm the only one watching them, but she's still startled. I wave. I can't help myself.

Chloe: Um, sure.

(Assessment: They're TOTALLY doing it.)

Jake

My palms were slick as I walked into class on Wednesday. They'd been slick on Monday, too, because Chloe and I had figured we'd be getting our tests back then. But Mr. Froggy had decided to take the weekend off and promised us we'd have our grades "theees Weeednesdeee."

"You ready for this?" Chloe asked, tucking her skirt under her as she sat.

"I think so."

But what if I'd been wrong? What if I hadn't done as well as I'd thought? If I got that test back with a big red C, or worse, a D, I was going to walk right out of here and never look back.

Or not. Because that hadn't really worked so great as a strategy before.

"Goot aufteernoon!" Mr. Froggy walked in with his briefcase. He put the papers down on the desk. And once again, they scattered all over the floor thanks to the fan. This time, for some reason, I was the one who jumped up to help. I practically flattened the front row girl as she started to get up from her seat.

"Ah. Meeester Grayton. Thank yeuu," Mr. Froggy said.

I couldn't help glancing at the names and grades as I picked up the pages. Darlene Robinson: B. Tanna Autufu: A. Gary Law: C minus. Poor bastard. And then, there it was. My name scrawled in my handwriting.

Jake Graydon: A.

Shut. The fuck. Up.

I dropped the rest of the papers back on the floor. Mr. Froggy said something under his breath that sounded vaguely like a curse word. I hit the floor again and regathered the pages, but I couldn't stop grinning.

I'd never gotten an A in English before. Not once.

Jake

"Mom! Mom, you're never going to believe this."

For a second, in the driveway, I'd considered not telling her. I mean, why make her think that I was excited? That she'd somehow done the right thing by grounding me for the whole freaking summer? But I couldn't help it. I was *too* excited to not say something.

My mother was at the desk in her office, just off the kitchen, going over some bills. She looked up when she saw me, and smiled.

I hadn't seen her smile all summer.

"Look," I said, holding up the paper and letting my backpack drop to the floor. "I got an A."

It felt really good to say that. Why had I never realized how good it would feel to say that?

"Jake! That's amazing! I'm so proud of you!" My mom got up and gave me a hug. I one-arm hugged her back. No need to go completely crazy here. "And there's more good news."

She turned back to her desk and picked up a folded page, which she held out to me.

"Your practice scores from last weekend," she said. She folded her hands and stepped back to watch me take it in.

I'd scored a twelve hundred. My best score yet.

"Wow." I looked at her. "Maybe I'm a genius."

She cracked up laughing. "See? I told you. All you had to do was cut out the distractions and apply yourself and—"

"Mom. You're ruining the moment," I said.

"Sorry." She held up both manicured hands.

Then she just stood there for a second, her eyes shining as she looked at me. I started to feel self-conscious.

"What?"

"I've just . . . never seen you excited about school before," she said. "It's nice."

I cleared my throat. Could she be any dorkier? But then it hit me. There was a slim possibility I could use all this goodwill to my advantage.

"Nice enough to get me ungrounded?" I asked.

The smile died and she pressed her thumb and forefinger into her forehead above her eyes. "Jake—"

"Come on, Mom. It's August already. I have to be in soccer practice, like, next week." She looked at me and shook her head, but she was considering it. I could tell. Something in her eyes said she wanted to cut me a break. "Just . . . let me go see a movie or something with Chloe. Come on. We're both bored out of our minds with all our friends down the shore."

She sucked in a breath through her teeth and blew it out. "All right, fine. One movie."

"Yes! Thank you, Mom!" And this time *I* hugged *her*, still clinging to my two best scores ever, one in each hand.

"But only because it's with Chloe," she said as I released her. "I think that girl's been a good influence on you."

The way she said it made my stomach flip. Like she thought

me and Chloe were together or something. She walked past me over to the junk drawer and removed my keys.

"Here," she said, dangling them in front of me. "You can drive her for once."

Whatever. Let her think what she wanted to think. If it got me my car back, I didn't care.

"Thanks, Mom," I said, grabbing the keys from her as I headed out to the foyer.

"Thank *you*, Jake!" she shouted after me.

I ran upstairs, grabbed the phone, and called Chloe.

Daily Field Journal of Annie Johnston
Wednesday, July 28

Position: Bed Bath & Beyond.

Cover: None. I'm actually shopping for pillowcases. I saw mine in the sunlight this morning and it was not pretty. I need to start washing my face before bed.

Observations:

12:35 p.m.: Subjects Victoria Mihook, Tandy Lassiter, and Corinne Law stroll over to the "Deck Out Your Dorm!" display. Uniform: sundresses, heeled sandals, wicker bags dangling from forearms. Subect Tori fingers a purple sheet, wrinkles her nose, and lets it fall.

Tori: I cannot believe Faith didn't invite us. I mean, what's she thinking?

Tandy: That party is going to blow without us.

Corinne: And suck.

Tori: Well, if it sucked and blew it might actually be fun.

They all giggle. I try not to upchuck my McNuggets.

Tori: Whatever. Faith's a loser anyway. Always has been. I have no idea why Chloe and Shannen have tolerated her this long.

Corinne: But it's the end-of-the-summer party. I've never not gone to one.

Subjects Tandy and Tori exchange a look of disappointed longing. I step out from behind a shelf full of discounted sheets and they actually jump they're so surprised—or is that appalled.

Me: I'm going to Faith's party.

Tandy: You?

Me: Yep. Got my invitation in the mail today and everything.

I whip it out for good measure. It's an actual coconut shell, hollowed out, with the invitation tucked inside. Jaws drop. Subject Corinne's gum falls out of her mouth and hits her bare toe with a plop.

Tori: Why did she invite YOU?

I snap the coconut closed and put it back in my bag.

Me: I don't know. Maybe she's developing more sophisticated tastes. Ta!

I walk away, leaving them stunned behind me.

(Personal Note: I know, I know. I don't usually interact with the subjects unless necessary. But that was just too much fun.)

Ally

I sat in my room on Friday night and stared at a page in *Wuthering Heights*, ignoring the multiple texts from Cooper. All I had done for the past few nights was hang out with him, get drunk, and hook up. I couldn't believe this was my life. Two months ago I hated drinking. Now it was a part of my daily life.

Well, not tonight. Tonight I was just going to sit here and read and not feel bad about myself. Although I would miss the hooking up part. The hooking up part was not at all bad. We hadn't actually had sex or anything. I wasn't about to give it up to a guy I'd known for two months. But we'd done a lot of other stuff. Stuff that made me blush whenever I thought about it. Like now.

There was a knock on my door and my mother stuck her head inside. I cleared my throat and wiped my palms across my face as if I could clear away the red. "Hey," she said. "Can we talk to you?"

My heart lurched and I sat up a little straighter. "We?"

She opened the door farther and my dad stepped into view. I was so shocked I almost fell off the bed.

"Dad!" I jumped up and ran over to hug him. "What're you doing here?"

"I just came to see how you're doing," he said.

I took a step back. There was something off about his tone. Like it was too chipper or something. Him and my mom were both looking at me with these sort of plastic smiles, and concerned eyes.

"What do you mean?" I said, edging back toward the bed. "I'm fine."

My father cleared his throat and looked at my mom. He was wearing a black polo shirt and his arms looked really tan for someone who'd supposedly been stuck inside a coffeehouse all summer.

"Well, your mother mentioned that you had a new boyfriend," my dad said. "How's that going?"

I sat on the edge of the bed. There was something all wrong about this conversation. Why hadn't I known my dad was coming down, for one? We could have made plans to go out to dinner—do something fun—just like old times. Instead this felt like an ambush, them cornering me in my room.

"It's going fine," I said. My eyes darted to my mother. "I'm sorry . . . when did you tell him about Cooper?"

"That's not important," she said.

"Yeah. It kind of is. Because if you've spent the entire summer avoiding him, but then called him just to talk about me behind my back, I'd kind of like to know," I said.

I heard a creak in the hall and caught a glimpse of Shannen's foot jumping back to the other side of the door. She was out there right now, listening. Probably trying to figure out if there was anything in this conversation she could use against me.

"Ally, we're just worried about you, that's all," my dad said, sitting next to me on the bed.

"Well, you don't need to be," I told him. "I can take care of myself."

"Really? Is staying out late every night drinking and doing God-knows-what-else taking care of yourself?" my mother blurted.

My face turned beet red. How the hell did she know? Whenever I came home she was either asleep or out with Gray and his Crestie friends, so she'd never smelled anything on my breath. All summer she hadn't even noticed my existence and now all of a sudden she was throwing around unfounded accusations?

"I'm not out late every night drinking!" I protested, standing up. "Why would you even think that?"

"I know what hungover looks like, Ally, and you've been the picture of it the past few days," my mother replied.

"I have *not* been hungover," I replied, shaking. "You just want to believe the worst about Cooper because he's not a Crestie. Admit it! You tricked me into coming down here this summer because you wanted to make me hang out with all your little friends' kids again. You just can't stand it that I don't want to be a part of Gray Nathanson's world!"

"In case you don't recall, I was perfectly ready to let you stay in Orchard Hill this summer, Allyson. You're the one who changed her mind at the last minute," my mother replied.

"Oh, yeah. Like you weren't praying the whole time I'd come with you," I shot back. "Can't disappoint Gray. Heaven forbid!"

"Ally, don't talk to your mother like that," my father said sternly.

I whirled around to face him, feeling as if he'd just slapped me across the face. "Don't tell me how to act," I replied. "You don't even know me. Maybe I've acted like this every day for the past three years when you weren't around to scold me! Ever think about that?"

My dad and mom exchanged a private look that made me

want to tear my hair out. As if there was still a "them." As if they were still a couple and I was the one on the outside. What a freaking joke. I'd been there for both of them more than either of them had been there for the other. And now they were ganging up on *me?*

"Maybe you guys should be concentrating on your own problems," I spat.

"Ally." My mom closed her eyes and rubbed her forehead. "We're not talking about us right now."

"Well, maybe you should be," I blurted. "I mean, have you even told him yet that you want a divorce?"

My dad's face went slack. My mom looked like she was about to faint. At that moment, Shannen strode through the door with her suede bag, looking all Friday-night-ready in low-slung jeans and a sparkly tank.

"Ally! You ready to go?" she said brightly.

"What?" I asked.

"We're watching a movie over at Connor's, remember?" Shannen said, widening her eyes slightly, telling me not to argue. "I promised I'd bring M&M's and I forgot to get them so we have to make a stop. Come on. We're already late."

"You're going over to Connor Shale's house?" my mom said, clearly baffled considering I'd just screamed my head off about not wanting to hang with the Cresties.

"See?" I said, picking up my bag. "You don't know what I do every night. Come on, Shannen."

I rushed past her out the door, just hoping neither of my parents would shout at me to come back. But I guess they were too involved in picking up the shrapnel from the bomb I'd just dropped, because neither one of them said a thing.

Ally

"Thank you so much, Shannen. You completely saved me."

I got out of her mom's car and leaned back through the open window. She killed the engine and unbuckled her seat belt.

"Wait. You're coming in?" I said, glancing over my shoulder at Chum and Howie's place. The lights were dim, but I heard a splat from the backyard, followed by a round of cheers.

"It *is* my brother's house. I figured I'd come in and say hi," Shannen said with a shrug.

"Oh. Right. I keep forgetting," I said, pushing my hair away from my face as we navigated the uneven front walk.

"Maybe you *have* been drinking too much," Shannen joked.

"LOL," I replied flatly.

If she got on my case about this, I had about a million comebacks, starting with the fact that she was the first person I ever knew to try wine coolers, and the only person I knew to ever black out. But she just smiled at me and reached for the door. I couldn't believe how cool she was being, first rescuing me from that awful scene with my parents, then agreeing to drive me here to meet Cooper. It was like a whole new Shannen Moore. Unless she had an ulterior motive. Always had to keep an eye out for one of those.

"Hey! Li'l sis!" Charlie loped over from the kitchen with two bottles of beer and handed one of them to Shannen. "What're you guys doing here?"

"Looking for Cooper," I said. "He's here, right?"

Charlie took a long pull on his beer, then sucked his lips and nodded. "Out back."

"Cool. Thanks again, Shannen."

"I'll come find you before I go," she said as I slipped out the back door.

"Okay." *Whatever*, I thought, keeping my defenses up.

As soon as I stepped outside, I froze. Cooper was standing behind the catapult with his arm slung over the shoulders of a wispy blond girl wearing a cutoff top and skinny shorts. She had her hand in the back pocket of his cargos. My head instantly swam. I was seeing things, right? I had to be seeing things.

"Crestie Girl!" he shouted when he spotted me. He raised the arm that was unoccupied and beckoned me over. "You're here!"

Everyone seemed to be watching me as I walked slowly toward Cooper and his arm candy, picking my way over the debris of shattered lawn ornaments and rotting fruit. The blond girl eyed me with obvious disdain as he pulled me into his side.

"What's up?" he asked, planting a kiss on my lips.

He still hadn't let go of the blonde.

"Nothing. I just . . . I wanted to see you," I said.

Wasn't he even going to introduce me to the girl who had her hand down his pants?

"Cool. Well, here I am." He let go of both of us simultaneously, lifting his arms up and over our heads. "Dudes! Let's try the barbells!"

"Dude! No way!" Dex shouted. "Too heavy."

"That's the point, asshole," Cooper shouted back.

He went chest to chest with Dex as if they really were fighting, and a bunch of guys got into the mix, yelling and cackling loudly. The blond girl sipped her punch and eyed me up and down. Who the hell *was* she? What was she doing here?

"So you're the summer girl," she said finally. Her voice was nasal and she didn't sound too impressed by me. Plus, the way she called me "the summer girl" made me feel about one inch tall.

"And you are?" I said.

She scoffed. "Not interested."

She tilted her head back and drank from her cup as she sauntered away. Clearly we were going to be BFF.

"Ally! Hey!"

Jenny came barreling up behind me, planted her hands on my shoulders, and jumped up like she was trying to dunk me underwater. I buckled and we both almost hit our knees. "You're here!"

"Yeah. I'm here," I said as she hugged me. "Who was that?" I asked, nodding toward the blond girl.

"That would be Jessie," Jen said with a grimace. "She was supposed to be in Louisiana for the summer, but she just got back."

"Oh." I took a breath and steeled myself. "Are she and Cooper . . . ?"

She rolled her eyes and pulled her hands into her long sleeves, shuddering. "They go to proms and stuff together. You know, they're like each other's fallback positions. So as soon as she got home, she fell back."

I swallowed hard. But Cooper didn't need a fallback position. He had me.

"Oh, but don't worry! They haven't hooked up or anything," Jen said, checking the end of one of her braids. "He's totally into you still."

I supposed that should have made me feel better, but it didn't. Probably because Cooper hadn't looked in my direction in five minutes. Plus, the "still" she tacked on the end sounded a lot like "for now."

"What's up with him tonight?" I asked, lifting my chin at Cooper. "He's being weird."

"He got into it with my mom," Jen said, rolling her eyes again. "He's been taking it out on the catapult all afternoon."

"Oh."

Suddenly I felt awkward and out of place. I looked around at all the unfamiliar, laughing faces—at Jessie's awful sneer—and wondered what I was doing there. But then, I remembered. Cooper was my boyfriend. I'd come here to talk to him. And it sounded like he might need someone to talk to, too. I screwed up my confidence, walked over to him, and put my arms around him from behind, standing on my toes to rest my chin on his shoulder.

"Hey," I said. "Wanna go somewhere and talk?"

He let out a sigh and tipped his head forward. "Hang on a sec, guys," he said to his friends.

I had to let him go so he could turn to face me, but his expression wasn't exactly encouraging. He looked down at me in much the same way Jessie had moments ago.

"Talk about what?" he said, taking a sip of beer.

"I don't know. . . ." I fiddled with the hem of my shirt. "Jenny said you had a fight with your mom. . . . I thought you might want to vent."

"No, thanks. I'm fine."

He started to turn away again, but I put my hand on his shoulder. "Well, then I need to talk. My dad came down tonight for some kind of, like, intervention. He and my mom just jumped all over me about what a huge disappointment I've been this summer and—"

"Oh my God! Enough already!" Cooper shouted, turning to face me.

The backyard fell silent and my stomach splattered all over my feet.

"What?" I croaked.

"I am *so sick* of hearing about you and your problems with your mother and how your dad bailed on you and wah, wah, wah," he said, his eyes blazing. "News flash, Crestie Girl, everyone's lives suck! The only difference between you and the rest of us is that we don't spend every waking second whining about it."

I felt like the very air was closing in on me. My eyes stung and I blinked back tears of shock. Why was he talking to me like this?

"Cooper," Jenny squeaked. "Don't."

"Shut up, Jen. I know you worship the ground she walks on, but God! Thank God you don't sound like her. I would've had to disown you years ago."

"Cooper," I said, my voice thick. "What's the matter with you?"

"What's the matter with me?" he blurted. "What's the matter with me is I thought you were different. I thought it was so cool that I finally found the one bennie who was chill and down to earth and only cared about having fun. But deep down you're just like every other female on the planet. Self-centered, whiny, and a prude."

"Dude. You are so outta line."

Charlie walked over and got between me and Cooper.

Shannen's hand was on my arm, but I barely felt it. I couldn't feel anything. I couldn't breathe. I couldn't move. Cooper blinked at Charlie like he'd never seen him before. Then he looked down at me and blinked again. For a split second he was Cooper again. The Cooper I knew. The sweet, carefree, kind Cooper. But then, his expression shut down.

"Whatever," he said. "I'm outta here."

He tossed his beer bottle over his shoulder and it smashed on an old, broken-down barbecue. As he walked out, he grabbed Jessie's hand and tugged her with him. A tear spilled onto my cheek and I swiped it away.

"Ally," Shannen said.

Her voice sparked this roar of heat inside of my chest that brought me back to life. I couldn't believe that she, of all people, had been here to witness that. First she'd brought down the worst humiliation of my life at her birthday party, and now, in one night, she'd been there for a horrifying argument with my parents, and the worst breakup scene of a lifetime.

"I wanna go home," I said.

"Yeah. I'll take you right now."

"No. I mean I want to go *home*," I said, my voice cracking.

But even as I choked out the words, I realized I didn't know where home was.

Ally

I needed to see Jake.

I knew it as soon as Shannen pulled into Gray's driveway

and I saw that my dad's leased car was still there. I had this vivid flashback to the night we'd come home from Shannen's party to find my dad on the doorstep and I'd thought, for a split second, that it was Jake. I had so, *so* wanted it to be Jake. And just like that, I needed to see him. Now. Jake was the one who actually cared about me. Jake was the one who had actually been there for me. I'd shut him out because I was angry and embarrassed and small. Now all I could do was hope that it wasn't too late.

Because Jake . . . Jake was home.

"Want me to come in with you?" Shannen asked as we both looked up at the brightly lit house.

"No. It's okay. Go to Connor's."

"You sure? Because it could get ugly in there," Shannen said.

That's fine, because I'm not going in there, I thought.

"I'm good. Really." I looked at her as I got out of the car. "Thanks, Shannen."

She sighed and shrugged. "Anytime."

She pulled out slowly, her tires crunching over the pebble driveway, her headlights flashing across the garage doors. I held my breath, waiting for someone to come to the window, having noticed the lights, but no one did. I stared across the driveway at the open garage. Gray's second car—a late 1990s BMW—was parked inside. My eyes glimpsed the drawer where he kept the emergency set of keys. If I could just get into the garage with no one hearing, I could be out of the driveway before they noticed. I looked down at the rocks beneath my feet. Damn these LBI driveways and their loud pebbly-ness.

Tiptoeing wouldn't work. Probably the best thing to do

would be to take long strides. The fewer footfalls, the less noise.
I took a deep breath, and started to leap down the driveway.

My right foot hit the ground.

Crunch!

My left foot hit the ground.

Crunch!

I stretched as far as I could on the next leap.

Crunch!

One more and my foot hit the concrete floor of the garage.
I paused to listen for the sound of the front door squeaking
open—for footsteps on the indoor stairs that led directly to the
garage from the kitchen. Nothing. I lifted my hands in victory.
Freedom was mine. I raced for the keys.

"What the hell are you doing?"

I spun around, my heart in my throat. Hammond stood at
the end of the driveway, an amused smile on his face. He wore
a white polo shirt with multicolored pastel stripes, the collar
turned up to graze his cheekbones.

Where the hell did he *get* these ideas?

"You scared the crap out of me!" I hissed.

"What?" he shouted. Of course. He couldn't hear my
whisper over the island wind.

"Shhhh!" I brought my finger to my lips.

Hammond rolled his eyes and strolled casually across to the
garage, making enough noise to wake the neighbors, let alone
my parents and Gray.

"I may have to kill you," I said, tugging the keys from the
drawer.

"What're you doing?" he asked. Then the smile dropped
away. "Are you crying?"

"No!" I replied. I wasn't. Not anymore. I was experiencing that total clearness of vision that came with waking up from a summer-long delusion. "And I'm going home. To see Jake," I added, knowing that, if he *had* been trying to kiss me that day at Take a Dip, this might not be the best news. I walked by him and my hands shook as I tried to key the security code into the car's door. It didn't unlock.

"Oh," he said. "Okay. I'll drive."

"What? No. I'm fine."

I put the code in for the second time and tried the door. Nothing. My skin prickled as I tried one more time, Hammond basically breathing down my neck. The code was 5885. Not that difficult. I hit the buttons and tried the handle. It stayed stubbornly closed. I groaned in frustration.

"What's the code?" Hammond asked.

"Five eight eight five," I said begrudgingly.

He nudged me aside, pushed the buttons, and opened the door. Then he turned and held out his palm. "I'll drive."

I hesitated. It was bad enough, me taking Gray's car without asking, but should I really let Hammond drive it? And did I really want to spend three hours in the car with him, there and back?

"Come on, Al. I'm not letting you drive all that way, by yourself, in the dark, when you're clearly freaking," he said.

I blew out a sigh and dropped the keys in his hand.

"Sweet," Hammond said. "Let's take this baby out and see what she can do!"

He slammed the door and I slumped down in the seat, wondering what I was getting myself into, and just hoping it would be worth it. Just hoping Jake still wanted me back.

Jake

"I can't believe you made me watch that crap," I said. But smiled.

Chloe held the glass door for the people behind us—a mother and daughter—which was who made up most of the audience for the awful movie we'd just seen. Every girl walking out was snorting and sniffling. I didn't get it. The whole thing was about a love triangle, and at the end, one guy ends up killing the other and the girl ends up alone. What's the point of that?

I'd spent half the movie wondering if Ally would have ever made me waste my time on something like this, and the other half trying not to check out Chloe from the corner of my eye.

"Are you kidding me? It was so romantic!" Chloe protested. She tugged a tissue out of her little bag, which was on the crook of her arm.

"Romantic? Murder is romantic now?"

We moved a little farther out onto the sidewalk so the rest of the crowd could get out. I spotted one other guy, a dude in a Valley baseball T-shirt with a weeper on his arm. We exchanged a look. *I feel ya, man.*

"But he did it for her!" Chloe said, turning her palms up.

"Great. So now he gets twenty to life and she gets to have conjugal visits with a psychopath. Sweet."

Chloe whacked me with the back of her hand, but I could tell she was trying not to laugh. I took a breath and looked up and down Orchard Avenue. It felt kind of good to be out. Like

I'd just been released from a twenty-to-life sentence. The air was warm, but clear. A rare nonhumid night. At the restaurant across the street couples ate at the outdoor tables. All around us, people talked and lingered. It was like no one wanted to go home.

"You want to get some ice cream or something?" Chloe asked.

It was like she read my mind. She lifted her light brown hair over her shoulder, and I watched the way it fell softly back down against her skin. I had this urge to touch it, but didn't.

"Sure."

We turned and walked up the street together toward Scoops.

Ally

"Why did I have to take Orchard Avenue?" Hammond moaned, revving the engine at the corner of Walnut, like a warning to the dozen pedestrians in the crosswalk. We caught derisive looks from a middle-aged couple strolling by and I looked away. "It's Friday night. What was I thinking?"

"That some of the guys from school might see you in Gray's classic ride?" I said.

"Oh," Hammond said with a grin, waggling his eyebrows at me. "Right."

There was an opening, finally, and he lurched ahead. He was right about Friday nights in Orchard Hill, of course. There were benefits and drawbacks to living in a town with more than fifty restaurants, a theater, and a ton of shops that stayed open late on the weekend. The benefit was, everything you wanted was within walking distance. The drawback was everyone else in Bergen County had to drive to get there.

"So, did you call Jake to tell him you were coming?" Hammond asked.

I looked down at my lap. "Not exactly."

He started to make the turn at the top of the Avenue, but then slammed on his brakes. My chest pressed against my seat belt and then it flung me back against the seat.

"Hammond!"

"What the fuck is this?" he said through his teeth.

I looked up, my heart pounding. Walking across Orchard on the other side of the intersection was Jake. He looked amazing. Tan and tall and filling out that light blue T-shirt like it had been sewn just for him. I had this odd feeling in the center of my chest, like I hadn't seen him in years, instead of weeks. He was walking with someone, and when I saw who it was, I stopped breathing.

It was Chloe. Chloe with date-hair in a date-dress carrying a date-purse. And was it just me, or had their hands just grazed?

"Drive," I said.

"What? They'll see us."

"Just make the turn. Go! Before someone honks at you!" I felt like I was going to hurl. "Go!"

Hammond cursed under his breath and hit the gas. He almost ran over a Lhasa apso and its owner, but swerved at the last second. I raised an apologetic hand and Hammond gunned it to the corner, weaving into an open spot right in front of the double-arched doors to the church.

"That wasn't—I mean, they can't—they're *not*—"

I stared up at the stained glass window stories above my head. Mary with a halo on and her arms outstretched. "I don't know."

"She's just doing this to get back at me," Hammond said. He slammed the wheel with the heels of both hands. "Fuck!"

"Hammond! Shh!" I glanced out at the church again.

"What?" His face looked like something that had just come out of a meat grinder. "You think God's gonna come down and thunderbolt me?"

I looked at him and, suddenly, I started laughing.

Hammond didn't move for a long moment, but I couldn't stop. All this disgust and tension and confusion had built up so suddenly at the sight of Jake and Chloe together, that it had nowhere to go except out my mouth. I held my stomach and laughed until tears came out the corners of my eyes.

"What? What's so funny?"

But then he choked, and he started laughing too.

"Thunderbolt you? Really?" I said through halting gasps. "Is that what he does?"

"Dude. Shut up!" Hammond said. His laughter was less belly-full than mine. And ended sooner. "We might have just seen our exes on a date."

I let out my last laugh with a wheeze. Was this the dirt Annie had been talking about all those weeks ago? Did she want to tell me that Jake and Chloe were together? But he'd come down the shore *after* that. Was he seeing her then, when he'd stood on the deck and tried to get me to take him back?

Cold stones crowded my chest. I put my elbow on the windowsill and rested my mouth against my knuckles. "I guess I should have called ahead."

"So what do we do?" Hammond asked. "Drive back?"

I groaned and leaned my head back. "And sit in this car for another two or three hours? I can't." I felt heavy, suddenly. Like my body was spreading out across the seat and onto the floor and into all the gritty crevices of the car, getting pinned there by its own gravity. "Can you drive me back to my house?"

"Sure."

There were no more surprises on our way back to the Orchard View Condominiums. When I opened the front door, the hot, stale air was almost suffocating. I went directly to the air conditioner and flicked it on, then picked up the phone to dial my mother. I had turned off my cell before we'd gotten on the parkway, but I knew by now they had to have realized what I'd done, and I knew that I was in for it.

"Hey, Mom," I said.

"Ally. Where the hell are you?" she said, her voice controlled but angry.

"I'm in Orchard Hill with Hammond."

"You took Gray's car back to Orchard Hill?" she shrieked.

"I'm sorry, okay?" I said. "I just couldn't stay there for another second."

"So you thought the best way to deal with those feelings was to steal Gray's car and not tell anyone you weren't coming home."

I closed my eyes. After everything that had happened today—the fight with her and my dad, the scene with Cooper, seeing Jake and Chloe together—I felt like screaming and throwing things and crying until the sun came up. I felt like I could explode. But I took a deep breath and held it together. I had to figure out what I could say to end this conversation as quickly as possible.

"I know," I said. "I've been a jerk lately. I get it, okay? But I just . . . Mom, everything sucks right now and I'm really tired and so's Hammond. Is it okay with you if I stay here tonight and he drives me back in the morning? You can give me whatever punishment you want to give me then."

Hammond was walking around the living room, looking at the photos in the frames, checking out our TV. I realized with a start that he'd never been here before. At least, not inside.

"Oh, I'll give it to you right now. You're grounded for the rest of the summer," she said. "No, scratch that. You'll be allowed to go out, but only to functions I'll be attending. How does that sound?"

In other words, she was going to force me to hang out with the Cresties. As punishments went, it was genius.

"Fine," I said, gritting my teeth. "Whatever you say."

"Good," she said. "Now we're getting somewhere."

"Mom? Can I go now? I'm really tired."

"All right. We'll talk more tomorrow." There was a long pause and I could hear her trying to get her breathing under control. "Ally . . . are you okay?"

My eyes welled with tears and I bit them back, holding one arm across my stomach and clutching my T-shirt at my waist. "Yeah, Mom. I'm fine."

"Okay. Call me when you're going to leave there tomorrow so I know when to expect you," she said.

"I will."

"Good night, Ally," she said, her voice tense.

"Night."

I took a deep breath as I hung up the phone, squelching the last of the tears. When I turned around, Hammond was looking right at me and I felt this sudden and unexpected thump of anticipation. Which made no sense. It wasn't like we were going to do anything. Even if he tried, I wasn't about to let him. I mean, he was Hammond. And he was clearly in love with Chloe. And I had just been dissed by two guys in one day—a new personal record.

Still, it was weird, wasn't it? My mother hadn't even asked me where Hammond planned on staying. That's how much she trusted me. Even after everything.

"So . . . you can drive back if you want to," I said. "I could maybe figure out some other ride. . . ." Though how, I had no idea.

Hammond pulled out his phone, hit a speed-dial button, and brought it to his ear. He didn't take his eyes off me until it connected. Then he turned toward the wall.

"Hey, Dad. I'm gonna stay at home tonight. Yeah. Yeah. I will. Cool. Bye."

Just like that. And then he was facing me again. The air conditioner flipped to a new cycle, groaning as it spurted cold air into the room.

"What do you want to do?" I asked.

He looked around at the couch, the chair, the TV. "X-Men movie marathon? I know you've got 'em around here somewhere."

I smiled. What could be better after a day like this than total immersion in a fictional world? "Perfect. Popcorn?"

"That works."

Hammond powered on the TV and dropped onto the couch with the entitlement of someone who'd lived here his entire life.

I located the popcorn and started the microwave, still smiling. But then, I remembered why I was here, and not at Jake's. Glancing over my shoulder at Hammond, who already had on ESPN, I fished my phone from my bag and texted Annie.

Am in OH. Can u meet up tmrw? 10ish?

The response came almost instantly.

Will be @ work. Stop by!

OK

The microwave beeped and Hammond looked up, his arm laid out across the back of the couch. I thought of Jake. Of Jake and Chloe's hands touching. Was it wrong for me to feel like this—like me and Hammond being here—was a kind of revenge? Was he thinking the same thing?

"We doing this or what?" he asked.

I grabbed the popcorn out of the microwave, tossed him the bag, and sat down on the opposite end of the couch. This was going to be a long night.

Jake

On the way home, with the top down, I felt very alert. For the first time, I noticed how hard the stick shift felt in my grip. How the air felt twenty degrees cooler when I was zipping through it. How the wind tugged at my hair, making my scalp tingle, even though it was cut short. As I turned up Chloe's driveway, she took out a tube of something and touched up her lips.

That was when I knew for sure, she wanted me to kiss her. And now, I was all *kinds* of alert.

I'd kissed dozens of girls. Maybe hundreds. Seriously. That was what I used to do. It was, like, my number one pastime. Before Ally. On weekends, I'd always hook up, usually with more than one girl. Before Ally.

Since Ally, I hadn't kissed anyone. Was it a good idea to start with her former best friend who'd just broken up with my best friend?

Probably not.

I stopped the car. Stared out the windshield. Chloe didn't move.

"You didn't have to drive up my driveway. It's about a thirty-second walk from your house."

"I know."

I glanced over. My eyes went to her bare knee. Bad move.

"Well . . . thanks," Chloe said. "I had fun."

"Me too."

My hand clasped the stick shift and the wheel. I refused to move them.

"Okay, well. I should probably go," I said.

She didn't say anything for a minute. "Yeah. Me too."

Then she got out of the car and it was over. Except for my . . . alertness.

She walked in front of my headlights and her dress was so sheer I could practically see through it. Or possibly that was my imagination. She did that twiddling thing with her fingers, then jogged to the door. Her skirt bounced behind her.

I blew out a breath. I hadn't inhaled in, like, five minutes. Then I backed out of the driveway so fast I'm lucky I didn't take out the stone planters. I was in my driveway, up the stairs, and in my room with the door closed before Chloe had probably closed the front door.

I needed to do something. Jog or swim or kick a soccer ball. Something. My eyes fell on my books. I was supposed to take another practice test tomorrow. I pulled out my chair, sat down, and opened the math study guide. My brain was completely clear.

I was about to have the most intense study session of my life.

Jake

I woke up sitting up straight in my bed. It wasn't until I heard the tires squealing that I realized I'd been startled awake. I jumped out of bed and was at the window in half a second—just in time to see Will Halloran flying out of Chloe's driveway and down Vista View in his father's truck. His brake lights illuminated for a split second at the bottom of the hill, then the engine roared, and he was gone.

Out of the corner of my eye, I saw the lights in Chloe's bedroom window go out. I looked at the digital clock on my iDock. It was 2:16 a.m.

What. The fuck?

I snagged a T-shirt off my desk chair and pulled it on. The first sneaker slipped on no problem, but I was still hopping with my toes jammed into the other and my finger hooked around the back of it, when I made my way out the door of my room. I rushed downstairs on my tiptoes and out into the warm night air.

This is a bad idea. This is a bad idea.

But I didn't stop. I jogged across the street, fueled by pure adrenaline. My eyes were still foggy, since I'd been asleep two minutes ago, but the rest of me was completely awake. I slowed to a fast walk up Chloe's driveway. As I rounded the bend, the security lights over the front door flashed on. I lifted my hand to shield my eyes and tripped sideways into the bushes.

Ow.

I looked up at Chloe's new deck thing, which overlooked Mrs. Appleby's English Garden she was always ragging on about. There was a trellis up the side.

This is a bad idea. A bad idea.

Crouching, I crept across the stone patio. I tried the trellis, giving it a couple of tugs. It held. It took a little grunting and groaning and a couple of splinters, but then I was up. And banging on the glass door.

This is a bad idea. A very bad idea.

Chloe shoved the curtain aside and her jaw dropped. She opened the door so fast it blew her hair back. She was wearing the tiniest nightgown I'd ever seen outside the Internet. And she'd been crying.

"Jake! What the hell are you doing? My parents are home!" she whispered.

"What the fuck, Chloe? I just saw Will Halloran peeling out of here like he was being chased." I walked into her room. It was as neat as a catalog. Every little pink and purple thing in its place. Except for the bed. The bed was a wreck. My stomach clenched. "Are you fooling around with that guy?"

She exhaled a laugh. "Not anymore."

I blinked. What the hell did that mean?

"Why do you even care, Jake?" She walked over to her

bathroom and lifted a robe down from a hook. She went to put it on, but then stopped. Instead, she hooked it over her arms and walked toward me. "You're not . . . I mean, you're not jealous, are you?"

My chest was heaving up and down, and not from the run. I couldn't answer her. Because I realized, just like that, that I was.

Which made no sense. Because I liked Ally. I was in love with Ally.

But shit, I really wanted to kiss Chloe.

And Ally was out there kissing loser surf posers. Telling me I wasn't good enough for her, not answering my texts. So why the hell was I even hesitating?

Chloe dropped the robe on the floor. That nightgown showed almost everything, and she knew it. She reached for my hand. I let her take it.

This is a bad idea. A really, really, really bad idea.

But when she stood on her toes to kiss me, I let her do that, too.

Ally

I woke up on the couch with Hammond's arm looped around my waist. The second I saw how close his hand was to my breast, I flinched, and the back of my head exploded in pain.

"Ow! Ally! What the fuck?"

I sat up, holding the back of my skull as Hammond brought his hands to his forehead.

"I'm so sorry," I said.

He squinted sideways at me. His face was all blotchy red. "It's okay."

"I just—"

"It's okay," he repeated.

Hammond sat up too, scooching back on the couch so that he was a few inches behind me. I was about to get up, when I felt his hand on my neck. He ran his fingers down from my shoulder, across my bra strap, and to the small of my back. My hands dropped heavily at my sides as my skin tingled.

"Hammond," I said. "Don't."

He scooted forward. His arm was around my waist, the back of my shoulder pressed into the front of his. He put his chin on my shoulder. His morning breath was surprisingly sweet. I didn't move.

"Don't what?"

His lips met mine and I instantly pulled away. I jumped off the couch and stood in the middle of the living room.

"We can't do this," I said.

"Why not?"

"Because." I grabbed the popcorn bowl off the floor and went over to the kitchen. I was shaking from head to toe, unable to believe I had almost just let that happen. I turned the sink on full blast and turned my back to him.

"What's wrong?" he said, getting up. "I like you, you like me, Chloe's apparently with Jake. So what's wrong if we—"

"I don't," I said to the sink.

"Don't what?" he blurted.

"I don't like you." I pressed the heels of my hands into the edge of the counter, my fingers rigid. "Not like that."

There was a long pause. "Come on. You just . . . I mean, we just—"

I turned around to face him. He looked bereft for a guy of his size. Lost. Suddenly, I wondered . . . was Faith right? Had he really liked me that much back then? Did he still?

"Hammond, I'm sorry. I really am," I said. "But I can't just hook up with you because I'm pissed at Jake."

Hammond's face turned bright red. I had a feeling I'd just said the wrong thing. Big time.

"I'm outta here." He grabbed his wallet and Gray's keys off the table and made for the door.

"You're taking Gray's car?" I blurted.

He paused at the door and blew out an angry sigh. "I'll be back to pick you up at twelve."

"I'll be here!" I shouted.

But he was already out the door, and all I got in return was a slam.

Ally

I decided to walk to CVS instead of riding my bike. It was a nice morning, warm and not humid, and I figured I'd use the time to delete all the angry mom messages from my phone. When I got to the last one, I was just turning the corner into the parking lot. My thumb was about to come down on the seven button for delete, when I heard Jenny's voice whispering through the ether. I quickly brought the phone to my ear. She was midsentence.

". . . wanted you to know that Cooper didn't mean what he said. He really had a bad night and he was a lot more wasted than he looked. He gets like that sometimes . . . scary like that . . . when he's mad at my mom. Usually he just yells at me, but— Well, anyway. He's not a bad guy. That's all. I know he really likes you. He just has, you know, stuff that gets to him sometimes and he needs to, like, blow off steam, I guess. Anyway. That's it. Sorry for rambling. Call me back if you want to. Okay. Bye."

I paused outside the CVS window, feeling shaky and not all there. It was weird, hearing Jenny's voice on my phone in Orchard Hill. Thinking about Cooper on the very spot I'd kissed Jake at least a dozen times when he'd picked me up from work. Being here made the LBI world feel like it didn't actually exist. And I guessed in a few weeks, it wouldn't. Not really. I got that chill brought on by deep thoughts and the anticipation of change—school and fall and seeing everyone again. Then I shook it off—we weren't quite there yet, and I had other things to deal with—and walked inside.

Annie was sipping Yoo-hoo behind the counter.

"Hey," she said, straightening up. "Whoa. You look like ass."

"Thanks." I shoved my phone into my back pocket and leaned my forearms into the red Formica countertop. Part of me wanted to tell her what had happened with Hammond, but I didn't feel like dealing with all the questions. Instead, I decided to get right to the point. "So tell me about Jake and Chloe."

My throat gradually closed over the words, so that the last syllable barely came out.

Annie took a long sip of Yoo-hoo and avoided my gaze. "Jake and Chloe?"

Something deep inside me squirmed. "I know you didn't tell me everything before, so spill. What's going on? Are they, like, together?"

Annie clucked her tongue and placed her bottle down. "I don't know exactly."

I scoffed. "Please. You know everything."

She preened a bit, cocking her head to one side. "Thanks . . . but this one's unconfirmed. All I know is they've been taking a class together, and she's been driving him around a lot, but he's grounded off his car, so that could be why. They *have* been spending a lot of time together." She reached for her bag under the counter. "I can give you exact stats if you—"

Someone walked by with a cart full of toilet paper, the wheels squeaking loudly.

"That's okay," I said, pinching the top of my nose. "I don't need the gory details."

"The weird thing is, Chloe's also been hanging out a lot with—"

"Ally!"

David and Marshall came swooping toward me and gathered me up in a two-way bear hug. They smelled so clean and looked so bright-eyed and healthy it made me want to cry. I'd really been hanging out with a lot of grungy, lazy stoners, hadn't I?

"What're you guys doing here?" I asked as they pulled away.

"I kind of told them you were coming," Annie said apologetically.

"We're taking you out for breakfast at the diner," Marshall said, slinging his arm over my shoulder. "Our treat."

"What? You can't go for pancakes without me," Annie whined, wide-eyed.

"We'll bring you back a doggie bag," David said as he tugged me toward the door. "So how's the shore? How's your mom? How's Shannen?"

Annie groaned and rolled her eyes, but I couldn't help laughing. It was nice to be among real friends again. No matter how briefly. If anyone could distract me from thoughts of Jake Graydon, David and Marshall could. In a few hours I'd be back at the shore, back with the Cresties, and seriously grounded. I could spend a couple of hours sipping coffee at the diner.

It would be kind of like the calm before the storm.

Daily Field Journal of Annie Johnston
Sunday, August 1

Position: Counter at the Apothecary.

Cover: Looking for a zit cream that won't dry out my face. (I have no zits at present, but the woman behind the counter is still willing to sell me fifty bucks' worth of cream to zap them.)

Observations:

1:15 p.m.: Subject Mrs. Appleby walks in. She passes by all the fancy displays, stops at the counter, and nods at the woman behind it. The woman hands over a bag. Subject Mrs. Appleby walks out. No words are exchanged. No money is exchanged either. (Query: Do the wealthy just get free stuff around here? Is that why they're so frickin' wealthy?)

1:27 p.m.: Subject Mrs. Shale walks in. Her skin looks like leather. She walks to the counter and is given an even bigger bag than the one Subject Mrs. Appleby got. Again, no words or money exchanged. (Assessment: Maybe the Apothecary is actually a front for a prescription drug ring!)

Jake

"Hey, Mr. Ryan."

I went over to the computer to clock out. He'd just come in the back door and was putting his stuff down on the desk.

"Jake. Off so soon?" he said. He sounded tired. He hadn't sounded like that once since I'd known him.

I hesitated. "My shift's over."

"Right. Of course," he said, waving a hand. "I apologize. I'm just out of it."

I hit the enter button and stood up straight. "Everything okay?"

He looked over at me, then down at some paperwork on the desk. "No, actually, since you asked. Turns out I'm getting a divorce."

My stomach kind of fell out of my body. "Oh."

Ally must have been freaking out. Shit. She must have been so upset.

"I'm . . . sorry?" I said, cracking a knuckle.

"It's okay. I mean, it's not okay. But it's going to be okay." He shrugged hugely and pressed his fingertips into the desktop. "I screwed up. Apparently there's no going back."

I tried to swallow, but my throat was dry. All I could think about was Ally. Ally crying, Ally curled up in a ball on her bed. My heart actually hurt.

"Anyway, I just figured I'd tell you because I know Ally's been having a hard time of it this summer," he said, turning to look at me. He folded his arms across his chest. "She could probably use a friend."

My heart skipped a beat. Was that his way of giving me his blessing or something? Did he not know that Ally and I hadn't even spoken since July Fourth?

"So what do you say, Jake? You gonna be there for my daughter?" he asked.

Suddenly, I saw Chloe's neck tilted to the side as my lips moved to meet her skin. Her light brown hair tangled around my fingers. That stretch of thigh that went on forever. I felt a prickle on my neck, and started to sweat.

"Yeah, I don't know if she really wants me to be there for her," I said, chewing on my lip.

"If you're worried about that kid she was seeing down the shore, don't be. They broke up."

"They did?" I said.

"Yeah. And I happen to know that she's grounded, so if you were to drive down there, say . . . this Friday night when you happen to be off, you'd probably find her home."

My brow knit. "Mr. Ryan, why are you telling me all this?"

He took a couple of steps toward me. "Because you're a good kid, Jake. And I know from what her mother has told me that Ally really likes you. I just think it'd be nice if something worked out for her. I couldn't give her her family back. Maybe I can . . . I don't know . . . "

"Give her me?" I said.

He laughed. "Something like that. Just think about it."

He turned and walked out onto the floor, leaving me alone in the office. I sat down on his rickety desk chair and blew out a sigh. I couldn't believe this was happening. Ally had broken up with that surf loser? When? How? Why hadn't I heard about it from Hammond or Faith? I wondered if this was before or after Chloe and I . . . Before or after we . . .

I felt like I very much needed to curl into a ball and die.

I hadn't talked to Chloe since that night. She'd blown me off for class both Monday and today, and I hadn't tried to call her, either. Every time I thought of her, I felt guilty and embarrassed. I shouldn't have gone over there. I shouldn't have done what I'd done. But what was I supposed to do with her standing there all half-naked and grabbing me and kissing me like that? I didn't know a single guy who could walk away.

"Okay, don't think about that," I whispered to myself. "Think about Ally. What are you gonna do about Ally?"

I imagined myself going down there. Knocking on her door. Her opening it and seeing me. And then . . . what? I beg her to take me back *again*? Could I really be that guy? And what if she said no? I had a feeling another rejection from her might kill me.

But I guess . . . I guess I could just do what her dad said. Not beg her to take me back, but just be there for her. Give her a shoulder to cry on or to hit or to yell at or whatever she needed to do. Because I knew her heart had to be broken and the thought made me sick. I wanted to help her fix it. Even if she didn't take me back.

Daily Field Journal of Annie Johnston
Tuesday, August 3

Position: Cream of the Crop denim boutique, Orchard Avenue.

Cover: None. They sucked me in with their designer discounts, okay?

Observations:

1:01 p.m.: Subject Jake Graydon walks in. Uniform: cargo shorts, gray T-shirt, Nikes w/o socks. Subject Mrs. Graydon is with him. Uniform: pristine white linen suit. Subject Jake immediately crosses to a rack of men's jeans that look like they just barely survived the beach at Normandy. Subject Mrs. Graydon drags him away to a rack of jeans that look as if they've been pressed to within an inch of their existence. (Assessment: This should be good.)

1:08 p.m.: After arguing through their teeth for a few minutes, and consulting the salesgirl, who looks like she just stepped out of one of the raunchier Miley Cyrus videos, Subject Mrs. Graydon shoves Subject Jake toward a dressing cube with two pairs of pressed jeans, two pairs of destroyed.

1:09 p.m.: Subject Chloe Appleby walks in. Uniform: khaki shorts, eyelet top, espadrilles. She spots

Subject Mrs. Graydon and freezes. Her eyes dart
to Subject Jake as he yanks the curtain closed
over the dressing cube. Subject Chloe turns green
and walks out, sprinting out of sight. (Assessment:
Yeah. Something DEFINITELY went down between
those two.)

Ally

The Kirkpatricks' party might have had a smaller guest list than usual, but no one would have known they'd cheaped out on anything. This year's theme was a luau, and if I hadn't known better, I would have sworn I was in Hawaii. Real palm trees decorated their sprawling deck, and a roasted pig turned on a spit outside. The waitresses wore colorful sarongs and leis made of real flowers, and the food was unbelievable. Plus, they had no problem handing over the piña coladas and strawberry daiquiris to anybody who asked.

Maybe these Crestie parties *were* good for something.

Although, as I stood at the tiki bar in the living room, my mother was partaking in a one-on-two hula dancing lesson with Mrs. Moore across the room and, from the looks of it, having the time of her life. It made me sick, really. I mean, how could she be having so much fun? She was getting divorced. Officially. She and my dad had told me last Saturday, after I'd gotten back from Orchard Hill. Apparently my mother had decided over a year ago that she wanted her marriage to be over—she just hadn't been able to track my father down to sign the papers. But now, here he was. And he was done fighting. I guess they had a long talk while I was gone, and she convinced him. Over twenty years together, if you count the few they'd dated, and it was just done. And she was acting like she'd never been happier.

She and Mrs. Moore tried a frantic hip-shaking move, then dissolved all over each other, giggling. I groaned and rolled my eyes. Didn't they see how ridiculous they looked? But at least my mom hadn't been on me all night long. Thanks to Faith, she was under the impression that the waitresses were only serving virgin drinks to the minors.

So maybe Faith was good for something too.

"Okay! I just saw one of the Idiot Twins hooking up with that Lindsey girl in the bathroom, but I don't know if it was Todd or Trevor," Annie said, looking frazzled as she joined me. "Hammond is nowhere to be found and neither is that sophomore chick with the punk hair. Not his type, I know, but they could be somewhere together and I'm missing it. And Faith totally just took off her bikini top in the hot tub even though her parents are, like, right upstairs. This party is either going to kill me or make my book a bestseller."

I downed the dregs of my third piña colada and grabbed another from a passing waiter. "I vote for the bestseller thing."

Annie narrowed her eyes at me, as if she'd just actually seen me. "How many of those have you had?"

"Not enough. Yet, anyway," I said, sucking on the straw.

"I thought you didn't drink," Annie said, looking suddenly concerned.

"I didn't. Then the shore happened," I said.

"Damn. These Cresties really know how to corrupt," Annie said.

I lifted my glass to her. "You know it."

Annie shook her head and looked across the living room full of laughing guests with their perfect teeth and their island gear and their twinkling diamonds.

"Gotta say, I never thought I'd see the day," she mused.

"The day that what?" I asked, taking a sip of my drink.

"The day Ally Ryan became a cliché."

My throat tightened and I almost dropped my drink on the hardwood floor. "Um, ouch."

Annie shrugged. She was about to say something else when the other half of the room got suspiciously quiet. Then I heard a happy shriek and a round of applause. A crowd had formed in the general area of the hula dancing. I stood on my toes to see what was going on, just in time to see Gray slip a humongous diamond ring onto my mother's trembling finger.

No. This was not— No.

My vision swam. For a second everything went fuzzy— all the colors and sounds and smells. Annie grabbed for my hand, but I shook it off. My mother threw her arms around Gray's neck and he twirled her around. Then Quinn was there, giggling and checking out the ring, and she didn't even look surprised.

She knew. She'd known all along. She probably even knew that day on the beach when I tried to grill her about whether my parents were breaking up. Oh my God, I was going to wring that girl's skinny little—

And then . . . then . . . then . . . everyone at the party was turning around slowly—turning around to look at me. Waiting for me to jump up and down and smile and kiss my new father. Expecting me to play the part of the perfect Crestie daughter.

Gray had proposed to my mother. My mother had said yes. My mother was getting married to someone who was not my father.

Don't be a cliché, Ally. All you've done all summer is storm out, avoid, turn your back. Don't be the cliché Annie expects you to be.

From across the room, my mother's eyes implored me even as her smile widened.

"Ally?" Gray said with a grin. He opened an arm out to me as if he wanted me to take his hand.

That was all I needed. I turned around, dropped my glass, and ran.

Jake

The flowers might not have been the best idea. For the past two hours they'd been sitting there on the passenger seat of my Jeep next to Faith's stupid coconut invite, taunting me. A few times I'd decided to toss them out the window, or give them to some tired-looking mom at a parkway rest stop and make her year. I mean, I'd decided it didn't matter whether Ally took me back. What mattered was being there for her. So wouldn't the flowers confuse things?

But no. Everyone liked to get flowers, right? At least, all girls. It was the kind of thing Chloe would know the answer to. If nothing had happened that night, if we had just gone on being friends and study partners, I could have called her and asked her. A couple of months ago, she wanted me and Ally to get together. She was, like, the only one who did.

And now . . . what would she think if she knew I was half an hour away from LBI? If she knew where I was going and why? Would she be mad? Jealous? Happy for me?

Did I even care?

I looked at the flowers again as I zoomed through the last tollbooth before exit sixty-three.

Screw it. I was going to give them to her. I loved the girl. Simple as that. It was time to stop fucking around.

Ally

Jenny picked up the phone on the first ring.

"Ally! Hey!"

"Where are you guys?" I blurted, wiping the back of my hand across my nose. Tears streamed down my face and my nostrils were so clogged I had to breathe through my mouth, but I did the best I could to sound like I was not crying.

"Actually, we're right up the beach from your place. Is someone having a party? Because it smells awesome."

I had been headed for the driveway—God knows why, since I didn't have a car—but instantly turned the corner and started up the plank walkway for the beach.

"Who's that?" I heard Cooper say in the background. My heart did a little pitter-patter, fluttery thing that made my stomach turn.

"It's Ally," she whispered.

He said something, but I couldn't make it out. I just hoped he wasn't telling her to tell me to kiss off.

"Where are you *exactly*?" I said as the wind off the water blew my hair back.

"We're up by that house I like," she said as a round of laughter erupted in the background. "The Applebottoms?"

The Applebys. "I'll be right there."

I shoved my phone in my pocket and turned left, headed up

the beach. The wind seemed impossibly cold and I hugged my bare arms as hard as I could, wishing I was wearing anything other than the tank top and long, gauzy skirt I'd snagged on sale at B&B. I guess I wasn't as drunk as Annie had implied. If I was, I'd probably feel a lot warmer than I did right now.

"Ally! Wait up!"

The sound of Annie's voice only made me walk faster. I squinted, trying to make out the figures up the beach. Why was there no fire? Cooper and Dex always had a fire. I was just trudging past Gray's house when Annie caught up.

"Ally! Come on! Stop for a sec!" her hand fell on my arm, and I turned to face her.

"Why are you following me?" I snapped. "I thought I was some huge cliché unworthy of your friendship."

"I'm sorry, okay? I was just talking," she replied, lifting the hood of her sweatshirt over her hair. "I didn't know that—"

"My mother was about to get engaged?" I replied, wiping my eyes. "Yeah. Me neither."

"Are you okay?" she asked.

I laughed into the wind and looked out at the ocean. "No. Not even a little bit."

"Come on." She hooked her arm around mine and tugged. "We'll go get something to eat and you can vent all over me."

I suddenly saw myself ensconced in a booth at Chicken or the Egg, the twenty-four-hour diner at the other end of the island, plowing through a plate of pancakes and telling her everything I hadn't had a chance to tell her all summer. It actually sounded kind of nice.

But then I heard Cooper's voice in my mind, mocking me for being a whiner. Telling me everyone's life sucked and I was basically a big, fat baby. Suddenly I didn't want to give Annie the satisfaction of watching me blubber over carbs. She'd basically insulted the crap out of me ten seconds ago and now she wanted to hear my sob story? Why? So she could put it all in her book?

"Thanks anyway," I said. "I think I'm done whining."

Then I turned around and kept walking. Much to my chagrin, Annie fell into step with me.

"Then where are we going?" she asked.

"To meet Cooper," I said. We were passing by Hammond's house now, where his mom's old-school weather vane creaked in the wind, spinning around like a top.

"I thought you guys broke up."

"Not officially," I told her.

Right now all I wanted to do was find Cooper and prove to him that I was *not* a whiner. That I was not self-centered and a downer. I wanted to be the girl he'd thought I was. The fun, carefree bennie. I wanted this summer to have never happened.

Finally, a few dark, nebulous shapes came into view up the beach, past the Shale's modern, gray monstrosity of a mansion. They were standing in the sand right in front of Chloe's house. Jenny let out a whoop and came running toward me.

"Alleeeeee!"

She threw herself into my arms. I gave her a quick hug, but kept moving.

"Hi, Annie," she said.

"Hey." Annie sounded wary for some reason. Why did she have to come? The last thing I needed right now was a judgmental witness.

I kept walking toward the guys. Cooper, Dex, and Stoner

were all there. Thankfully, Jessie was not. Cooper took a sip of beer and eyed me as I approached.

"Hey, guys," I said, lifting a hand.

I really hoped that it was dark enough to keep them from telling I'd been crying.

"What's up, Al?" Dex said.

"Hi, Cooper," I said tentatively.

"Hey." He looked away briefly. "Been a while."

Yeah, well, you kind of ripped me to shreds the last time I saw you, I thought but didn't say.

"So what are you doing here?" he asked.

I took a deep breath and walked up to him, so close our toes touched in the sand. My skin tingled with warmth, just being close to him again. "I wanted to tell you I'm over the drama. My family, the Cresties, all that crap. You were right. At the beginning of the summer I did just want to have fun. And I still do."

To prove it, I took the beer out of his hand and took a long swig. I felt both seriously cool and completely gross at the same time, but it had the desired affect. Cooper slowly smiled and my whole body tingled.

"Yeah?" he said, reaching one arm around me.

"Yeah," I said.

He leaned down and planted a kiss on my lips. When he pulled back again, there was a spark of something dangerous in his eyes and my heart thumped nervously.

"So prove it."

I smiled and took a step back. "How?"

"We're gonna break into this house right here," he said, pointing up at Chloe's. "That should be *super*fun."

Ally

"Ally, no."

My stomach was in knots as Annie pulled me away from the others, but I managed a casual laugh. I didn't want Cooper to think I was going to chicken out—that I might let my buzzkill friend talk me out of it.

"What's the big deal? It's not like they're actually going to take anything," I whispered to her, glancing over my shoulder.

No one seemed to be in a huge rush. Cooper and Dex were chugging beers while Stoner tried to open a package of jerky for Jen. I shivered violently against the wind and hugged myself, hard.

"How do you know that?" she asked.

"Because! I won't let them." I took a sip of the beer I'd stolen from Cooper, trying to look like this whole thing wasn't bothering me, too. "You should come with us. You hate Chloe. This is the perfect chance to get back at her."

Annie crossed her arms over her chest and raised her eyebrows. "How, exactly?" she asked dubiously.

"You can . . . I don' t know . . . go into her room and mess things up," I improvised. "Or snoop! Maybe she has a diary in there or something."

I took another slug of beer, holding my wind-whipped hair back from my face with my free hand.

"Right. Right. Because everyone keeps their innermost thoughts recorded in a diary that they leave at a house they only go to for two months out of the year," Annie said, glancing up at the darkened windows. "If they go there at all."

"God. Where do you get off?" I said. The sarcasm and put-downs were getting old fast. "This from the girl who spends her entire life stalking innocent people and recording their every move."

Annie's jaw dropped. "Since when are they innocent people? Have they totally brainwashed you?"

"I'm not the one who's brainwashed. You're brainwashed!" I shouted. "You think every single person who lives on the crest is evil, no matter what! Well, guess what! It looks like *I'm* gonna be living there soon again, Annie! So I guess now I'm too cool to be friends with you."

"Oh my God. You are so far off the deep end," Annie said through her teeth.

"Whatever. Why don't you just go away already? I don't remember asking you to come along."

Behind me, the guys reacted to my diss with a loud chorus of "oh!" Annie's face burned red. I felt suddenly hot and guilty and wanted to take it back, but why? She'd insulted me first.

"Wow. I really hate you when you're drunk," Annie said, her eyes narrowed into angry slits, her arms crossed over her chest. The guys shouted again. Dex even slapped his knee. My face was on fire.

"Yeah? Cuz I really hate you when you're all self-righteous and know-it-all," I retorted. "Oh, wait! That's *all the time!*"

Annie's face completely fell. She glanced at the others uncertainly as they basically cackled in her face. A thump of regret hit my chest hard, but I didn't take it back. I was too furious, too embarrassed, too far gone.

"I'm outta here," Annie said, her mouth a tight line. "At this point, I think I'd rather hang out with Faith anyway."

My eyes stung with tears. The guys didn't know it, but that was actually the biggest insult yet. Annie turned and walked away, her feet spraying up sand in her wake. This night simply could not get any worse. I chugged the rest of the beer and threw the bottle in the sand. Suddenly my stomach swooped and I felt like I was about to lose my dinner all over the beach, but I managed to hold it back with a few deep breaths.

Okay. So maybe I was drunker than I'd thought.

"All right, are we doing this or what?" Dex asked, clapping his hands together.

"You really staying?" Cooper asked, moseying up behind me and slipping his arms around my waist.

"I can do better than that," I told him. I turned around and covered my mouth to keep from burping in his face. I swallowed hard, then spoke. "I know the security code to kill the alarm *and* open the door. No breaking in needed."

Cooper's head flinched back in surprise and then he grinned a grin that flipped my heart. "This is gonna be epic."

He turned around, slinging his arm over my shoulders. "My girl knows the code!"

"Shut up!" Dex shouted.

"Omigod! Let's go!" Jenny said, running for the stairs.

Stoner and Dex were right behind her, Stoner gripping the side rails and swinging himself up three steps at a time like an orangutan. Cooper kept his arm around me as we navigated up awkwardly, our hips bumping and our feet tangling. My stomach turned again as we reached the deck, and when I opened the flap over the alarm pad, my teeth started to chatter. Cooper put his big, tan hands on my shoulders and kneaded them lightly.

What are you doing, Ally? What are you doing? This is not you.

And then I saw Chloe and Jake crossing Orchard Avenue together. Saw their hands touching. Imagined it was their lips.

I swallowed back bile and closed my eyes for a moment while my brain righted itself.

Screw Chloe. Screw Jake. Screw my mom. Screw all of them.

I typed in Chloe's birth date and heard the telltale beep. Then I closed the flap and nodded at Cooper. He held his breath and tried the door. It slid open, and nothing happened. No sirens, no flashing lights. Nothing.

"Whoooohooo!" Cooper shouted, leading the way inside. The others followed, jumping over the threshold like little kids. I had to steady myself on the doorway for a moment, then tripped inside.

Chloe's house was exactly how I remembered it. The décor was all shabby-chic beach cottage with slatted ceilings and weathered wood chairs and cushions in stripes and florals and plaids. Her dad's sailboat collection was displayed proudly on the bay window that faced the water, and Dex went right for it, smashing the two-hundred-dollar-and-up wooden models into each other like they were at war. Cooper made for the liquor cabinet and opened a bottle of something brown, drinking straight from it and sloshing the liquid onto the pink-and-white dining room rug. Stoner was in the pantry, rooting around through bags and cans. Jenny instantly disappeared around the corner and up the stairs. I knew she was looking for Chloe's room and the fabulous clothes she figured she'd find there. I started to follow, but the metal dolphin sculpture on the coffee table tilted in front of me. Then the boat-wheel chandelier tilted the other way. I found myself stumbling sideways into the overstuffed couch, too dizzy to take another step. I sank into the cushions gratefully and held my head between my hands. The crashing and banging and shouting jabbed at my brain like violent stabs of a very sharp knife.

"Hey. Are you all right?" Cooper asked me, sitting on the coffee table across from me, clutching the neck of the bottle.

I nodded, but the action brought chunks up the back of my throat. Before I could do anything to stop it, I threw up all over his feet.

"Oh, shit!" Cooper jumped up and away from me. "Fuck! Ally! What the fuck!? That's disgusting."

"M'sorry. M'sorry." My eyes burning with humiliation, I lay back on the couch with my arm over my forehead. My mouth tasted like bile and banana. Citric acid burned the back of my throat and my nostrils.

But I was not going to cry. I would. Not. Cry.

Cooper slipped and slid over to the kitchen, leaving puke prints on the tile floor. The squishing and slurping made me want to hurl all over again, but I managed to hold it back this time. I heard him complaining to Dex about me. Heard them groaning as they cleaned his feet and flip-flops in the stainless steel sink.

Cooper's disgusted moan was the last thing I registered before I fell asleep.

Jake

I left the flowers in the car. I was still going to give them to her, but I didn't need to carry them into a house filled with all my friends, plus Ally's mom. When I opened the door to Faith's house, the party was raging. Parentals danced like no one was watching, which was never a good idea. At first it seemed like there weren't a lot of people my age around, but once I got downstairs I found them. Everyone was either in the hot tub or around it. The first person to spot me was Shannen.

Great.

"Hey!" she said as she walked over to me. Either she'd forgotten the last time we talked or didn't care. She looked good. Her hair was brushed back from her face and she looked . . . pretty. "What are you doing here?"

Yeah. She didn't want to hear the answer to that.

"Looking for Ally?" Faith asked. She was wearing a wet, white bikini and had a see-through sarong tied around her waist. She took a swig of champagne and rolled her eyes. "She's probably halfway to California by now."

"What? Why?" I asked.

"Oh, you didn't hear?" Shannen snorted a laugh. "Dr. Nathanson popped the question to Mrs. Ryan. Looks like Ally Ryan's moving back to the crest."

My heart fell. "You're kidding."

"Nope. He did it in front of everybody," Faith said, waving her glass around. "Except me, of course. I missed it because of Connor."

"You mean because you were trying to seduce Connor in the hot tub," Shannen said.

Faith blew out a sigh. "Whatever. *He* started with *me*."

I shook my head. Did they not realize there were more important things happening here?

"So . . . what? Ally bailed?" I said. "Do you know where she went?"

"Todd saw her on the beach with Annie, that's all I know. But that was, like, fifteen minutes ago," Faith said.

"Thanks." I shoved between them and started for the door.

"Good luck!" Shannen called after me.

I paused for a second, my back to her, wanting to ask her what the hell she meant by that—because she couldn't actually wish me and Ally luck, could she?—but I shook it off. It wasn't about that right now. It was about finding Ally before she completely went off the deep end. I wove through the crowd at the open glass doors, ignoring the shouts from my friends, and hit the sand. Of course, once I got there, I had no idea where to go.

"Dude."

Hammond came jogging down the steps from the deck. Connor Shale, Josh Schwartz, and the Idiot Twins were behind him. I reached out to slap hands with him, but instead he grabbed my shirt and pulled back a fist. My stomach hit my shoes.

"Hammond!" Shannen screeched from the basement door. I saw her and Faith out of the corner of my eye, running toward us.

I stared at Hammond's cocked fist. "What the fuck are you—"

"Jake! Hammond! Stop!"

Hammond released me as Ally's friend Annie ran up behind me. She looked panicked.

"It's Ally," she blurted, wheezing for air.

All the tiny hairs on my neck stood on end. "Where is she?"

Annie bucked forward, bracing her hands over her knees.

"God. It's a lot . . . harder to . . . run in the sand . . . than it looks," she gasped.

"Where's Ally?" Hammond demanded.

"She's . . . at Chloe's," Annie said between breaths. She pointed back over her shoulder, up the beach toward my house and Chloe's. "Her and those guys . . . those local guys . . . are breaking in."

"What?" Hammond blurted, his voice like a woman's screech.

"She's pretty drunk," Annie said, hands on her hips as she straightened up. "She's being a total bitch, in fact. She wouldn't come with me, but . . . she's gonna get in a lot of trouble."

"Shit," I said under my breath.

"I just want to make it clear," Annie said, holding up her hands, "that I would *not* be asking you guys for help unless I had no other choice."

I exchanged a baffled look with Hammond. Whatever that meant.

"So let's go get her," Hammond said, slapping my shoulder.

I guess whatever reason he had for wanting to punch me in the face was temporarily forgotten. He jogged up the beach with the other guys and Shannen, of course, went along too. I started to follow, but then a hand closed around my wrist.

"Wait."

I looked down at Annie—at her fingers on my arm. They looked very wrong there. A few yards up, Shannen paused. "What?" I said. "Let me go."

"I don't think you should," Annie said. "Let them handle it."

"Why?"

My adrenaline was slamming through my veins. I couldn't

believe those guys were getting such a head start. Shannen moseyed back toward us, eyeing Annie. Finally, the girl let go of me and wiped her palms on her denim skirt.

"Because she knows."

My heart thumped extra hard. I had no idea what she was talking about, but it didn't sound good. My eyes darted to Shannen and Faith. Clueless.

"Knows what?"

Annie pressed her lips together. "She knows about you and Chloe."

Jake

There was no way I was about to deal with that. Not with Annie's revelation, not with Shannen and Faith's reaction. Not with any of it. All that I cared about was getting to Ally. Getting her away from that surf loser. Getting her safe.

But how did she know? How had she found out? Had Chloe called her or something? Had she posted it on Facebook? I mean, how the hell could Ally possibly know?

All of this went through my mind as I sprinted up the beach toward Chloe's alone. Shannen had apparently decided not to come after all, which was fine by me. One less person to worry about. When I got there, I heard a crash and someone screamed. I took the stairs two at a time and vaulted through the door, fists clenched.

The first thing I saw was Hammond and Ally's surf loser wrestling on the living room floor. There was a broken

343

bottle of scotch next to them and some girl stood over them, screaming at them to stop. Todd and Trevor were whaling on a skinny dude in the kitchen and Connor and Josh were nowhere to be found.

Part of me wanted to rip Hammond off the asshole that had kissed Ally and take a swing at him myself, but then I heard a moan. I looked right and saw Ally lying on the couch. She had puke on her shirt, and there was a puddle of yellow and brown on the rug at her side.

I jumped over the puddle and knelt near her feet.

"Ally?" I said, taking her hand. "Ally, wake up. We have to get out of here."

Her eyes fluttered open and focused for half a second. "Jake?"

Then the front door burst open and two guys in rent-a-cop uniforms came barreling in.

"Everybody freeze!"

"Omigod! Omigod! Omigod!" The girl started wailing and shaking, like she was having a fit. One of the security dudes reached down and hauled Hammond off the local dude by the back of his neck. Hammond started to swing, but then froze when he saw the guy's face.

"Charlie?"

"Hammond? What the hell are you guys doing in here?"

The surf loser took the moment to grab the screaming girl and run. His friend in the kitchen wasn't far behind. Then Charlie, whoever he was, looked over at the couch.

"Oh, shit, is that Ally?"

"She's kind of out of it," I said.

He came around the table, grimaced at the puke, and leaned

toward her. I did a double take when I finally recognized him. It was Charlie Moore. The dude in all the pictures in Shannen's room. Her long-lost brother.

"Get her out of here," he said, standing up straight.

"What?" his partner said from the other side of the room.

Charlie ignored him. He looked me in the eye. He looked exactly like Shannen, but with a beard. "Get her out of here now." He took out his radio and glared at Hammond and the twins. "All of you, get the hell out of here. You have about two minutes before the actual police show up, and then I'm gonna have a hard time making them believe I didn't see anything."

I didn't ask questions. I scooped Ally up in my arms, stepped over the puke puddle, and followed Hammond and the Idiot Twins outside. Surf loser and his friends were nowhere to be seen. Nice that he cared so much about Ally to just bail like that. The twins sprinted ahead of us, back toward the party, cackling like they'd just had the best night ever. We had passed Connor's house and were almost to Hammond's when we met up with the girls.

"Oh my God! Ally!" Faith said, running over to me. "Is she unconscious?"

"I think she's just asleep," I said, out of breath. I jostled her in my arms, trying to get a better grip, and she opened her eyes again.

"Jake?" she said.

"Yeah. I'm here," I told her.

I imagined her saying something dramatic. Something like "you saved me" or "thank you" or even "I love you."

But she looked me right in the eye and said, "You hooked up with Chloe."

And then she turned her head and barfed on Faith's feet.

"Nice," Annie said with a grin.

Faith shrieked louder than any seagull I'd ever heard. She turned to glare at Annie, her fingers curling like claws. I swear I thought she was going to tear the girl's eyes out.

"What?" Annie said happily. "You can't tell me you didn't deserve that."

Faith groaned and ran for the water. Shannen bit back a laugh. Hammond shot me a vicious look, then took off up the beach. Clearly, he already knew about me and Chloe, and clearly this was why he'd wanted to pummel me. I expected Shannen to follow him, but she just looked sorry for me.

"We have to get her home," Annie said.

Ally groaned and rested her cheek on my chest.

"Her mother's gonna kill her," Shannen replied.

"So, what? Should we take her to a hospital?" Annie asked.

Shannen scoffed. "The ones down here suck. She'll end up getting a kidney replaced or something."

"Fine," Annie said firmly, taking charge. "You get her back to Gray's. I'll go tell her mom to meet us there."

"Okay," I said finally, starting up the beach again.

Faith trudged back from the water, her feet, legs, and sarong wet, her sandals dangling from her fingers. I walked with her and Shannen toward Dr. Nathanson's house. For a second I wondered where the hell Connor and Josh had gotten off to, but it didn't exactly matter. All that mattered was getting Ally into bed and making sure she was okay.

That, and figuring out how the hell I was going to explain about Chloe.

Ally

My mother was sipping tea by my bedside when I woke up the next morning. All the blinds were closed and the entire room looked gray. Even my mother's skin looked gray.

"Mom?" I croaked.

My throat was dry and felt like it was covered in sour-tasting fuzz. She put her tea down on the bedside table and leaned toward me as I rolled onto my side. There was a huge bouquet of colorful flowers in a vase next to my bed. Where had those come from? Was I sick enough to merit flowers?

"Are you okay? Do you need to throw up again?" my mother asked.

My eyes rolled in disgust as the memories of last night came flooding back, and just like that, my head began to pound. It was like someone was playing a timpani drum at the center of my skull, radiating sound waves out to every corner of my head.

"I don't think so," I said, bringing my hand to my forehead.

She lifted a glass of water from the nightstand and I tried to push myself up. I couldn't get there, though, and settled for leaning back against the pillows at a forty-five-degree angle, where I slowly sipped the water. My mother sighed through her nose and pushed the hair back from my forehead with the palm of her hand. The way she was studying my face made me sad. She'd never looked at me that way before. In that *what am I going to do?* helpless kind of way.

"You're getting married," I said finally.

She tilted her head. "Oh, Ally."

My lip started to tremble and a tear plopped from my eye onto my hand. "I'm sorry. I don't mean to cry. It's just—"

"You've had a rough few days. A lot's gone on," my mother said. "We don't have to talk about it now."

I took a deep, broken breath and looked toward the window, trying not to cry for real. I choked a little, though, and a few sobs came out. I felt like such a loser, all hungover and gross, with my mother waiting on me. And like I didn't know which way was up. Who were my friends? Who was my boyfriend? Where was I going to live? Would my dad move away again? And all the while, that timpani drum was pounding away, trying to shatter my skull.

"Here. Take these."

My mom held out a couple of Tylenol. I swallowed them gratefully and lay back again.

"We don't have to talk about it now, but we *are* going to talk about it," my mother assured me, smoothing my hair again. Her hand felt cold and steady, comforting and perfect. "You and I are going to be doing *a lot* of talking over the next few days."

I nodded slowly. "I know."

"Good," she said. "Right now I think you should try to get some more rest."

"Okay," I replied, my voice thick.

I shakily put the glass down on the table, next to the flowers. She picked up her tea and started to go.

"Mom?" I said when she got to the door.

"Yeah?"

"Was . . . was Jake here last night?" I asked.

"He's still here. He's asleep in the guest room," she replied.

My heart pounded against my rib cage. I had this odd memory of him holding my hand, looking into my eyes, but that was it. What was he doing here? What had happened between us? What had I said?

My mother turned to face me. "Hon, you know that I love you, right? No matter what."

My throat closed over. "Yeah."

"Good. And I have to tell you . . . I think that kid does too," she said.

I blinked, confused. "What kid does what?"

"Jake. After what he did for you last night, it's pretty clear to me that that guy is in love."

Then she smiled and quietly closed the door.

Jake

I was in and out of sleep all night, confused about where I was, worried about Ally. At one point I could have sworn that Annie chick snuck into my room and took a picture of me with her phone, but I hoped it was just a dream. I finally woke up for good at ten, got dressed in my jeans and a T-shirt Ally's mom had left for me, and then basically hid out in the guest room all morning. Every now and then a door would open and close. I heard Ally's mom whispering to Shannen's mom at some point, and around eleven someone brewed coffee downstairs, making the whole house smell like work. A few minutes after that, Annie left, even though Ally's mom kind of begged her to stay. That conversation was full-volume and Annie did not sound happy. Finally I thought I heard Ally's door open and my heart skipped. I peeked out into the hallway just in time to see her slip into the bathroom at the other end.

She took a fifteen-minute-long shower, then went back to her room. I watched the clock, waited five minutes—long enough for her to get dressed—then rushed over to her room. My pulse pounding in my ears, I knocked quietly on her door.

Nothing.

I knocked again. A second later, it opened a crack. Her hair was wet and combed back from her face. I could only see one eye.

"Hey," I said.

"Hey."

"Can I come in? Just for a sec?" I asked.

She cleared her throat and stepped back. "Sure."

As I walked inside, she turned around and headed for the end of the bed. Then she paused and turned to face me. She was wearing her Orchard Hill basketball T-shirt and sweatpants and she looked tired, but beautiful. I had no idea where to start. For a long moment we just stood there, looking at each other. Ally toyed with her fingers. I shoved my hands under my arms.

"So are you, like, *with* Chloe?" she blurted all of a sudden.

"No," I said. "No. Definitely not. We just—it was one time. One . . . thing. And it didn't matter. It was stupid. But we're definitely not together. We haven't even talked since we—"

I didn't have time to finish my sentence because Ally closed the space between us and kissed me. Pure relief rushed through me, cooling me from the inside out. I pulled her toward me and held her as close to me as I possibly could. Her mouth tasted minty and clean, like she'd spent that entire fifteen minutes in the bathroom brushing her teeth.

Finally she pulled away. She rested her forehead on my chest and looked down. All I could see was her wet hair.

"I missed you so much," she breathed.

I tilted my head back and put my hands on her shoulders. I could hardly believe this was happening. I was finally getting to touch her. To kiss her. It was all happening. "I missed you, too."

She turned so that the side of her face was against my chest, and wrapped her arms around me tight. "Thanks for last night. Shannen told me what you did."

"She did?" I asked, running my hand over her hair. "When?"

"This morning. Before she left to meet Charlie for breakfast," she said.

"Oh." It was all I could think to say. Shannen was helping me out with Ally now? What the hell had gone on down here this summer? But then I realized, it didn't matter. I'd decided something last night. Something important. And it was time to man up. I cleared my throat and pushed her away gently, holding her at arm's length.

"There's something I have to say," I said seriously, looking her in the eye.

She smiled. "Ooookay." She was mocking me—mocking my tone—but I didn't care.

"Okay. Here it is. I love you," I said. "And I never, ever wanted to hurt you. It's, like, the number one thing I never want to do, but somehow, I keep doing it. And I'm sorry. I just . . . that's all I wanted to say all this time. All I was trying to do . . . with that thing with your dad, not telling you . . . was *not* hurt you. And I'm sorry that I did."

Ally stared at me.

"And I'm sorry that I did it again. With the Chloe thing. Which was stupid. Like, really, really stupid. And I—"

"Can you just stop, for a second?" Ally said, holding up a hand.

"What?" I said.

"Can you say the first part again?" she asked, rolling her fingers around for a rewind.

I racked my brain.

"Um . . . I love you?" I said.

"That's the part. Cuz I love you, too."

And then she smiled. A slow, happy, blissful, perfect smile. I leaned in to kiss her, and for the first time all summer, everything was right.

Daily Field Journal of Annie Johnston
Friday, August 13

Position: CVS (God, I feel like I'm ALWAYS here).

Cover: None. This is my life.

Observations:

11:57 p.m.: The place is dead when the doors slide open and Subject Chloe Appleby walks in. Uniform: oversize OHH T-shirt, gray sweats, rubber flip-flops, messy ponytail, sunglasses, baseball cap. (Note: See time stamp. Assessment: Someone's undercover.) Subject Chloe walks slowly down the makeup aisle. She picks up CoverGirl powder, puts it down. Inspects a Neutrogena lip gloss, puts it down. (Assessment: She's not really shopping. Girl would never let drugstore cosmetics near her perfect self.)

12:01 a.m.: Technically we're supposed to be closing, but my manager has a strict policy against kicking anyone out.

12:05 a.m.: Subject Chloe finally arrives at the back of the store. Where, as has been established, the condoms live. Suddenly, I am very awake and happy behind the counter.

12:06 a.m.: Subject Chloe speed walks toward the

front of the store. She emerges from the end of the aisle, a box tucked under her arm. All I can see is that the packaging is white. (Query: Which condoms have white packaging? Note: Check that later.)
She sees me and freezes. Her skin, behind those sunglasses, goes frighteningly pale. And then, before I can even think of a quip, she turns and sprints out the door. The alarms go off. My manager runs up from the back. Subject Chloe's car zooms out of the parking lot.

Manager: Did you see that girl? Do you know her?

My mouth just kind of hangs open. (Note: I could get Chloe Appleby arrested right now. The knowledge of this, the sheer power, makes me heady with glee.)

Manager: Annie? What did she take? Does she go to your school?

And then, I hear myself say it.

Me: I've never seen her before in my life.

(Assessment: I need my head examined.)

Ally

And suddenly I was packing again. Packing to move in with Gray and Quinn. We'd been home for just over a week, and already I'd picked out my very own room in the Nathanson house. It had a window seat and built-in bookcases and a king-size bed, but I still hated it. I was trying not to, but I did. I just could not wrap my brain around how this was going to work. Living with Gray. Living with Quinn. All of us eating dinner together and spending weekends together and holidays and birthdays and the wedding.

Ugh. The wedding.

I picked up a framed photograph from the day my parents had renewed their vows at the shore. My eyes prickled with hot tears and I clenched my teeth. Before I could start blubbering, I wrapped it up in newspaper and shoved it into the bottom of a box.

It's over, Ally. Get used to it.

Out in the living room, my mother and Gray laughed, and my shoulder muscles curled. At least Gray's house was huge and my room was as far away from theirs as it could get. One of its biggest selling points.

My cell phone beeped and I lunged for it, hoping it was Annie. She hadn't returned my calls or texts since that night at the shore, and I'd been too chicken to go to CVS and corner her. I guess whatever I said to her that night on the beach had been pretty bad. But still, from everything I'd heard from Jake and Shannen, things might have been a lot worse if she hadn't

355

been there for me. Why would she save my ass if she was so mad at me? Was this a temporary freeze out, or were we really not friends anymore?

The text was from Shannen. She was packing too. She and her mom were moving into the condos, three doors down from the one we were vacating. The whole thing was so ironic it made both of us want to vomit on an hourly basis.

Found old bball jersey of urs. Want it?

I texted back.

Def. Gotta walkin closet now. ☺

LOL. F U. :P

I laughed and dropped the phone back on my bed. Tomorrow I would track Annie down at work. This could not go on. She'd said some mean things to me that night too, but I was willing to forgive and forget. Maybe she would be too.

The doorbell rang and my heart pitter-pattered happily. Jake was here. For a real date. Our first since Shannen's party. Who knew that all I needed to trust him again was for him to drive to the shore, save me from getting arrested, and tell me he loved me?

My stupid heart was a very silly thing.

I had decided not to ask him about the Chloe thing, not to know how far they'd gone or where or when or how. In my mind they had only kissed and nothing more. And they were both drunk. And sad over losing me and Hammond. Maybe Jake was actually passed out and Chloe had just taken advantage. That was the version I liked best.

When I opened the door, he was standing there all smiles.

"Hey," I said.

"Hey."

I smiled. He smiled back. Just standing there, all goofy like that, made my heart full.

"So where're we going?" he asked.

"Nowhere you can't walk to!" my mother shouted from the kitchen.

I gritted my teeth. "I'm still grounded, but my mother said we could go out as long as we don't take your car."

"Oh." He knocked his fists together. "Pizza?"

"Pizza's good," I replied, reaching for his hand as I stepped outside. "We're walking to Stanzione's!" I shouted.

I tugged Jake down the stairs toward the parking lot. He looked over his shoulder at my mom and Gray, and waved.

"Good to see you, Mrs. Ryan . . . Dr. Nathanson."

"Have her home by eleven, Jake," Gray said.

I felt warm all over and had to bite back a retort. Something about him not being my father, not making the rules. Yeah. Living with him was going to be interesting. But as the door closed, I vowed not to think about it. Not tonight. I would not let Gray Nathanson ruin this. I swung Jake's hand back and forth as we crossed the parking lot.

"What are you so smiley about?" Jake asked, grinning as well.

"Just happy to see you," I told him.

"Do you realize when you move, I'll be able to get to you in two and a half minutes? I timed it."

Wow. Could he be any cuter? I leaned my head against his shoulder as we passed by the Orchard View Condominiums sign. "Thanks," I said.

He squeezed my hand. "For what?"

"For being the one good thing about moving back to the crest."

Jake

Five weeks. Ally and I had been together for five weeks. In that time I had kissed her, like, a thousand times. Held her hand, like, a hundred. Watched her chew on the inside of her cheek while concentrating, wrap her hair around her finger when she didn't know what to say, dribble ice cream on her shirt while laughing with her mouth full.

And I wasn't bored. Of any of it.

Every time we hung out, it was just the two of us. And every time we hung out, I didn't want it to end. Even if we were just lying on my bed watching a movie, my arm around her with her head on my chest—even that went by too quick. I'd spent the last few weeks of summer not wishing I was down the shore but just sort of floating.

And now, it all had to end. Because tomorrow, school was going to start. And there would be no more long afternoons of just me and Ally. Tomorrow the shit storm would begin.

Or maybe tonight. Because tonight was Connor Shale's back-to-school party. Ally pulled her mom's car to a stop behind Jessica Cox's Sebring Convertible, which I only knew was hers because she'd chosen the unfortunate vanity plate that read j coxxx. We both looked up at the window walls of Connor's house. There were already tons of people inside, and the glass vibrated from the reverb coming off the speakers.

"We don't have to go in," I said.

"No. We really don't," she replied.

We'd talked about it a million times—whether or not to go

to this party. Neither of us had spoken to Hammond or Chloe since LBI. Ham and I had been at soccer practice together every day for two weeks, but basically ignored each other. Ally had explained that she and Ham had seen Chloe and me that night in town, and assumed we were together. She'd told me it was what I'd said, when she'd mentioned it, that confirmed we'd hooked up. For all we knew, Hammond still just *suspected* it. He may or may not have spoken to Chloe. Who knew? All I knew was that I wasn't in contact with a single one of my old friends.

And that I didn't much care. All I cared about was Ally.

"But we do," Ally said, unbuckling her seat belt. "I mean, it's better to get it over with, right? Before school starts?"

"Do you not remember what happened here last year?" I asked.

A shadow passed over her face as she looked back at the front door. I could see it playing out before her eyes. How Faith and Shannen had attacked her. How I hadn't defended her. How she'd left the place near tears.

"Ice cream?" she suggested suddenly, plugging the seat belt back in.

"Sounds good."

I was just about to snap my own seat belt tight when my door was flung open and I was yanked out onto the grass. Ally screamed. I looked up to find Hammond standing over me, his arms down at his sides like a boxer's, his hands curled into fists.

So I guess we knew how Hammond was feeling.

"Hammond! What the hell!" Ally shouted, getting out of the car.

"Get up," Hammond spat.

I pushed myself up awkwardly and shoved him as hard as I could. "What the fuck are you—"

Slam. His fist hit my cheek so hard I was flung sideways. My eye popped, gushing blinking stars across my vision. I held on to Ally's car for dear life, blood seeping down my face. My jaw felt crooked and when I tried to move it, tiny slivers of pain crackled toward my temple.

"Hammond!" Ally shouted, her voice cracking. "What's the matter with you?"

He ignored her and got right in my face. I could smell scotch on his breath. His eyes looked possessed.

"That," he said, spitting all over my cheek as he shoved a finger into my chest, "was for knocking up my girlfriend."

acknowledgments

Even though I spend most of my day alone in front of a computer, typing my fingertips off, I always feel like I have a squad of cheerleaders behind me, keeping me going. I'd like to thank the following people for always having my back, especially where these books are concerned: Emily Meehan, Sarah Burnes, Justin Chanda, Julia Maguire, Logan Garrison, Paul Crichton, Lucille Rettino, Elke Villa, Krista Vossen, and Jenica Nasworthy.

To all the librarians, teachers, readers, Facebook friends, Twitter followers, bloggers, and fellow authors who supported *She's So Dead to Us*, my heart swells with gratitude. There are too many ever-changing screen names, handles, and nicknames to mention here, but you know who you are. A very special thanks to Laura Leonard, Courtney Sheinmel, Elizabeth Scott, Jenny Han, Sara Shepard, Gayle Forman, Susane Colasanti, Heidi R. Kling, Kay Cassidy, David Levithan, Jen Calonita, Caroline Aversano, and Christi Aldelizzi for everything you've done and continue to do to help me get the word out about these books.

HUGE thanks to Jaimee Mulholland, Molly Brown, Anna Hickey, and Geralyn Hickey for helping me make certain bits authentic.

And, as always, thank you to my family and friends for tolerating my craziness, listening to my rants, and telling me, always, how fabulous you think I am (especially on those days I don't agree): Matt, Mom, Erin, Ian, Wendy, Shira, Ally, Meredith, Sona, Liesa, Jessica, Courtney, Aimee, Manisha, Lynn, and Lanie. . . . I may not see all of you as often as I wish I could, but I always know you're with me, and that's enough.

And, of course, special thanks to Brady and the little one to come, for lighting up my life.